RIGHTEOUS SUFFERING

Righteous Survival EMP Saga, Book Five

By: Timothy A. Van Sickel

Dedicated to my Lord and Savior, Jesus Christ, who
inspired me, and my wife, family and friends who encouraged me.

Contents

Author's Foreword

For those who have read the first four books in this series, you have seen how the scope of action increases with each book. That will continue in this book. If you have not read any of the previous books in this series, it's recommended that you do so, but I have tried to write enough back story into this novel to not only reorient the series fans but also allow a new reader a glimpse into what has already transpired.

This book portrays more of the militaristic and governmental posturing needed to survive. Some of the emotional and family-oriented sentiments are lost as the scope of the story grows.

As the title suggests, there is a religious overtone to the story. The main characters in the story are Christians, and they try to follow the tenets of their faith in the chaotic situations of societal collapse that they encounter. But remember, like you, they're flawed, fallen.

For the EMP, apocalyptic fan; this is an epic adventure of survival and the rebuilding of society after a total societal collapse. I'm sure you will have questions as to why certain things work and other things don't. And you may have questions as to how the intrepid survivors manage to get things done. I'm not an electrical engineer, nor a military strategist. I try to explain all the steps needed to make things work and come back on line, how all the pieces come together to begin to form a new society. Amidst all the violence and chaos, good people work together to defeat tyranny. The tale relies on American ingenuity and can-do spirit.

For the Christian reader, this is a PG 13 novel with "minor" swearing and graphic violence. The message of reliance on God to see us through humanity's darkest hours is inspirational to many readers. This may not be your normal "Christian Fiction" series, but I encourage you to dive into this dystopian future epic tale.

I hope you all enjoy this novel.

You can contact me at vansickelauthor@gmail.com

Roster of main characters

Righteous Survival, Book 5 of the Righteous Survival EMP Saga

In this saga it will take many people coming together to survive the chaos. The focus of the saga will be on Mark Mays, his family, and his community. But many other characters are involved in the tale. This is a list of characters carried over from books 1, 2, and 3, as well as some new characters introduced in book 4.

Some characters are brought in to carry out a specific objective, and then may fade into the background once their story has been told. Mark Mays and his family will continue through the entire saga.

Mark and Rebecca Mays
    Brit & Bennie, Zach & Janie
Zach and Janie
    Rusty, Blake, James (Jimmy), Mark, Sarah
Brit and Ken
    Larson, Grace (Grayson)
Reverend Wysinger   Baptist Church Minister
Paul and Eva Mays (Mark's brother and sister in law)
Herc and Leesa, John Jr.
John Fisher   Army Ranger First Sergeant (retired), Central City
    Colonel, XO
Sgt John Anders,Former Lt Col, communicationsLt, S2
Hairy   Large bad man, converts to Mark's side
Daneel,   Security Marine
Buck, E6 MP   Family in Orlando
Captain John AlbrightSomerset Militia Commander
Sarah Farmer   Mark's Sister
Mary Dugan   Refugee Doctor

Captain Regis	Jennerstown Militia
Terry Barnes	Local Evangelical Christian
Lt Jerry Hasselrig	Johnstown refugee clan leader
Lt Colonel Adkins	PA National Guard General Staff, Bedford militia leader
Sgt Merkle	Bedford County NCO, now militia captain
Dean Chaffe	Billionaire banker
Carl Chaffe	Dean's son
Major Jeffers	Chaffes hired security, retired Special Forces officer
Dan Farmer	Mark's well-connected brother-in-law
Lucas Thomas	Independent Farmer
Mr. Ted Zearfoss	Fulton County Commissioner
Captain Warfield	Fulton County Militia commander, oath keeper
Cpt. Sheila Mathews	Specials forces, Major Jeffers' XO
Colonel Jenkins	Letterkenny commandant
Colonel Miller	Center County Militia Commander
General Mills	82nd Airborne Div. Commander
Prof. Dombrowsky	Richland civilian leader
General Smythe	Martial Law Corps Commander
Shelly Clinton	Martial Law President
Admiral Van Hollern	Third Fleet Admiral
Admiral Barnes	Martial Law Admiral, Fifth Fleet
Major Higgins	Task Force Commander
Dr. Sam Gray	Roanoke Militia
Admiral	Ninth Fleet Commander
Jim Robertson	Dover civilian commander
Colonel Tiani	Dover Air Force Commander
General Watkins	Fort Hood Commander
General Travis	Minot Airforce Base Commander
Susan	Missionary leader from Winchester

Summary of Events, Righteous Survival EMP Saga

It's recommended that you read the previous novels in this series to grasp the totality of events that have played out so far in this epic saga.

Even if you have read the entire saga, a brief refresher may be helpful before diving into this novel. Here is a brief summary for each book.

Summary of Events

Righteous Survival EMP Saga

It's recommended that you read the previous novels in this series to grasp the totality of events that have played out so far in this epic saga.

Even if you have read the entire saga, a brief refresher may be helpful before diving into this novel. Here is a brief summary for each book.

Righteous Gathering, Righteous Survival EMP Saga, Book 1

Mark Mays gathers his family to his farmstead and starts to rally the local citizens to fight against the rising anarchy

Righteous Bloodshed, Righteous Survival EMP Saga, Book 2

A bloody, gruesome tale as neighbor fights neighbor for food just to survive and warring factions start to square off over the available food.

Righteous Sacrifice, Righteous Survival EMP Saga, Book 3

Tough decisions are made as control of the farms becomes essential for survival.

Righteous Soldiers, Righteous Survival EMP Saga, Book 4

Paramilitary groups form including Oath Keepers, to fight against forces trying to implement martial law.

Chapter 1, Patriots

Blue Ridge Mountains

November 22nd

Sam nudges his son-in-law, Alan. He whispers to him. "That's the second time I've seen helicopters in the past two days." The two men are perched twenty feet in the air over a thicket, hoping for a deer to come by. In years past, Dr. Sam Gray would have been waiting for a monster buck. Today he will gladly take any game that will put meat on the table. He has Alan with him to teach him hunting skills.

Dr. Gray is a retired family practice doctor. He lives twenty miles west of Roanoke, on twenty-four acres of land. In his retirement, he planned on being a hobby farmer, church elder, and good grandfather. That all changed two months ago. Now he spends most days as a volunteer helping the sick and injured while still trying to provide for himself and his wife.

A week ago, one of his daughters and her husband arrived home. Against long odds, they made the four-hundred-mile trek from Atlanta to their homestead in the foothills of the Blue Ridge Mountains. The couple had stayed hunkered down in their suburban home for four weeks, surviving on stashed food and keeping a low profile. Then the military began to move in. At first, they were relieved. But as martial law started to show its dire effects, they realized they were in trouble and needed to flee.

With minimal supplies, two hand guns, and a twenty-two rifle, they loaded up their two bicycles and headed north. A trip they could have completed in six hours in a car, took them a month. They don't talk about what they've seen. Their daughter,

Beth Ann, has scars on her face that mar her beauty; Alan is similarly disfigured.

Sam and his wife have survived the chaos fairly well. Sam is a Captain in a local militia, a militia set up many years ago. All their members are well armed and well supplied. But none of the militia members were really prepared for the total societal collapse that happened. By the third week, chaos reigned. The militia fell apart as the people migrated out of the piedmont and into the mountains and their leadership feuded about what to do.

At that time, Dr. Gray and his wife Katy hunkered down. They were far enough off the beaten path that they could possibly make it on their own. They hired two local hands along with their families to help maintain their small farm. They formed a loose alliance with other locals. They prayed daily for deliverance.

His family and small farm were also protected by the fact that Sam is a Doctor. Sam helped the sick and injured from the many factions fighting for control of Roanoke and its surrounding farmlands. Neither side wanted to tick off the doctor, so they're off limits to raiding parties.

When Beth Ann and Alan showed up, it gave them hope. They have four grown children dispersed across the country. They never expected to see any of them again. With their arrival, a renewed push to survive permeated the small farm.

A group of local farmers have been meeting to try and find a sane path forward. Dr Gray has started going to those meetings. Whether the local farms are controlled by the anarchists, martial law or the militia, the sentiment from the farmers is the same: "These bastards only take from us. We ask for security, and they blow us off."

"Your right," Dr. Gray responds, "we're providing food in return for security. But that ain't happening, there is no security. There has to be a better way forward. The way things are going, our farms will be wrecked, and next spring will be bleak. We need to form a new alliance. The daily chaos has to stop." But no one has an answer to the problem. The chaos is too entrenched, the powers in control are too ruthless.

* * *

Ten weeks after the attacks, Roanoke has fallen into complete chaos. It has fared no better than any other mid-sized city. Half of its population of two hundred thousand people have died from lack of medical care, starvation, disease or violence. The city proper is basically a vacant warzone, controlled by a hodgepodge of gangs, the police, and military units trying to implement martial law. Most of the residents have fled to the countryside in search of food.

South and east of the city, in the rolling hills of the fertile piedmont, martial law forces are the controlling faction and they help to keep those still in the city supplied with food. They try to control the flow of refugees from the east coast, but starving parties raid and ravage the farms daily. The military patrols that are detailed to protect the farmers have grown immune to firing on desperate people seeking help. They have also depleted the farms to fill their bellies with no regard for the future. The farmers plead for their future, knowing that winter is coming, and they will need to have enough resources to plant next spring. The pleas fall on deaf ears and their hope for the future wanes.

South and west of the city, in the foot hills of the Appalachian Mountains, a wily drug lord has taken control of the farms. Soon after the power went out, he ransacked every store, warehouse and trucking depot he could find. With control of so much food and goods, he gathered together an army. When he

realized his supplies would run out, he used his loyal army, fed by the supplies he controlled, to take control of local farms.
Conditions are harsh and his people are brutal. The farmers and refugees cringe at the sight of his patrols. His lands are less chaotic because there are fewer raiding parties and his people rule with no pity. Any dissension is dealt with forcefully; none dare to confront him. Human trafficking has sprung up, sex slaves are the newest commodity as moral norms fall.

To the north and west are the Blue Ridge Mountains. The militia loosely controlled this area. But the militia fell apart due to poor leadership and lack of tactical skills. They worked well as small groups but managing large scale operation utterly failed. Over a half dozen militia groups fend for themselves across the hills and valleys of the Blue Ridge Mountains. Tens of thousands of refugees from Roanoke have fled to these mountains. In some areas they're accepted and fairly put to work. In other areas they're rejected, fired on as the enemy. In a few areas they're brought in to be used as slave laborers. The one redeeming aspect of the mountainous area is the leaders realize that the farms are the key to the future and must be kept viable.

* * *

Sam and Alan sit down at the dinner table. Fresh venison with stewed cabbage is the meal. Alan downed a good doe shortly after the flyover. Most of the meat is being smoked, some of it's being dried, and some was traded for potatoes and cabbage. The backstraps are tonight's dinner.

The meal is mostly eaten in silence after a grace has been said. After two months of survival, even with fresh venison on the plate, not much is said. Chaos and death do not make a great dinner conversation. But the flight by of helos are something worth bringing up.

"We saw a helicopter flying south today. Just one. I told you I saw three heading north yesterday. One headed back south today," Sam states.

No one says a word. The clanks of forks and knives against dinnerware is all that is heard. The people around the table have been beaten down, defeated. A helicopter flying over means nothing to them. They're more worried that a raiding party will attack them again, stealing precious chickens or even worse, one of their three remaining sows.

Sam continues his one-sided conversation. "So, three helicopters flew north yesterday, and one flew back south today. I wonder what that means?"

"Two got shot down," One of the farm hands states bluntly.

"Maybe," Sam replies. "But why are they flying? We haven't seen anything flying since they stopped the sky cap missions six weeks ago. Those helicopters were military. They came out of Bragg, or Benning. Who could have shot them down?"

"Any crazy bastard could have shot them down, Lord knows we have plenty of crazy bastards out there," the farm hand replies.

"Watch your language, there is no need for that kind of language," Katy, Sam's wife, states.

"Yes ma'am," the farm hand states, more to his plate than to Katy.

"It would take a missile to shoot down one of those birds. No one has missiles like that. Katy, we need to start monitoring the ham radio again. I think something is happening."

"We have too much to do to keep someone listening to that chatter box. Besides, it can be so depressing. Jamie was listening to one operator while he got over run and killed. I listened to a woman as her family farm was raided and her two grown daughters were carried off. I can't do it Sam, I can't do it." Katy begins to sob as she thinks of what she has heard from across the country.

"I'll do it," Janie states. She was the office manager for Dr. Gray's practice before she quit to be a full-time mom. She brought her family to the Gray's farm when things got too bad in her suburban neighborhood. Her husband works as one of their hired hands. She's a middle-aged woman with a twenty-year-old son and seventeen-year-old daughter who also help out around the farm.

"I'll make sure the kids help too. With all the canning finished and the crops brought in, we have more time on our hands. I know there's still lots to do, but we need to know what's going on out there. We can't survive in a vacuum."

Alan and Beth Ann agree to help monitor the Ham as well. While it's not a breakthrough, Sam is pleased that they've made a small commitment to get engaged. Later that night, as he snuggles into bed next to his wife, his mind churns slowly about how to bring peace to their fractured lands.

Chapter 2, New Allies

Bakersville

November 22nd

"He's meeting with General Mills right now? This wasn't part of the plan. How the hell did he get to Fort Bragg?" Dan Farmer exclaims. Dan was a well-connected business man prior to America being attacked and the world thrown into chaos. Now he's in charge of the Laurel Highlands Militia's effort to monitor communications and help set long term strategies. He has over a hundred people working for him monitoring ham radio networks and any other transmissions they can pick up and record using equipment scavenged from preppers with Faraday cages and any other older equipment that is still functional.

His brother-in-law is Mark Mays, the elected general of the Laurel Highlands Militia. Over the past two months, General Mays has assembled an army of veterans, woodsmen, and Oath Keepers. Cooperating with the local farmers and civilian councils, they've secured the Laurel Highlands as a place of stability. The Laurel Highlands Militia and its allies managed to take control of the massive Letterkenny Arms Depot.

Before the winter storms set in, a task force was sent to Winchester to free the fertile and productive Shenandoah Valley from tyranny and martial law. Meanwhile, Dan found out that an assassin team was assigned to take out General Mays.

The last Dan knew, General Mays and his wife, Rebecca, were in Winchester to work out a system to implement a civilian government and help the farmers establish sustainable methods to feed those in need. Now he hears that Mark is meeting with General Mills in Fort Bragg, four hundred miles south of Winchester.

"Get me the sat phone," Dan orders. The sat phone was recovered from an elite family of bankers that sought safety after their million-dollar shelter was compromised. It uses hardened satellites and gives Dan direct communications with hundreds of elite players around the world. There were a few thousand people that had these special phones. But over half the phones have gone unresponsive. Billionaires and world leaders had these phones as well as key military leaders deemed faithful to the world's elite.

General Mills has one of these phones because some of the elite thought his resources at Fort Bragg could help them. But he's an Oath Keeper. He would not help them implement martial law. He would not help rescue those who wished to impose tyranny. It ran counter to his moral code. Now he has an assassin team after him for betraying the elite.

Dan finally reaches General Mills. "Hey Dan," The general says kindly. The two have talked several times and are on friendly terms. The line is secure, so they talk openly. "I thought you would be calling. We've learned a lot in the past few days, so it's good you called."

"I hear Mark is on his way to meet with you. How did that happen?" Dan asks.

"Well, your general managed to refuel my birds and decided a face to face meeting would be good. Besides that, an assassin team was moving in on him, so he decided to get out of town. I understand that he claims the birds I sent north as his new air force. I'm not so sure I agree with that. There are only a few dozen of those birds on the whole east coast and I'm supposed to give three to you hillbillies?"

"You're three steps ahead of me general. Fill me in."

"I forget that information doesn't flow the way it used to, sorry brother. We got wind that an assassin team was assigned to take out General Mays. These are people we trained. These are

19

professional killers. But they have allied with the martial law people. I have no control over them. So, we sent three elite teams to help out your good general, only to find that he wasn't in Central City, but was down supporting your mission in Winchester. By the way, you all got balls for that move.

"Anyway. Our birds flew to Winchester. They found Mark, but they also found that the assassin team had moved to Winchester too. So, Mark got the birds refueled and flew out of Winchester. He sent two birds back your way, but he decided to head down here. We expect him within the next thirty minutes. We now have line of sight radio communications with them."

"That explains a lot," Dan replies. "Do you know Mark is my brother-in-law? He's a bit quirky, and way smarter than he lets on. Don't expect to get your birds back. If he has them, he's keeping them. Treat him good, general, he has done a lot of good around here. He sees things other people don't. Have him call me when he can."

"Will do Dan. Thanks for the info. Stay safe my friend."

Chapter 3, New Allies, Part 2

Fort Bragg, NC

November 22

Fort Bragg sits squarely in the middle of the North Carolina Piedmont, the vast coastal plain between the Appalachian Mountains and the lowlands of the east coast. The piedmont is rolling hills of forests and farmlands. The closest major cities are Charlotte, Raleigh and Columbia. All are metropolitan areas of over a million people. All three cities are in chaos as the starving masses seek survival. Fort Bragg has been insulated from the madness because it's over a hundred miles away from the closest of these cities.

But General Mills knows the chaos is out there. He has established firm control of the sprawling fort and the surrounding lands, including the town of Fayetteville. The shear presence of the strong military force that he has sent to protect the local farms and communities has stopped any refugees from even trying to cause any problems.

They've made their hospital semi functional using generators and their stocked supplies. They've been generous to the locals with their supplies and provisions. Anyone within twenty miles of the fort is extremely loyal to the general.

He has a sent a heavy brigade, with a strong supply contingent to Charlestown to help the fifth fleet land. That mission is still underway. Camp Lejeune is located just south of Charlestown and there are many retired vets in the area who can help rally the people. The chaos and depravity that the task force reports are horrendous. The closer they get to the city; the worse things get. But if his task force can secure the port, a nuclear-powered reactor will be able to dock in that city. Progress is being made, but too many people are only thinking of today. Their only thought is how to feed themselves and their families. The long-term benefits of a nuclear-powered aircraft carrier moored in their city doesn't register in the minds of the starving, jaundiced and emaciated people that the task force encounters. This is the Fort Bragg that Mark Mays flies in to.

* * *

I grab my crutch as the doors of the helicopter open. Becca stands and I reach out to her. She helps me up. I smile and she smiles back. "This is a whole new adventure, babe."

She looks away for just a second, then focuses back on my eyes. "The Lord put us here, Mark. Let's go do His work." That word of encouragement gives me strength.

"If God is with us, who can stand against us?" I state, paraphrasing one of my favorite Bible verses." Let's go meet General Mills."

Becca and I negotiate the narrow steps from the helicopter to the tarmac where there is a royal greeting. A dozen staff officers along with General Mills are there to greet us. I think of our bare bone's operation, where General Adkins has maybe six staff members and a few NCOs. Our welcoming party is bigger than her entire staff.

General Mills steps forward to greet us. He's of average height but fit. His hair is short cropped but wiry. His skin is bronze, and he has a well-groomed mustache. He's a handsome man obviously of mixed raced, and proud of his heritage, like my wife. General Mills hugs my wife first. "Welcome to Fort Bragg," he states. Then he turns to me. He looks me up and down, then steps back and salutes. "Welcome to Fort Bragg, General Mays."

I return his salute. "Thanks for having us, general. Let's go swap stories and figure out a way to make the country work again."

"Interesting. A few years ago, the slogan was Make America Great Again. Now we just hope to make America work again. By the way, did you bring a windmill generator with you?"

"Well, no," I say laughing. "But as we speak, they're moving the crane to the next windmill. If they get the chance, they'll bring down another generator. We've lost good people on that project, but their work is astounding. It worries me that you know of their success."

We exchange news as the general takes us to his main mess hall. It's mainly small talk to fill the time until we can discuss more serious issues. My security detail stays by my side. General Mills takes note and offers them a chance to stand down. They politely turn him down. After lunch we convene to the general's office.

His headquarters building is the size of a corporate office building and despite the grid being down, the facility is fully operational. Most of his computers are fried, like the rest of ours; communications systems are fried too. But like Dan Farmer's system, they're doing their best to monitor communications and determine what is going on in the world. They also have a few hardened systems that let them communicate with other major military units from all the other armed forces branches.

We enter the general's office. It's a large office worthy of his position. Maps adorn the walls. We all sit down at a small conference table. My two guards stand upright against the walls, arms at a ready position. Becca and I sit in two comfortable arm chairs. General Mills sits behind his desk in an expensive swivel chair. One of his senior officers sits opposite me at the conference table.

"What the hell have you stirred up, general? You got a first team assassin squad after you. You're higher on their hit list than I am. How did you pull that off?"

"It wasn't my objective, general. I didn't know there was a hit list until yesterday. I was just trying to help people. I guess when we finally took control of the arms depot, that ruffled a few feathers."

"You might say that," General Mills responds. "The fact that you managed to keep it really got people riled up. Do you realize how much equipment is stationed there?"

"Yes and no. Most of its cold war era equipment, out of date and obsolete. Which makes it highly valuable because a lot of it still works. We didn't just happen upon Letterkenny. It was a decision we made over a month ago. We just beat everyone else to the prize."

"They want you dead for more than taking Letterkenny. You're disrupting their plans. You're bringing stability. They want chaos."

"What do you want, General Mills?" I ask. "Do you want the chaos?"

"Hell no, not at all. It's ripping our country apart. I'm with you. You're one of the few that has it figured out. That's why you need to see the bigger picture. I sent some of my best assets to save your butt, general. Don't go all righteous on me. I'm all in," the general replies, with a bit of indignation and surprise that I would challenge his motives on his home turf.

I look to Rebecca. She has a great sense of character. I tend to trust everyone. She's more wary of people she doesn't know. She nods and smiles. She likes the man. That is good enough for me, that and the fact that I'm sure God has my back, God is leading everyone in this room.

"Okay, general, we're both all in. Now what? What is the bigger picture? How do we make sure we make it through the winter? How do we ensure stability wins over chaos?"

"The one-legged general gets right to the point. Stability over chaos. As I said, they want chaos. Then desperate people will gladly accept the martial law to bring back stability. They are a few elites who want to control the world. They've been pulling strings, manipulating markets, influencing elections around the globe for years. They're the ones who have the shielded SAT phones. They're the ones who built the massive bunkers. They're the ones who don't care if billions of people die. They're the ones who knew something bad would happen and planned to ride in as the saviors.

"The cost of salvation will be enslavement. Humanity will revert to a feudal system where the elite live in luxury and the plebeians will be enslaved. My people were enslaved for hundreds of years. Throughout human history, people of all races have been enslaved. The victor enslaving the defeated. But I believe in America and its founding principles of liberty. Mankind has never been freer and more prosperous than it has been in the past two hundred years. So 'they' must be defeated. Liberty must be defended."

"We're with you general. But what is the bigger picture?" I respond. "The major cities are in chaos, lost. We can't even approach Harrisburg, let alone a city like Atlanta or Chicago. Those hordes of people are flooding into the farmlands around them, where there is food.

"They're so desperate that they destroy the farms, like a horde of locust. Then they move on to the next farm. Meanwhile, violent fights break out between people who have found food and those still starving. The farmers are helpless against these masses of people. Even if the farmers could join together, you would have farmers fighting their fellow Americans. So how do we bring stability? Don't tell me your troops are going to fire on starving Americans to save the farmers. Your people won't do that. We've seen similar situations. The soldiers will walk away, despite the chaos that will ensue."

"Your assessment is very accurate, General Mays. The cities are in chaos. Unfortunately, at this point the only option I see is to avoid the chaos as much as possible. But your people have implemented a simple plan on a simple theory. America is an exporter of food. There is enough food to feed everyone. We need to quit fighting over the food and start cooperating on keeping the food safe and distributing the food fairly. That's easily said but not easily done.

"And then there are those who want to stop that from happening. There is no federal government right now. The attack on DC killed or maimed most of our leaders. The helos we sent your way saw that Camp David and Greenbriar were overrun and the vaunted Mount Weather was unearthed and rendered useless. There are a few places in the Midwest and the Rockies where elements of the federal government still exist. And there are still many civilian police forces allied with Army units that are trying to implement martial law."

"We have come across that," I state. "But we have been able to rally the local populace to rise up. The martial law forces fold as soon as they face real opposition. The problem is that organizing the opposition takes time and arms. Bottom line, martial law can be sent running."

"We're special ops, General, that's what we're trained to do. We have a mission to free the naval station at Charlestown. We're upending the martial law people every day. But you're right, it takes time. And meanwhile chaos reigns and people are dying."

"So, the third fleet is returning home?" I ask.

"The Third Fleet is off the coast of Charlestown right now; the Fifth Fleet is approaching Norfolk and the Ninth Fleet is trying to secure the San Diego Naval Station. The Ninth Fleet has given up on landing until the naval station can be secured. The naval station has been overrun and any approach by them has been met with hordes of people.

"The Third Fleet has committed to helping us. They've reconnoitered the mainland and have ignored orders from the elite. We have a full brigade heading to Charlestown. But their movement has been slow. We have been securing farms and recruiting people to lead a food drive. But this is a live food drive, moving cattle, pigs and chickens into the city. Most of the people have fled or already died. If we can bring livestock into town, with a few skilled people, we can start to turn things around.

"Couple that with the nuclear fired generators on some of those ships, along with their medical facilities. We can turn Charlestown around right quick, if properly supported. The Fifth Fleet commander is watching us, to see how it turns out."

"Sounds promising. But who is leading the elites? I know first-hand that many of them have been killed and their supposedly safe bunkers unearthed," I ask.

"Apparently Senator Shelley Clinton has laid claim as president. She's a niece of the well-connected political family that has run New England for many years and was not in DC at the time of the attacks. She has many loyal factions and the support of many military leaders. She's pulling the strings for the elite. She has unleashed the hit squads and has implemented the martial law decree. She's staying low key right now, but we think she will make a move to assume the presidency this spring, when no one will be strong enough to oppose her."

"Which is one of the reasons that she has hit squads out to take down any emerging leaders." I state thoughtfully.

"The commander of the Minot Air Force Base in North Dakota was killed yesterday. A Clinton loyalist was put in command. Several senior officers revolted. There is a battle raging on that base right now. Planes are being blown up so that they can't be used against American citizens. They've vowed to destroy the base and its assets rather than let it be used to impose martial law."

"Wow, that's a strong statement. How can we help you secure Charlestown Harbor? That seems to me to be a crucial step right now."

"I hear you give a rousing speech general. With your half leg you have credibility. I'm about to send another battalion to help secure Charlestown. Believe it or not, you're becoming well known. We couldn't believe that you took Letterkenny. And the fact that you've got the power turned back on in some towns, you're an inspiration."

"I tend to get a bit religious in my speeches. And I'll send them off with a prayer," I respond. "Christ is my savior and God provides me with my armor."

"Every man who has been under fire has talked to God. I like you and I trust you," General Mills responds.

* * *

Twelve hundred men and women, and their equipment and trucks are spread out across the large assembly area, ready to start their resupply and support mission to Charlestown. There are tradesmen, farmers, merchants, medical professionals and missionaries along with their military escort. General Mills quiets them as he mounts a small stage. "Thank you all for your attention and service at this time of need. Before you go out on this mission a special guest has been asked to give you a few words of encouragement. Please give a warm welcome to the commander of the Laurel Mountains Militia, General Mark Mays."

A smattering of applause starts along with a lot of buzz. As I hobble on to the stage the applause grows louder. I make my way to the center of the stage and toss one of my crutches aside as I grab the bullhorn. This act of self-determination brings the large crowd to its feet and they roar with approval. I nod and wave, waiting for them to quiet down.

As the crowd grows quiet, I begin my address. "You are a missionary force, not a military force. Remember that. Food, security, medical supplies, that is what will win the day. You cannot fight your way through the chaos. You must bring stability to the chaos. General Mills has farmers with herds of cattle, swine, and poultry ready to follow you into the city. Not just food for today, but the ability to breed more food. There are farm tractors full of grain and hay that you will be protecting so that the livestock can be fed and used to reproduce.

"The Bible says, 'Give a man a fish and he's fed for a day. Teach a man to fish and he's fed for a lifetime.' You're the protectors of those who will teach these people to feed themselves."

A thousand soldiers are sprawled across the large parade field. They're loaded and ready to head east. They know their mission and are ready to move. They sit quietly as I speak.

"My name is Mark Mays. I'm the elected general of the Laurel Highlands Militia. I got this here stump leg defending my family's farmstead. The guy who cut me is rotting with his anarchist followers on the lower end of my farm.

"That was two months ago. Since then we have gathered an army of veterans, reservists and Oath Keepers. People who hold your same values. We have secured our homeland in the Appalachian Mountains. You may have heard that through devine inspiration, we have also secured the massive Letterkenny arms depot. During that time, we have freed thousands of people from martial law. We have fought many battles and have come out victorious in most cases. We fight for freedom over tyranny. We fight for good over evil. We fight with Christ in our heart, seeking peace first. Always first reaching out with a hand of friendship to our foes. That is why escorting these farmers and their herds is so important. They're the hand of friendship.

"We have also started efforts to rebuild our society." I pause for a moment.

"If you have heard rumors that the power grid is being turned back on, those rumors are true. Where we bring stability, we try to reestablish the grid. It's slow going, but we have a team of engineers and technical people working to turn the power back on, one town at a time.

"You all can have that hope of bringing power back to your fellow Americans. The third fleet has several nuclear-powered ships. Once docked, those ships can be used to start to repower Charlestown. You literally can help bring light to a darkened city.

"While on this mission, you will come across chaos. Tough decisions will need to be made. Your mission is to defeat the chaos by bringing stability. There will be times that you will encounter people not interested in stability. They will only be interested in food. Feed them, calm their fears. Then teach them to feed themselves.

"When you meet evil, deal with evil forcefully. Do not allow evil to stop your mission. Your mission is to bring peace and stability. You may find at times that your mission will require force and violence. Realize that your mission is a good mission, a righteous mission.

"I ask you all now to turn your faces to the sky." As I say this, a break in the clouds brings sunlight beaming down on the parade grounds, warming the chill air.

I see the soldiers look up to the sky and the brief glimpse of sunshine. I look up too. "Dear Lord, have compassion on our nation. Clear a path for these soldiers that they may help bring stability to Charlestown. Grant these soldiers and the officers that lead them wisdom and compassion. I ask that Your light be in their hearts and that they bring light back to the city. May your hand guide each and every one on this mission. In Christ's name I do pray, Amen.

"Your mission is a mission of light." I say strong and clear across the hushed assemblage of men and women.

"Be that mission of light!" I say this strong and loud. It evokes cheers among the soldiers.

"Light! Light! Light!' starts to resound across the parade grounds followed by "USA! USA! USA!"

I hobble off the grandstand and glance at my wife. She has a tear in her eye as the cheers continue.

I look to General Mills as he gets ready to give his address to his men before they head out. He smiles broadly and gives me a thumbs up.

Chapter 4. Thanks Giving

The Farmstead

November 26th

The wind blows cold, driving a freezing rain. The tiny pellets tink against the windows. The sky has grown darker all day long as the temperatures dropped. The day before was clear and calm. The sky grinders had even managed to finish bringing down one last generator. But this night is bleak and cold, the winds howl, rattling the windows and causing the trees to sway violently. The freezing rain turns to snow and it begins to accumulate on the grass and cling to the trees.

Becca walks up behind me and hugs me warmly as I stare out the window. There is a dim light coming from the front house. Other than that, it's complete darkness. The usual warning lights on the radio towers are gone. The same with the flashing lights on the windmills. There is no glow on the horizon from Central City. There is nothing but the dark and the cold and the sleet and the snow.

"We're blessed, Mark. Come and join us. I need you to carve the turkey."

"I'll be there in a moment, dear," I respond absently.

She hugs me tighter. "Mark, you have done what you can. Thousands of homes across the region are filled with people eating a good meal in a warm house. Rejoice in what God has inspired you to do, inspired us all to do. Even Paul and Eve are enjoying the moment. You know they're missing their kids. But we have seen miraculous things accomplished over the past few months. We need to give thanks."

My mind lingers on the millions of people without food, without shelter, drifting through each day wondering if today will be the day they will die, maybe even wishing that today will be the day they die. And now winter is truly setting in. The suffering will be great. Our nation has lost millions of people already. With winter upon us, the death toll will rise exponentially. I can't wrap my mind around it. Millions of dead already, and tens of millions will be lost soon. The fight for survival will become more desperate. A chill runs up my spine. Bad times are coming. Why God? Why?

"You're thinking bad thoughts, Mark. I can see it on your face," Becca says. "We can't save everyone. Come, you have a family that misses you, that loves you." She grasps my hand and I follow her into the great room where our extended family and friends are gathered.

As we enter the crowded room, Brit comes bustling from the back porch. "Make way, make way," she hollers as she brings in a twenty-pound turkey roasted on our outdoor spit. "Mark, that one needs to rest for half an hour, but you can start carving the other one. Mom, Mom," she hollers. "Make sure the mashed potatoes are ready. Let's get ready to eat everybody! Ken, gather everyone up for grace."

Ken, a quiet man, tries to bring the large crowd under control. With our farm hands and security people there are over thirty people gathered, not counting those out on patrol.

Herq whistles loudly and the room goes quiet very quickly. "All yours Ken," he says, smiling.

Ken is a bit red faced but has the attention of us all. "As usual, kids and moms eat first. We have turkey and stuffing and gravy and all the fixins. Be sure to take your plates and silverware to the kitchen when you're done."

Ken looks to me. I nod as I want him to say grace.

After an awkward moment of silence, Ken speaks up. "It's Thanksgiving Day. Let's give thanks to God for our blessings. Father God, we thank You for food and shelter. We thank You for family and friends. But there are many tonight who don't have food and shelter, whose family and friends are sick or dying. Father God, we ask that you give them comfort. Father God, we pray that we can help those in need in any way we can. Inspire us, lead us, protect us. We're blessed Dear Lord and we thank you. We ask that we may spread those blessings. May the food we eat tonight nourish us that we may glorify your kingdom. In Christ's name we do pray. Amen"

"We should sing now," Paul states. He begins singing the doxology. "Praise God from whom all blessings flow. Praise Him all creatures here below." The rest of the room picks up on the familiar homily.

"Praise him above ye heavenly hosts. Praise Him Father, Son and Holy Ghost."

"We should sing another song," young Mark exclaims. "I know which one we should sing, see if you can guess it!"

The eight-year-old starts to belt out Jesus loves me. We all join in, smiling, singing loudly. "Jesus loves me, this I know…"

Brit clangs a spoon on an old pot as the song dies down. "The feast is ready people. Save room for dessert. We got pumpkin pie and apple crisp."

* * *

This feast is not the norm across the country. In the farm belts, far from the cities, similar feasts are being held. But along the East Coast and West Coast, outside of Atlanta, Chicago and other cities large and small, there is no feast. On this very day, tens of thousands perish from malnutrition and disease. Thousands more die to exposure to the cold and wet weather. The suffering has only just begun. Twenty-five percent of America's population has decreased due to lack of medication, violence, or starvation. That number will grow as the oncoming winter begins to grip the nation.

The southern part of the nation won't be hit as bad by the cold and the exposure. But as survivors move south, the violence will increase. The devastation wreaked upon the world by the despots and religious fanatics will have a severe toll on all of mankind. Meanwhile, the deer hunker down as usual, the bear go into hibernation, the coyotes and other scavengers are fattened, and cats and dogs go feral. Nature takes its course. The world will be a different place for those who survive the winter.

* * *

Hairy, with one of his biker recruits comes bustling through the door and stamps his feet, trying to shake off the wet and the cold. "It's a nasty night out their folks," he says as he sets his rifle down and begins shedding equipment and wet clothing. He looks through the doorway from the mudroom into the great room. "Quite a feast laid out I see. I told Larson and Rusty to come in out of the wet and cold. They should be here any minute. Who would attack us in this miserable weather?"

Daneel, our resident security chief over hears this comment. "You Fool! This is exactly the kind of weather that encourages an attack. They would already expect us to be lax due to the holiday. The bad weather is what they would hope for. That black ops team is still out there. They want the general and our team dead. We can't let up on our security, Hairy."

"Herq, Buck, Joe, gear up. It will be a long cold night." Daneel goes over the security detail making sure everything is covered including the ops room to monitor our security cameras.

As Larson, Rusty and the other guards come in the door, more people head out to replace them. Some of them are the

35

special ops people sent by General Mills; they smile and nod at the diligence of the security team. As they take up their positions and begin their patrols they often stop to look deep into the thick woods. Did they see movement? Did they hear a snapping twig?

Already an inch of snow covers the ground. The wind blows strong. The trees creek and snap. One of the special ops team presses deeper into the woods after hearing the snap of a branch that seemed out of place. He comes across boot prints in the snow, already partially covered. He and his team member begin to track the prints. But the snow begins to fall harder, and the winds blow stronger. The boot prints are lost in the quickly accumulating snow. The sergeant calls in this development over his local coms.

Grace, manning the operations center, acknowledges the report. In the great room of the farmstead, the day of Thanks Giving continues. Grace looks up for just a moment and thanks God. Then he returns his attention to the security cams displayed before him. All six screens show the heavy snow coming down. He shivers as he gobbles down a piece of pumpkin pie.

* * *

At Roxbury Park, just a half mile from Conemaugh Hospital in Johnstown, Alex, Jerry and the rest of the clan that volunteered to reclaim the city are having their own feast. They have much to be thankful for. Their dam and waterwheel have passed the brainiacs inspection. A generator will be arriving within the week.

Thanks to a turkey farm in southern Somerset County, thousands of turkeys have been made available across the free lands of the Appalachian Mountains. Over a hundred fresh turkeys were delivered to Letterkenny alone. Through Lucas's connections, three dozen turkeys are being roasted on open spits at Roxbury Park. Corn bread and apple crisp is being made in make shift outdoor ovens. A few specimens get burnt in the trial and error operation. Many pots of boiling water are brimming with potatoes to supply the required mashed potatoes. Thanks to the dairy farmers, butter is available in unlimited supplies.

Many large fire pits are well stoked to keep the several hundred people warm in the cold weather. Despite the cold and the snow, people congregate and celebrate. The Hassleriggs and Cashaws started this movement. But now more locals have joined in to reclaim the city. A crew of linesmen has already showed up to establish an isolated grid, and they take part in the Thanksgiving feast.

Lucas shows up again, just as dinner is to be served. He brings with him a few cases of Appalachian Clear and a few people who are now free of the Davidsville socialist. A local pastor says a blessing over the meal and the people line up to be fed. Despite the cold, snow and wind, there is joy in the air. Unannounced and unplanned, four people mount the stage of the large stone bandstand. One man has a fiddle, another has a guitar, a third has a garbage can that he skillfully uses as a drum. They begin to play up a storm of music. Their fourth compatriot is a woman and she provides the vocals.

By now over five hundred people occupy the park; despite the cold and the snow, they celebrate. They will soon have power, and their hospital will be partially reopened. They're reclaiming their city from anarchy and bedlam. Yes, many have died. Many more will die. But hope is growing. Where there was nothing but anarchy and starvation, now there is hope.

* * *

At a large modern farmhouse twenty miles west of Roanoke another 'feast' is being served. Two dozen people share a twelve-pound wild turkey that Dr. Gray shot the week before. Two rabbits supplement the meal. Katy has made a large rice dish and thanks to a local dairy farmer, they have lots of butter. They manage to feed everyone at their table. The bones will be used the next day to make soup.

After the meal has been eaten, Dr Gray confers with a few of his closest friends. "Something is going on people," He states. "We need to take control of this city. If things start to turn around, we don't want to be a city in chaos, passed over. We want to be a city in control, worth helping. I'm not sure what we can do, but right now, Roanoke is in chaos."

Many of the local militia leaders are present. Sam's plan is to somehow unite this group. He has no idea of how to do it. But he figures that getting them all in the same room would help or blow it all up.

One of the militia captains begins to speak. "We had a plan to stick together, to be ready for an event like this. We had a cohesive group. Somehow that all fell apart. Now we're a bunch of small groups trying to survive. I kicked some rogues out of my valley and the next day they raided a farm three miles away. If we were working together, that wouldn't have happened."

"So why aren't we working together?" Dr. Gray asks.

"Lack of communications is part of the problem," another militia leader states. "We got no way of knowing what's going on."

"We got CB radios for communications," Dr. Gray states. "That was protocol from way back when. I think it's that we don't communicate rather than that we can't communicate."

Katy has been listening quietly. Now she speaks up. "So, if a farm gets raided in your valley, you could let Hank know with your CB radios, but you don't. That's not lack of communication. That's lack of a will to communicate. What's going on here?"

The room goes silent and wary glances are exchanged.

Katy stands and looks between the two men. "What is going on? You two were the leaders of our militia. Hank, you're the one who sold us our AR15s." She turns her glare to George, the other militia leader. "You recruited us into this militia. You talked us into stock piling supplies. The rice dish we had tonight is from rice I stored and vacuumed packed, six years ago. Now that we need to be united, you're divided. What's going on? I demand an answer now!"

The two men look at each other. There is obvious discomfort. No one talks for several tense moments. Katy glares at the two men. They had painted a picture of unity as the militia would protect the community during a time of chaos. That time of chaos is upon them, and the disunity in the militia is part of the chaos.

Hank's wife breaks the cold silence. "Our daughter is pregnant with George's grandson."

Katy looks at the woman in disbelief. She looks at the two militia leaders. One is a well-established lawyer, the other the owner of a previously prosperous manufacturing company.

"And that has caused a problem?" Katy asks, dumbfounded. "They've been dating for two years."

"George doesn't want a mixed raced grandson," the lawyer's wife states. "He wants his grandson to be a black man."

"You have got to be kidding me!" Katy exclaims. She turns and faces the distinguished lawyer. "The world is crumbling around us and you, George, don't like what God has created. Out! Out of my house right now! I'll not tolerate that kind of bigotry. God has used the love of your daughter and Hank's son to create a new human being. Who are you to judge! Oh my Lord, please help us!" Katy exclaims as she begins to cry.

"George, you're a good man, how can you let this come between your families?" Dr. Gray asks. "This is not just about you. Our militia was strong. We could be helping thousands of people, but we're helpless because of your DNA preference?

George hangs his head. After a moment he looks up. "My daughter is smart. She would have ended up at an Ivy League School. I want those genes passed down to make more smart black men. It sounds racist, it sounds stupid. But I want my grandchildren to be black."

The room is in stunned silence for several moments.

Dr. Gray is the first to speak. "George, don't leave. My wife is angry, and I understand that, but anger won't solve this problem. You're a lawyer, George. You think things through, so follow my logic. Your DNA is not being diluted, it's being amplified. Mixed race children are more and more common place. You know that. In less than a hundred years almost all people will be of mixed race. You're part of that now. Don't push it aside, embrace it."

George, with his head in his hands, his wife sitting next to him, begins to cry. "I just love black people," he says through his tears. "I love my brothers. I wanted my daughter to love a Black man. But that didn't happen. Now I have let my own ambitions for my daughter wreck our militia. Everything we planned to prevent I have let happen, due to my selfish desires."

He stands and walks across the room. "Hank, I've been an ass. Our grandbaby will be a beautiful child. Your son is a good man. I've known that all along. I have been struggling with this, but I have to put those struggles behind me."

Hank stands and slaps George across the face. George steps back.

"That's for insulting me and my son, and for letting our militia fall apart. I ought to take you outside, but you'd probably kick my ass." Hank smiles and opens his arms wide. George, a bit shaken, steps in and wraps his old friend in a big hug. Hank whispers in his ear, "We'll have beautiful grandkids my friend, beautiful children.'

Trying not to sob, George says, "I know, my friend, I know. Now let's make sure they have a future. Let's get our militia working again. I feel what Sam feels. Something is happening and we want to be part of it."

* * *

In Asbury Park, New Jersey, four people walk aimlessly down a residential road; two adults and two children. It's a miracle that they're still alive. They survived by using common sense. They had some food stored and they figured out ways to collect water. The father joined in with a local militia that basically forced their neighbors from their homes and took any food they had. For several weeks, that kept his family fed.

He did not feel good about what he was doing, but being part of the gang kept his family alive. But soon the raided food began to run out. The gang turned on each other. He fled with his family and a few possessions. They've been wandering the dangerous streets for several weeks, hunkering down at times, moving on when things got too dangerous, too chaotic. Cats, dogs, even rats and pigeons have kept them alive. He thinks that today may be Thanksgiving Day, but he's not sure. It doesn't matter, what do they have to be thankful for? They're homeless, starving. Maybe they might come across a rouge dog that he could kill for a big meal. Maybe a collie, or even just a beagle.

But the dogs are very wary now, they travel in packs and get aggressive. They're hunters too. The last time he killed a dog, he had to fight off two other dogs to claim the meat. That was four

41

days ago. He and his family have not eaten in two days. Two months ago, he was slightly overweight at five foot ten and two hundred and twenty pounds. Now he's skin and bones, his excess skin sagging where there once was fat and muscle.

They stop for a minute to rest. They have no destination. They only have a quest, find food. He looks at his family, gaunt, shriveled, dirty. Why him? He asks inwardly. Why did this happen? He was not raised in the church. He does not know God. It does not even occur to him to ask these questions to God. He asks these questions to the cosmos. The cosmos has no answer.

It begins to rain. He knows his family won't survive in the cold and wet. He rallies them to a nearby house. The doors and windows have been broken, but they can get out of the wind and the rain. He uses what little strength he has left to rig up a system to collect the rainwater from the downspouts. His wife searches the home and finds good quilts and bedding. The four refugees go to sleep tired and hungry. They're suffering, but they're alive; for now.

* * *

Across the country, similar scenes play out. In some cases they run into hoodlums who kill them on the spot for whatever measly possessions they might have. In another situation a family might kill a dog or a cat and feast on the roasted meat. In a few situations, the father gives up, and three murders and a suicide take place.

Even in the countryside where food is plentiful, the situation is grim. The millions of people who have fled the cities fight over every chicken, pig and cow. In their desperation, they rape the farms, fight over the farms. Food providing animals are killed in the skirmishes fought to control a farm. One day the refugees feast. For two days they eat well. Then another, stronger more desperate group of refugees comes roaring in. More people die. More farm animals get killed. Crops get trampled on, unharvested. And by now, the animals themselves are starting to starve because the farmers have been killed or run off their lands.

In a few places, like the Laurel Highlands, the value of the farms is understood. They protect the farms. But that takes place far from the population centers, in the farm belt of middle America. But without a viable transportation system to get the food to the cities, they sit on a cornucopia of food while millions starve.

While a family is starving to death in Ashbury Park, New Jersey, a farmer outside of Peoria, Illinois must let thousands of turkeys go free range. He can no longer feed them all. His family feasts on turkey on this Thanksgiving Day, as do all his neighbors.

The suffering can only escalate as winter sets in.

Chapter 5. The Navy

Charlestown

December 7th

It takes four powerful tugboats to dock an aircraft carrier. The massive ship can get close to the pier, but the powerful harbor boats are needed to position the nearly one-thousand-foot-long ship into its final mooring station. In the past decades, those tugs have become highly computerized and very complex. With just a few old harbor tugs, it takes two hours to secure the massive ship to its moorings.

A gang plank is secured, and Admiral Van Hollern walks ashore. It's a new America and he knows it. He's met by General Mills, the commanding officer of the 82nd Air Born Division. They exchange salutes.

"Welcome home admiral," General Mills states, smiling.

"Glad to be on dry ground, general. I've never had to wait for a port to be secured. This is all new territory to me. Update me on the situation."

"Chaos, admiral, mainly chaos. As you know, there is no governing authority left. The succession of leadership is gone. Most of our civilian leadership in D.C. died in the initial attack. I have confirmed reports that Mount Weather, Green Briar and Camp David have all been compromised.

"So, who's governing the country? Who do we report to?" The admiral asks.

"The last orders that came out were to implement martial law. Those orders came from Senator Clinton, who is claiming leadership of the country, as you know. But what claim does she have? And martial law is stifling recovery rather than helping it. Martial law pits us against the citizens we're sworn to protect. I can't ask my troops to fire on innocent civilians. I can ask them to stop the tyranny and chaos. But I can't have them implement martial law."

"I agree, general. We were asked by forces allied with Senator Clinton to launch missions against you and areas in the Appalachian Mountains, as well as targets in Texas and Nebraska. Texas and Nebraska are out of our range without refueling capacities, which we have not brought back on line yet. But why do they want us to attack you? And why attack some rural lands in western Pennsylvania?"

"The one legged general really has got their attention," General Mills muses, thinking out loud.

"Who's this one legged general?" the admiral asks. "Why are they after him?"

General Mills focuses back on Admiral Van Hollern. "There's a quirky guy leading a bunch of Oath Keepers and veterans up in Western Pennsylvania. They managed to take control of Letterkenny Arms Depot. Since then, he and his group of freedom fighters have carved out a large swath of land that they call the area of stability."

"I've heard rumor of this guy," the admiral states. "General Mays of the Laurel Highlands Militia. He's been mentioned on the ham networks. But that's all fairy tales, right? Who takes over an arms compound like Letterkenny?"

"Well, if he's a fairytale, then I'm a leprechaun. I had lunch with him and his wife last week. Your fleet is docked here, and safe, due in large part to him and his people and the recommendations they made. They recommended we recruit farmers and use their herds to supply the city as our way to move in and secure the port. He and his wife pointed out that the quantity of food is not the problem. The problem is how to get the food to the people."

45

"Well, that's smart, that was a good move."

"He also recommended that the nuclear reactors on your ships could be used to start to repower the city, especially the hospital."

"Now that's nuts. Our power plants are not like a nuclear reactor on land. We can't power up a city like Charlestown."

"Using the model that the one-legged fairytale suggested, we have line crews working right now to establish small grids. Engineers are working out load capacities and limits. Within a few days they should have several isolated grids established."

Admiral Van Hollern pauses for a second as his engineering mind churns through what he's been told. "Seriously? Confined grids? That's brilliant! That could work. We can't fire up the whole city, but we can fire up parts of it. That's a great idea, general."

"They've been doing it for a month in the Appalachian free lands. They take generators off the tops of windmills and then power them with watermills. They've been turning on the power in small towns using the same technique."

"Now I call that bullshit," the Admiral states reflexively. "You're telling me you got some hillbillies turning on the power using water wheels and reclaimed windmill generators?"

"It's not bullshit. What I say is true. General Mays has recruited what he calls his Brainiac squad. It's a bunch of engineers and technicians dedicated to bringing things back on line, like water and sanitation systems. And the power grid, in small steps. My people have seen first-hand what they've done. I have three sky crane helicopters still operational. I have a crew getting ready to deploy to Johnstown to assist in bringing down and moving the generators. There are hundreds of them clustered across the ridges. Right now, they're using a reclaimed trellis crane and literally horse drawn wagons and farm tractors to bring down and move the generators. One of my brigade commanders was there. He'll give you a full briefing.

"This all is happening, it's real. And the forces against us are real too, admiral. You were asked to attack us. You were asked to attack your fellow soldiers. That is wrong. If I can prove what I say, will you commit to us? There is an alternative to martial law. We can help rebuild a stable and free America."

Admiral Van Hollern is a true patriot and a very intelligent man. A Commandants List Graduate of the naval academy he also has a master's degree in engineering from the University of Maryland. He had to play the political game to rise to his current position. But he always had a deep-felt resentment that he had to kiss the butt of his commanders and the politicians if he wanted to rise in command.

Today, there is no command. He's the Admiral of a fleet more powerful than any military on earth. He can be a king maker. Or he can be a king. Why submit or ally with these plebes? Why not just unleash his power? He could take out Letterkenny in one sortie. He could decimate Fort Bragg within a few days.

But that would not be right. He already has ignored commands to attack his fellow men-at-arms and the citizens of his country. He's very well versed in the intestinal fortitude that it takes to lead men in wartime. His people have launched strikes against Syria, Pakistan and Libya. As a flight commander he led attacks against Iraq and ISIS. And most recently, his fleet launched the nuclear strikes that decimated Iran after the EMP attacks. Nuclear holocaust was almost unleashed against Russia and China as well. He was part of the command group that helped bring the world down from nuclear annihilation.

Which is part of the reason he refused orders to attack unknown targets in America. He couldn't see how attacking anyone in America would help stop the chaos. He chose his own route. By talking with General Mills through their secure communications, he has now arrived on shore to make his own determination of how he can uphold his sworn oath to defend the Constitution.

"Let's get airborne general. I need a bird's eye view of the situation on the ground. You ever done a catapult takeoff from a carrier?"

* * *

The heart pounding rush of the catapult launch is almost too much for even General Mills, who has jumped out of planes from thirty thousand feet and repelled from helicopters into hot landing zones. Admiral Van Hollern kept up his flight credentials through the years. His last combat mission was only six years ago. With two wing men, he and General Mills begin a fly-over of the east coast.

The first thing they notice is the fires. Even after two months, fires still burn. But not in the cities, those fires have burned out. Now the fires are in the countryside. They're fires of chaos as people fight over food and shelter. As they quickly pass over Myrtle Beach, they see it's mainly vacated. Half of the resort town is burned down. But the small harbor remains functional and there is activity. Fishing has replaced tourism as the main industry for the few remaining residents.

Soon they see the chaos around Richmond. The farmlands are a battle zone. Even from ten thousand feet they can see a large group of people rush a well defended farm. They see the two groups of people engage in hand to hand combat with shovels and boards as weapons. The scene is shocking as some can barely walk, but they continue to press the fight. No word is spoken as they fly over the chaotic scene.

To the east they can see the pickets of the fifth fleet, hoping to gain harbor in Newport News. Two F16s fly nearby. "Don't worry, general. I sent word to them of our flight path," the admiral states. "They're just saying hello, letting us know they're still here."

Next up the coast is Washington DC. The chaos in the rural lands is repeated. But what they see when they fly over the capital turns their stomachs. It was reported that a nuclear bomb had detonated on a yatch or barge in the Anacostia River near the National Mall.

That looks to be true. The National Mall and all the buildings around it are leveled. The capital building is only recognizable because of the large steps leading up to the rubble that used to be the seat of government. The bases of the pillars that made up the porch of the Whitehouse can be seen through the debris. The stones of the Washington Monument and the Lincoln Memorial lay in a distinct pattern radiating from ground zero. Anyone not in a bunker would not have survived. There was no warning of the attack. No one was in a bunker. No one survived.

"Sons-a-bitches decapitated us," the admiral states, a tear forming in the corner of his eye as he takes in the devastation. "I've heard it was bad but seeing is believing. Our capital has been destroyed. Let's turn west, toward Weather Mountain. That's where my orders to launch nuclear strikes against Iran came from."

"My people say it's been compromised," General Mills responds.

Within minutes after turning west, the Blue Ridge Mountains come into view. Their flight makes a slow circle around Mount Weather. "The place is unearthed," the admiral states in quiet disbelieve as he takes in the massive destruction. His mood turns sour. "Is this the work of this Mays guy?" he states angrily. "If so, I'll have ten sorties flying on him tonight."

"Keep calm, admiral," General Mills responds. "Anarchists, survivalists did this. It will be detailed in your briefing. From what my people told me, the Laurel Highlands Militia defeated the people who did this when they moved into the Shenandoah Valley. Look to the east, Winchester is part of their area of stability."

Sure enough, as they fly over the valleys and ridges of the eastern reaches of the Appalachian Mountains, they notice much less chaos. There are very few fires and no major groups of people fighting each other. They pass over Winchester.

"That's a military occupation at the hospital," the admiral states.

"Those must be Oath Keepers, General Mays' troops. Notice the mess station and the herd of cattle grazing nearby. Look to the west, there's a convoy coming, ten farm tractors hauling goods. Do you see that admiral?"

"I do," Admiral Van Hollern replies slowly, as he takes in the scene. "They have pickets spread out far into the farmlands. They're hard to see, but they're there. And the airport is fully defended."

"They secured the airport to refuel the birds I sent this way a few weeks ago," the general responds. "They have this whole valley secured. A very fertile valley. Just look at the beauty of those rolling hills. Next spring those valleys will be lush and green; food producing dynamos."

The admiral's mind quickly assesses what he has seen. He realizes the stark contrast between the chaos on the coastal plains and the stability he sees below him. He knows what he needs to do. "Let's fly north, general, over the 'free lands."

"That's okay with me. I would have suggested it. Are we good on fuel?"

"We're good. We'll gain altitude and straight-line for Fort Brag when we're done."

The sun is setting as the flight turns north. In just a few minutes they're flying over the Stoneycreek River valley.

"Son-of-a-bitch" the two men say almost simultaneously. Darkness envelopes them, The entire horizon is dark, other than obvious fires burning from the chaos. But they see pinpricks of light emerge. Not vast swaths of light. Just points of light in distinct patterns, distinct man-made patterns.

"They have power," the admiral states. "Your man did turn the power back on. I'll be damned."

General Mills looks at the pin pricks of light shining from below. A tear forms in the corner of his eye. His people had told him this was happening, but to see it, the joy of hope cannot be suppressed, even in a hardened man like General Mills.

He chokes back his tears. "Never underestimate the American spirit to survive."

Chapter 6, On The Map

Laurel Highlands

December 8th

The bacon has been cooked and the eggs crackle and hiss on the hot pan. Several tins of corn muffins are set on the counter, ready to be served. The morning kitchen crew has been up since five getting ready to feed the dozens of people that keep the Mays' farmstead working and secure.

The first to be fed is the security detail that will be heading out to replace the overnight shift. A mixed group of Special Forces, local vets and some of Mark's own people make up each security shift. Some will take up secured locations, others will walk the perimeter of the farm and the neighboring woods.

As the security detail heads out the door, the farm hands come in for their meal. These are the men and women who keep the farm running. Even on this early winter day much needs to be done. Their small herds of steers, dairy cows, hogs, chickens and ducks will need fed and tended to. Firewood is still being stockpiled for the winter. Fences need checked and mended, coops and stalls cleaned out, the list goes on. Mark and Rebecca have learned a lot about the ongoing maintenance and chores that need to be done to keep a farm running. Rebecca has organized the operation well. Every day brings a new challenge, but they find ways to continue on.

As the farm hands head out, the overnight security detail comes in. After stowing their gear, they warm up in front of the fireplace. Leesa, Herc's wife, brings them their meals. Then the best part of the morning happens. Rebecca's grandchildren and the other children supported by the farmstead come in for breakfast. Some are grumpy and sleepy. Some are talkative and energetic. Soon they will all walk to the front house to have school. It brings her joy to see them all healthy and active. She has seen enough of the chaos to know that they're truly blessed.

* * *

I emerge from my office, which is also our command and communications center. "Been smelling this awesome breakfast for two hours now. Let's eat." I sit next to my wife as the kids settle in around the large table. They all know not to start eating until we pray.

"Shawn Jr., will you say grace this morning?" I ask Herc's seven-year-old son.

He nods, "Okay, Mark." He bows his head. "Dear God, keep my daddy and mommy safe. Keep us all safe. And make the bad people go away so we can always be safe. Amen." He looks up. "Was that good?"

"That was great Shawn," Leesa responds, as she brings over plates of food. "Do you have all your homework ready for school today?"

"Yes, Mom, you know I do," Shawn junior responds.

The conversation turns to homework and school and the upcoming big math test. No talk of soldiers, chaos, or security details. I enjoy the break from what has become my normal routine. As soon as breakfast is over, I'll be mired in the latest developments and seeking more ways to help stop the chaos that envelopes our world.

Thirty minutes later, I kiss my wife goodbye. "I got to go to the headquarters at the American Legion in town. That fly over last night was General Mills with this Admiral Van Hollern. I may end up needing to meet with Dan Farmer to use his secure phone. I'll be back by dinner time."

Becca gives me a disappointed look, she hates me being away from the family and the farm. But she knows the work I'm doing, she knows that our people are helping to bring about good things. She hugs me. "Don't do anything stupid," she says with a smile and a quick kiss.

Six of us gear up and load into our old Econoline van and an old hummer with an M60 mounted to its roll bar. Fifteen minutes later we're at the American Legion.

I'm met by Colonel Fisher, my Executive Officer, and Lieutenant Anders, my intelligence and communications officer. Before they can start with questions, I cut them off. "Staff meeting in the conference room in fifteen minutes. Is Major Jeffers around? I want him there too, or his XO."

I turn to my grandson, Larson, part of my security detail. "Get our vehicles topped off and be ready for a trip to Somerset or Bakersville. If you see that sweet young girl with the cheese, get a few pounds for us. But be quick about it."

He stands tall and salutes. "Yes sir," he says smiling. "I'll make sure to pick up some good cheese." He and my two security shadows head off to carry out their orders.

Our staff meeting is brief. It's confirmed that the fly over the previous evening was by General Mills and Admiral Van Hollern. It's also confirmed that they flew over Winchester and Mount Weather. I have Lieutenant Anders relay a message to Dan Farmer that I want to meet with him in Somerset at noon. We only have one secure satellite phone. Dan is our man in the know. He has set up a communications monitoring system utilizing ham radios and this prized hardened and secure sat-phone.

Lt. Anders is a former Lt. Colonel in the regular army. He's a West Point graduate and had formerly specialized in cyber security. Since joining our militia, he has been helping us build a communications system. Local communications are by CB radio and relay stations. We use ham radios when needed but avoid their use for security reasons. His work has been essential to our mission. With our militia allying with stronger forces, his position needs to be elevated.

"Tell me Anders," I say, "How are the wife and kids doing?"

"Adjusting, general, adjusting. The wife is helping at the new school in town, and both kids are happy to be going there. But sharing an old three-bedroom house with another family, that's a major adjustment. I'm not complaining, but it's a big change from our McMansion."

"Is the heating system working? Can you keep the house warm enough?" I ask. Heating homes is one of our biggest concerns. A major part of getting the windmill generators operating was to provide power for heating systems. A house could have an operational coal or oil-fired furnace, but with no way to turn the pumps or blowers, the heating system is useless. By bringing down the windmill generators and turning them with the consistent power of a water wheel, we have brought vital heat to thousands of homes.

But the closest generator is miles away. The little town of Central City was not incorporated in the isolated grid that it powers. Two five thousand-watt generators have been hauled back from Letterkenny to power the bare essentials in town. Any house outside of town is on their own. This has brought about the doubling up of families in homes that have heat.

"Our quarters have electricity with an oil burner. So we have heat, sir." He replies. "We have to cook outside over a fire pit, and that is tough with winter setting in. Me and the homeowner are helping to tear down an abandoned house so we can use the salvaged wood to enclose our outdoor kitchen."

"Good to hear that you're making do." I state. "We have scavenger teams searching abandoned homes and siphoning heating oil. That's a long-term problem we're working on."

I turn to Jerry Devers, a local vet, church deacon, and very resourceful man. "Captain Devers, get two men over to Major Anders' house and get this outdoor kitchen made."

The newly promoted communications officer looks at me a bit sideways. "Major Anders?" he asks.

"Our team is growing; your team is growing. You're going to be dealing with other staff level officers. Besides, you've earned it, Major. Promote your three best men to lieutenants and fill out a company. The pay is the same. Help protect the farmers and the community, and you will be fed. That's the best I can offer right now."

The middle-aged man stands proudly and salutes. "Promotion gladly accepted sir."

"Major Anders, I expect we're going to be upgrading our comms soon. You will be coordinating with General Mills' people and Admiral Van Holern's people. Hell, I might have to promote you to Colonel. You'd be back to your former rank."

"Since you're going to get my wife an outdoor kitchen, again, I accept the new position and responsibilities general," Major Anders replies with a smile. "You didn't need to bribe me with the outdoor kitchen, general. You know how I feel about what we're doing."

"It wasn't a bribe, major. I can't have you tearing down an abandoned house to build a kitchen when we need you here. I need you to find a building here in town to turn into a new communications center."

The major smiles. "About time, general. That basement store room don't cut it anymore. There's an abandoned hardware store just across the railroad tracks. We'll start cleaning it up today."

"You got twenty minutes to get it going, because you're coming with me to meet with Dan in Somerset."

The meeting breaks up quickly as people have things to do. One of the Special Forces guards turns to one of the Oath Keeper guards. "That was quick. No pissing matches, just get done what needs done. I like what I see. I ain't never seen a staff meeting go so fast."

* * *

Our four trucks roll into Somerset. Colonel Fisher, Colonel Brit, Major Anders, Captain Mathews and I walk into Dan Farmer's intelligence gathering complex. This is where the thousands of notes that are jotted down from our ham radio monitors are turned into useful information.

Dan smiles warmly as he greets us all by name. We all settle into a large conference room, dimly lit by recessed LED lighting.

"So, Dan, we had a flyover last night," I start. "I assume the third fleet has made anchorage in Charlestown and that was a reconnoitering mission."

"Correct, Mark," he says smiling. "More importantly, General Mills and Admiral Van Hollern flew the recon mission. I've verified that. But now, unfortunately, we're famous. Listen to this." He hits the play button on an old cassette recorder.

"Jumping Jeffy reporting once again. Hey all you preppers and survivalists. I mentioned before that something was happening

57

in the mountains of Pennsylvania. I can confirm that it's real. Now follow me on this. It gets complicated

"I told you that the 82nd Airborne Division forced their way into the Charlestown Naval yards. That happened after reports that three armed transport helicopters were seen flying into and around Western Pennsylvania from Fort Bragg. Those three helicopters have been operating in Western Pennsylvania since then. That says something folks. Fort Bragg wouldn't give up three operational helicopters for no reason.

"I also reported two weeks ago that there are black ops people trying to assassinate freedom fighter leaders. Well, there is a freedom fighter leading what they call the Laurel Highlands Militia in Western Pennsylvania. The guy's name is Mays, and from reports we have received, the guy lost a leg fighting anarchists. This Mays guy is on the hit list.

"Do you believe that? Some Podunk militia leader is on the elitist's hit list? Makes me think he has something going on that the elites don't like. This Mays guy making the hit list makes me like him.

"So yesterday it was confirmed that the USS George Bush laid anchor in Charlestown harbor. Late in the day a flight took off from the decks of the aircraft carrier and headed north. I have several ham radio reports that the flight flew north over DC and then headed west, over Mount Weather and then over the areas that this one-legged general controls.

"The very first flight from this powerful naval unit didn't fly over Atlanta, or Charlotte, or Miami. It flew over DC, then the mountains of Western Pennsylvania. Keep an ear out for what you hear from Western Pennsylvania.

"I'll add this commentary. Western PA is a black zone. I have ham operators feeding me information from across the country. But Western PA broadcasts rarely, briefly and cryptically.

And keep in mind, it was reported that an arms depot in that area was taken over by a militia. It could all be related.

"Now on to other news. Praise God, we have reports that parts of Idaho have established power, as well as small cities in Iowa, Nebraska and Texas.

Dan turns off the recorder.

"Makes no difference," Brit states. "We knew we would become a target and a destination. As Mark said a month ago, we have the mountains to protect us. There is already six inches of snow on the ridges. The masses will try to hunker down where they are. If they run out of food, then they may try to come over the mountains. It's a nonissue as far as the refugees are concerned."

"But it might bring other militias this way," Colonel Fisher states. "We need to consider that."

"That's a good point," I state. "Captain Regis and Captain Albright as well as General Adkins' people need to be informed that likeminded militias may be heading our way."

"Or opposing militias." Major Jeffers states. "But overall, it does not change our stance. The more important thing is that the admiral chose to lead the flight. Van Hollern is a hands-on guy. I deployed to some sketchy areas under his command. I never met the guy, but his people always gave us solid support. I'm sure General Mills had some influence on the mission. But the fact that we got checked out is definitely significant."

"Dan, have you heard back from General Mills?" I ask.

"He told me to get in touch with him about now. We'll give him a call." Dan pulls out the secure phone and dials up General Mills.

A few seconds later the phone is answered. "Dan, how are things in the mountains? Hope our flyover didn't get you all roiled up."

"It's not every day, even before the attacks, that three F18's fly over the Laurel Highlands. So yeah, you got things roiled up. Mark and his staff are with me right now. Can we talk?"

"Fire away, my friend. My XO and Admiral Van Hollern's Flight Officer are with me, so this should be good."

"Well, that confirms that the fleet has arrived in Charlestown harbor and you all have hooked up," Dan states. "How was it getting into Charlestown?"

"Yes, the aircraft carrier George H. W. Bush has anchored in the harbor and its attending boats are there too. Getting into the city was a chore. The advice Mark gave us about bringing along the farmers and their crops took us a while to adjust into our mission. But once we figured out the mind set of bringing salvation not oppression, things happened quickly. We now have a wide path of cooperation between the farmers, the refugees and the army."

"Good to hear my advice was helpful," I chime in. "What about involving the churches in helping bring civility to the areas you have liberated?"

"They're fully engaged, general. In fact, our movement wasn't going well until we started engaging with people of faith. Their attitude and willingness to help changed everything."

"I knew they would be helpful. They're more key than you know," I respond. "What about the fly over? A heads up would have been nice. I assume the admiral wanted to get a report from his own people as to what's happening on the ground."

"Well Mark, the admiral himself flew that mission. I was in the gunner's seat with him. It was an impromptu mission. I guess he wanted to see things for himself. What we saw confirmed what we have heard and what you've told us. It's chaos across the country, Mark. Our government has been decapitated, rendered useless.

"We flew up the coast to D.C. It's leveled. The Vice President was at the Pentagon when a nuke detonated, probably on a yatch or barge in the Anacostia River. The Pentagon, the Capital Building, the White House, they were leveled. The Washington Monument and The Lincoln Memorial are piles of stones strewn across the National Mall. That nuke probably wiped out ninety percent of our elected leaders and most of the top levels of government."

"Knocking out our electrical grid wasn't enough. They knocked out the leadership that could have helped us rebuild," Colonel Fisher states.

"But they couldn't knock out the American spirit," I reply.

"No, they couldn't," states the admiral's flight officer, Captain Dravis. "After we flew over D.C. we headed west. We flew over Letterkenny and confirmed it's in control of Oath Keepers. Then we scouted Mount Weather and confirmed your reports that it had been compromised, unearthed really. Finally, we flew over Winchester before heading farther north."

"The Shenandoah Valley looked far different than the coastal plains. We saw more of the Oath Keepers there. Things looked much more stable. It was getting dark as we crossed the Mason Dixon line. But the admiral wanted a first-hand look at your area of control. General Mills is asking us to ally with you, we wanted to know why.

"I'll tell you what, General Mays," Colonel Dravis continues. "It was inspiring. In the vast stretches of darkness, we could see lights in the towns of the areas you control. The admiral did not believe this windmill generator conversion story. But after seeing the lights in your remote mountain towns, he's a believer."

Major Jeffers speaks up. "Captain Dravis, this is Major Jeffers responding. We met before, on a mission that you supported into Pakistan. I want to clarify something. You talk of the Oath Keepers in Winchester and Letterkenny as if they're independent of the Laurel Highlands Militia. You need to know that they're organized, supported and led by General Mays and his staff. Those soldiers are loyal members of his militia. What you scouted is the results of his leadership. I want to make sure you understand that."

Things go quiet on both ends of the conversation for a few moments. Major Jeffers knows how the slightest inference can change a situation. He knows that Captain Dravis was trying to downplay our significance in what has happened. That could lead to us being pushed aside as decision makers, 'players', in the future. All these thoughts run through my head during this lull in the conversation.

I speak up. "I almost wish I wasn't the guy leading this militia, captain. Then I wouldn't have a black ops team targeting me. But Major Jeffers is right. General Mills, you can confirm that both the Letterkenny and the Winchester missions are Laurel Mountains Militia operations."

We hear General Mills address Captain Dravis. "You need to know, the admiral needs to know, that General Mays and his people came up with the Letterkenny operation and the move into the Shenandoah Valley long before we allied with them. Not only that, they initiated the talks with us that led to us opening Charlestown Harbor. In many ways, you have a safe harbor due to the Laurel Highlands Militia."

Captain Dravis' little powerplay has been halted before it could get any traction. Truth and loyalty have trumped an attempt at deceit.

"I was unaware of the general's influence on these events," The captain says humbly. "I'll make sure the admiral is aware of the influence of your militia.""

"I hope so," Major Jeffers responds pointedly. "This militia deserves credit for what it has done."

Dan speaks up at this point. "Okay folks, I'm glad we hashed that out. Now we need to move forward. Captain Dravis, I know we're an unknown entity. We're hoping that after seeing what we have done, our offer of alliance would be more appealing to you. America is in chaos. It will take leadership, strength and compassion to restore our country, restore stability. The third fleet can help bring all those things to the table. If we break down into warring factions, America falls. If we unite, there is the chance that we survive. That is the message we want you to deliver to Admiral Van Holern."

"And what would the third fleet be committing too?" Captain Dravis asks.

"Support us in securing the farmlands first." Dan states. "The farms are the key to survival. Second would be to help us defeat martial law. This may require your people fighting other soldiers. It may even pit you against the fifth fleet outside of Newport News."

"We would not fight our brothers in the fifth fleet," Captain Dravis states definitively.

"Good to hear;" I state. "They were ordered to attack us, just as you were. They refused to attack American civilians just trying to survive. But there are elites ordering our execution. What if the Fifth Fleet begins following the orders of martial law?"

"By law and tradition, United States Military do not execute combat missions in the homeland. The martial law decrees need to be implemented without our assistance," The executive officer of the third fleet states. "If the fifth fleet is ordered to attack the homeland, I would hope that they ignore those orders as unconstitutional."

"It would only take a half dozen planes from the deck of the USS Ronald Reagan to wipe out everything we have accomplished." I state. "There are confirmed reports over the ham radio that the ninth fleet, off the coast of San Diego, has laid precision attacks on the homeland. Our fear is real, Captain Dravis. There is someone out there that does not want us to rebuild. Someone who wants us to remain in chaos."

"I understand your concerns, General Mays," Captain Dravis states. "I cannot commit the third fleet to your defense at this time. I assure you, we do not view you as a threat. I'll bring all of this to the admiral's attention. We understand the gravity of the situation."

Chapter 7, A Great Loss

Central City

December 10th

Over the past three months, the loss of life has been numbing to the mind and the soul. Good people have died. The elderly, the sick and the most vulnerable to disease have perished at an alarming rate. Everyone in the community has buried a family member, friend or neighbor.

Many times, a proper burial in a graveyard is performed. More often, a hole is dug in a back yard or remote farm plot and an impromptu service is held, with only a handmade wooden cross marking the grave. Work crews have been formed to dig graves, with the expectation that they will be compensated with food for themselves and their family. It's a grim task, but dozens of people make a living as grave diggers.

Some of the deceased get a wooden coffin. Most are just wrapped in a sheet. In some instances, the bodies are laid bare into the earth. Everyone knows to keep the graves on high ground. The disease of a decaying body close to a water source is well known. It's the reason for some of the burials.

Today, another funeral is being held. This is not an impromptu service on a remote farm. This funeral is being held at the VFW in Central City. The funeral is not attended by any family members of the deceased. He has no family members, no descendants.

But over two hundred people attend the ceremony. I'm one of them, along with my wife and most of our family. A man who knew me, probably better than I knew myself, is being laid to rest. A man who poked and prodded us to do the right thing finally succumbed to the cancer that attacked his body.

We lay the body of the Commander to rest in a solemn ceremony. A Vietnam War veteran with a silver star for heroism and three purple hearts is given a full military honors burial. He fought for his country honorably, only to be defamed and ridiculed on his return. I don't know if he knew Christ. I pray that he did. He was a good man. I hope to see him again. The world needs more honorable people like the Commander.

Chapter 8, More Chaos

Kankakee, IL

December 14th

The construction site fifty miles south of Chicago has been vacant for three months. The bountiful supplies have now been discovered. At first, a few survivors pilfered what they needed to help secure their homes against the weather and the ruffians that roamed their rural neighborhood. Now, open warfare has erupted around the construction site.

As the winter winds start to sweep down from Canada, the need to secure warm quarters begins to be of prime importance. The stockpile of building materials becomes a target of the survivors. A group of locals, who have survived by trading scavenged goods and labor with some of the local farmers, have used this construction site for supplies. They have a loose control of the area.

Today, the construction site becomes a war zone. A militia scout from Momence, twenty miles to the east found the site three days ago. She had been looking for abandoned or distressed farms that her people could raid. After finding the vacant construction site, she quickly pedaled back to her hometown. She reported to her bosses what she discovered; a raiding party was quickly established. They scavenged fuel to fill up their few running farm trucks, tractors and vintage vehicles. They will loot anything they can to insulate and secure their homes.

They left their compound before sun up. It's a mixed group of locals and refugees. They have a few vets and national guardsmen in their thirty-man crew. The scout had reported that the site was vacant, so the scavengers don't expect a fight. But they travel well-armed. They have dealt with bands of road warriors and desperate refugees often enough over the past few months, so they always travel well-armed.

67

They make sure to bring clubs, pikes and knives since their ammunition is running low. Many in the crew wear makeshift armor; shoulder pads, elbow pads, a football or hockey helmet. Three months ago, they could have been cast as extras in the Walking Dead. Today, after surviving attacks by the starving refugees and crazed anarchists, they wear anything they can find to protect themselves.

They travel warily. A quad leads a mile ahead of the main group of eight vehicles. The quad stops at a highway overpass and scouts the site, a half mile to the west. Using his CB radio, he reports back to the crew leader. "The site is massive, sarge, just like the chick said. Looks like they were building a Walmart or something. There's a bunch of supplies, and a bunch of equipment too. This could be a goldmine. But it ain't vacant boss. I see two trucks on site. Farm trucks. Maybe four guys.

"Two trucks, four guys? That ain't nothing," the crew leader replies. "It's a free country, let's go make some friends, share the bounty. Move in slow, wave the white flag. They can take what they want as long as we can take what we want. Everybody stays alert. We stay friendly with the other scavengers. But if they turn on us like what happened before, we let loose. We don't let none of our guys get caught in the cold, ya hear?"

He hears several double clicks over his CB.

As his scavenger crew crests the overpass, the smaller crew on the construction site takes notice. They set up a hasty strong position. The Momence leader notices that the defenders do an effective job of taking strong positions. He suspects they have an overwatch position too. He pulls up next to his scout's quad, only fifty feet from the small hasty position. He steps out with a white flag.

"We're neighbors. We're from Momence. We were told this site was vacant. We ain't lookin for a fight. Any chance of sharin'? Maybe not just the supplies, but also news, maybe get some trade goin'?"

The men defending the construction site talk amongst themselves for a bit. Finally, one of them hollers out. "How's DaShawn Williams and his family doing?"

The raiding party leader goes a little pale. DaShawn was his nephew, the star running back for their High School football team. He was good enough that scouts from both Illinois and Indiana were looking at him.

After a moment he responds, "DaShawn didn't make it. He got killed raiding a pharmacy trying to get insulin for his sister."

There is silence from the other side for several moments.

Finally, another voice rings out. "Come on in. We can't be neighbor fighting neighbor. We'll step out if you all lower your weapons."

The two sides converge and begin making introductions. A few people know each other through work or distant relations. They have a reunion of sorts, exchanging news and hugs. The construction site is a Godsend. It's a large strip mall that would have been anchored by a Lowes at one end and a Publix at the other end. The small group of locals show the newcomers about.

There is an abundance of useful materials from pallets of wood and bagged concrete to piles of insulation and crates of caulking. Old friendships are renewed, and an alliance begins to form. The sun beams down briefly, warming the frigid air. They start to load up the farm tractors with supplies and lay out a plan for the two communities to start working together.

They don't notice the distant rumble coming from the north, or dismiss it as bad weather moving in.

A crackly loudspeaker interrupts their revelry. "You're all under arrest," a voice blares from a loudspeaker, as three Urban Fighting Vehicles position themselves along a small rise only a quarter mile away. "You are looting and have weapons banned for civilian use. You're in violation of the martial law declared by the governor of Illinois and the acting president of the United States. Lay down your arms and raise your hands over your heads,"

The four scavengers from Kankakee don't hesitate in their reaction. Their leader grabs the leader from Momence and shouts out, "run! run! run!" The Momence people are caught by surprise as the fire from the Urban Fighting Vehicles begins strafing the construction site. The well-armed rogue military unit lays fire on what they see as rebels, criminals. A few try to give up, raising their hands in surrender. But pillaging is a capital offense under martial law. Those who try to surrender are mowed down by the SAW's mounted on the Urban Fighting Vehicles. The survivors flee the carnage anyway they can. Their hunting rifles and shotguns are no match to the fire power on the crest of the hill. Only eighteen people make it out of the firestorm. Sixteen people can no longer be counted as survivors. Hundreds more will die because homes cannot be properly sectioned off and insulated for the winter. The valued building materials would have been used to seal off unnecessary wings of homes, keeping heat confined to crowded but functional living quarters.

The sixteen lives lost help to unite the two communities. They begin an underground resistance to martial law and set up trade relations that will help them survive the cold Midwest winter and its howling winds that scream down from Canada. More lives will be lost before the long cold winter is over. Unfortunately, now they must fight martial law, as well as the cold, in order to survive. The next day an early Alberta clipper brings another six inches of snow as the temperatures drop down to the low teens.

* * *

Fifty miles east of Newport News a Navy Seal Lieutenant reports to Admiral Barnes and his staff on the Fifth Fleet flagship. "We made shore easy enough, sir. We actually had a good reception committee meet us. Things were going well for the first day. But as we started to roust out the looters and squatters from the naval base, that's when things started to go sour. There are thousands of survivors encamped on the naval station. There was no sign of our people, they've been killed or fled.

"What we encountered was worse than anything I have seen in all my deployments. You must understand, admiral, these people are both desperate and pathetic. They have some type of order established in which they disperse the supplies that keep them alive. As we started to move in on the base, it became very apparent that they were not going to willingly give up control. We threatened to use force against them. That backfired immediately. They rose up and attacked us. I lost six skilled fighters and an entire platoon of Seabees. They came at us with a vengeance. They're Americans, sir, trying to survive. We hesitated in firing back. We retreated. Half of us that is. Some stayed behind, consider them AWOL sir. I'm sure they headed out to help their families.

"I've seen chaos before, admiral, but in my twelve years serving this country, I have never seen anything like this. There is no way to retake Newport News without a significant fight."

The admiral chews on his unlit cigar for a few moments. "Van Hollern managed to secure safe harbor in Charlestown. Are his people better than your people? When we make harbor, we can implement martial law and bring stability to these people. Your mission is to secure that naval station, Lieutenant. If some of these squatters, looters I should say, have to die, so be it. Let the XO know what you need. We got a damn fleet supporting you. We need to kick these looters off our base and begin to set up some

71

badly needed law and order. I want you back on the beach by o-five hundred hours. Make it happen."

Chapter 9, Christmas

America

December 24th-25th

On the North Pacific coast, a low-pressure system brings cold and rain to Seattle, the home of many high-tech companies. The sprawling metropolis is hit hard by disease and violence. The cold wet conditions are a breeding ground for pneumonia, tuberculosis and influenza. Already the city has experienced a heavy casualty toll. Millions have fled to the mountainous countryside, but limited resources have led to skirmishes and more mass casualties in the fight for survival.

The local pastors and ministers make sure the bells are rung, hoping to attract people to their doors on Christmas Eve. Many heed the call, more in the hope of a warm dry place and a hot meal than to hear a message. The churches that open their doors find large crowds willing to hear the message and get a hot meal. Unfortunately, they do not all get a hot meal. The churches' resources have long since been depleted and getting food from the countryside is nearly impossible due to the raiders and looters.

But across the region, God is working, the message is strong. Christ came to forgive our sins. It's the greatest gift ever. Place your faith in Him and the miseries of this world will be replaced by the promise of a seat in heaven. Many people do take that leap of faith, some out of desperation, some looking for new hope. It's the beginning of a Christian Revival. The churches may not be able to offer food, but they provide love, compassion and hope. What few resources they have they willingly share.

* * *

In the mountains of Western Montana, at a rural church, white clapboard siding with a bell tower and steeple, the parking lot is full. A dozen farm trucks and vintage vehicles take up part of the parking area. Makeshift horse drawn wagons, bicycles, farm tractors and any other form of conveyance, takes up the rest of the available space. Inside the church, the ushers break out the folding chairs for the overflow crowd.

The young pastor delivers a strong message in the candle lit church. The salvation offered by Jesus Christ is timeless. Christ does not rely on lights or cell phones or cars. Christ's salvation only requires love. He came with love and only asks for your love. They sing Silent Night. They light their individual candles which slowly causes the church to grow brighter. "Be a light, spread the light," the pastor proclaims. "In the darkness, let Christ be your light."

* * *

Northwest of Houston, five hungry souls celebrate Christmas as best they can. The leader of the group, a quick thinking handsome young man with fair skin, blue eyes and blond hair had shot a wild boar the day before. They stopped and made a makeshift smokehouse, preserving enough meat to keep them fed for over a week.

The young man pulls a ham out of the smoker. "It's Christmas eve or Christmas Day," He states. "I'm not sure which. But we'll feast today, and rest too. No limited rations today. Let's eat to our heart's content. We have a long way to go, let's replenish our bodies as best we can."

The six-month-old baby that his sister has been carrying throughout their intrepid trip starts to cry. He's semi-malnourished. The group has been trying to make sure the mother gets enough food and water to keep her milk flowing. But the stress of the trek has made feeding the baby troublesome. They've scavenged some

74

formula and traded for more to keep the baby healthy. The fact that they all managed to escape the chaos of Houston and its millions of densely packed citizens is a miracle.

The father of the baby stands as they get ready to eat their meal. "God has led us out of the chaos, he has kept us all alive. Let's give thanks before we eat." They all bow their heads as they give thanks to God for the meal before them.

After the Amens are said, the young leader chimes in. "We still got eight eggs. Bacon and eggs in the morning people. Let's enjoy the day and lay tomorrows worries aside. My friend's ranch is less than fifty miles away. We can make that in just a few more days," Curt Mays states confidently.

* * *

At the Farmstead, deep in the Laurel Highlands, a feast is being prepared. Another local turkey farmer has butchered and delivered several thousand turkeys to the local populace. Thanks to the stability that encompassed his farm, his flock was unmolested by the looters and refugees. He made sure that his mature birds got distributed far and wide. As usual, he kept some brooding hens and a few good toms to make sure the flock propagates for the next year.

Our cooking staff, led by Rebecca, produce a feast that fills all bellies who come to the table. It takes three shifts to feed everyone, including the six Special Forces soldiers that remain as extra security. Before the meal is served, I have everyone gather in the great room of the main house. I know I need to give thanks to our Lord and God, even if many present do not believe. Ben helps me step up onto the fireplace stoop where I can be better seen by the large gathering.

"Today is Christmas, and we celebrate the birth of the Prince of Peace," I state as the people quiet down to hear me. We have many people here who have not been to a Mays Christmas

75

before. We do this every year. Christmas to us is not a time to just eat and watch football. Christmas is a time to celebrate the birth of Jesus. And since there is no football to watch, Jesus gets center stage, as it should be. "Please enjoy our short service as we recognize the birth of our Savior."

All eyes are on me. "We always include our children in this short service. Rusty, will you please do our bible reading?"

Rusty steps up next to me. "Make sure to speak up son."

Rusty reads Matthew, 2:1-11, the birth of Jesus to the Virgin Mary.

After his reading, I speak up. "The world is in chaos. We know that. So how can we still be so faithful to our Lord? We have all lost friends and family members. How can our loving God let so many people die? Why has He let so much misery be unleashed on His creation? I don't know the answers to those questions. But we have remained faithful. And He has blessed us. We have food, we have shelter, we have friends and family around us. We live in peace while most of the world is in chaos. But true peace can only be found in trusting Jesus. When you know you have a place in Heaven, that is when you know true peace on earth. That place in heaven is secured by Jesus Christ. Today we celebrate his birth. Let's joyfully sing his praise."

I bring Grace and Larson up to the front of the room. Grace speaks up, "We'll be singing 'Go Tell It On The Mountain', followed by 'Joy to the World'. Please make a joyful noise to the Lord." Grace nods to Becca and Janie. Janie begins playing the tune on the piano and Becca starts singing. Quickly the entire group picks up the song and a joyful noise begins to ring throughout the homestead.

I see some tears in a few eyes as Joy to the World is vigorously sung. After the singing is over, we have Hairy say a grace for the meal. He almost breaks down in tears as he blesses the food. He has not celebrated a true Christmas in his entire life.

By design, no gifts had been opened in the morning, mainly because there are very few gifts to be exchanged. As the children are being served dinner, some of the adults exchange gifts. Herq gives his wife a good pair of fur lined boots that he had made for her to keep her feet warm as she continuously treks between the front house and the main house.

Ken gives Brit a beaver hat to keep her warm as she helps lead the militia. Janie gives Zach a hand knit scarf. "I wanted to make you gloves or a hat, but a scarf was way easier," she states, smiling. Georgeanne, the nurse from Pittsburgh, gives Hairy a hand knit infant's blanket.

"What's this?" the former biker gang leader states. "A wash cloth? A hand towel?"

"You silly man!" Georgeanne exclaims. "It's a blanket."

"A blanket? You could barely wrap a baby with this blaaaaa." Hairy stops in mid-sentence. A smile breaks out across his face that could melt a glacier. He wraps Georgeanne up in a huge hug. "I'm going to be a daddy? We're going to have a baby?"

Georgeanne wipes a tear from her eye seeing the joy in her lover's eye. She was not sure how Hairy would handle the news. "You're going to be a daddy Hairy. Lord help us, you're going to be a daddy."

Hairy jumps from his seat. "I'm going to have a baby!" He proclaims to the entire crowd. "George is pregnant! She's going to have our baby!"

* * *

In Charlestown, several local farmers bring in dozens of hogs and over a thousand turkeys. Realizing how the stability brought to their area has helped them, they want to give the people a feast in recognition of their help. Many of the local churches help in distributing the food or host major feasts in their social halls. The Christian revival spreads, as many destitute and starving refugees see the love and hope offered by people of faith. It's not a wave of conversion. It's people talking with their neighbors and sharing their stories of how God has seen them through these dark hours.

Charlestown, a city of almost a half million people, is an anomaly. Less than a hundred thousand people still live in the city. Several hundred thousand have fled to the countryside. Many of them have died in the chaotic fighting. Unfortunately, many have died due to lack of medication, disease, or starvation. If not for the food that the local farmers bring in every day, and the Third Fleet making harbor, Charlestown would just be another city in chaos.

Admiral Van Hollern is with his men, helping in the serving line for a while, before he sits down with a few young sailors under his command. He introduces himself as he sits down. "You all know me as Admiral Van Hollern. But for now, I'm Jim. Is that okay with you all?" The six men and two women at the table nod.

"So, how's the grub?" the admiral states as a way to break the ice.

"Food's good. Sir. I mean Jim." A young man states. "I got two good slabs of turkey and gravy on my potatoes. I haven't seen real potatoes and gravy in a month. We get good breakfasts and dinner here sir, but nothing like this."

Admiral Van Hollern eyes the young seaman up. "You got family, young man?"

"Mom and Dad in St Louis, and a little sister too, thirteen years old," the young seaman responds.

"You ever think of trying to head out and find them," The admiral asks.

"Yeah, I have. But I can't cross a thousand miles of chaos. We've seen how bad it is here and heard how bad it is across the country. My best bet is to stick with the fleet. I hear rumors that good things are happening. That we have hooked up with the 82nd Airborne. That they cleared the way for us to come to port."

One of the women speaks up. "I hear the entire country is in chaos. We ain't got a president, ain't no government, nothing. What are we going to do? Who do we even work for?"

The admiral turns to the young lady. "You come right to the heart of the matter miss. As we announced several weeks ago, the country is in chaos and our civilian government has fallen. No one has rightfully assumed the presidency. But you're a member of the United States Navy. We swore an oath to the constitution. We'll do our best to establish peace and order, biding by the tenets of the constitution. Right now, I have no commanding officer, so you work for me. But I assure you, I'll do everything I can to help our country survive. Right now, we do that by helping this city survive and rebuild and by helping anyone else out there who is willing to work with us following our constitutional oath."

The young man speaks up again. "You mean we won't side with the orders to institute martial law?"

"We're here to defend and protect, not govern," the admiral says, looking back to the young sailor. "General Mills, of the 82nd Division agrees with that sentiment, and yes, they helped clear the way for us to gain the port. So did a lot of free trading locals and many farmers."

The admiral addresses the whole table. "We're working on plans to help Charlestown and the surrounding communities become a safe zone. There are other safe zones in the mountains and the plains. I have personally seen areas where stability has been established. It's working where there is freedom. I have seen where martial law has been established. There is no progress taking place in those areas, only suffering and chaos."

"You're speaking pretty freely, admiral. I assume we can talk with our bunkmates about what you've said," a corpsman asks.

"Speak as freely as you wish. I trust the American people. Look, we didn't put this feast together. We, along with the 82nd division are protecting the farmers, in return, they're making sure we're taken care of. That would not have happened under martial law. You all are smart, think about it."

The admiral stands to leave, and all eight seamen stand to attention. "As you were" he says with a salute. "Stick with us, this country will rebound. We can and will protect the free people of this country as best we can., with the help of sailors like you."

* * *

Unknown to anyone celebrating Christmas, be it those with food or those searching for food, the death toll in America reaches a milestone. Through disease, starvation, violence and exposure over one third of the population has died. Those numbers are the same around the world, since the attacks were worldwide. Asia, Europe, the Middle East, most of South America, Northern Africa and the Indian sub-continent are devasted by the chaos.

Rural areas fare better than the cities. In any areas where subsistence farming is practiced, the chaos is minimal. Australia, spared from the attacks, carries on, trying to figure out its path forward. Shelley Clinton and her elite allies are working diligently to pave the path forward, using the strength of the Island Continent to impose their new world order. The mullahs and the Korean Dictator, although no longer with us, have succeeded in bringing the modern world to its knees.

Chapter 10, Confrontation

USS George H. W. Bush & USS Ronald Reagan

January 3rd

"Jim, we have to take the port by force," Admiral Tom Barnes states over the hardened and secure radio to his counterpart, Admiral James Van Hollern. "We have to move in and institute martial law. The country is in chaos. We need to quash these rebels and restore order. I have a brigade of marines that I can land at Newport News. They can roust the squatters in two days."

"I advise against sending your marines to fight against the civilians," Admiral Van Hollern replies. "You'll regret it, and so will your marines. You need to find a way to bring the civilians to your side. You may think your marines are tough and loyal, but as soon as they come up against their own countrymen, things will change."

"I got orders to take back our port, Jim. I don't know who you're reporting to, but the acting president has ordered me to establish martial law at Newport News and then work my way to Richmond, then on to D.C. I also have orders to take out any forces that resist martial law, including the rebels that took over the Letterkenny Arms Depot."

"Tom, those people at Letterkenny can help you gain entry to your port. They're not the enemy. Who are you taking orders from? Who is the acting president telling you to do this? Is this coming from Senator Clinton?"

"Jim, her mother made sure I got confirmed as Fleet Admiral. She's the highest elected official that survived the attacks. I owe her my loyalty."

"Tom, we're to protect the country, not govern the country. You know this. Her orders are unconstitutional. We have known each other for years, Tom. I'm telling you, going in with force is not going to work. Let's work out a plan to get the people at Letterkenny to work towards securing Newport News."

There is silence for several moments.

"It's two hundred miles from Letterkenny to our port, across a lot of mountains and through a bunch of small towns and cities. I don't care how good these people may be, they can't get here till next spring. My ships need to make port before then. We need maintenance, our reactors need to cool down and be serviced. You want me to rely on some hillbillies who took control of a remote arms depot I never even heard of until a few weeks ago?"

"Tom, the situation on the ground is way different than anything you have ever seen. Don't send your people in to set up martial law. Let me work things from my end to bring you to port."

Again, there is silence.

"Two days, Jim. Give me a good plan in two days" Admiral Barnes states firmly. The line goes dead abruptly.

Admiral Van Hollern looks to his flight commander. "Commander, starting now, our sky cap missions include Fort Bragg and the Laurel Highlands. Make sure our flights extend up towards the fifth fleet, so we can keep an eye on them, but no hostile actions. Our allies will be defended. We'll not take part in martial law. This needs to be handled delicately. Are you onboard with me?"

The forty-six-year-old flight commander in charge of air operations looks at his commanding officer sternly. "Sir, I'm one hundred percent with you. I've been sending flights over the laurel highlands for more than a week. Our pilots know the situation. They will be glad to be protecting their homeland."

"Good," the admiral says as he turns to his fleet commander. "I want two cruisers and six destroyers sent out of port as soon as possible, set up a dispersed picket. We're sitting ducks here all bunched up in this harbor."

"Aye, aye sir," the commander of his fleet responds. "It's been a good shore leave sir, but we're sailors, we all feel more comfortable in open water."

Admiral James Van Hollern can see the writing on the wall. His fleet may be involved in protecting the homeland. He won't be caught flat footed. As of now, his fleet is on a war footing.

Chapter 11, Seriously?

Letterkenny Arms Depot

January 4th

The snow falls steadily, creating a winter wonderland. It's not a wind-blown dry snow, it's a heavy wet snow. It starts as flakes that are big and fat, like the flake's children try to catch on their tongues. As the snow falls more steadily it becomes a great snow for playing in, great for making snowballs, snow men, and snow forts. It clings to the trees and piles up quickly on the frozen ground. By mid-morning four inches of snow has fallen, bringing an eerie quietness across the Susquehanna valley. Tree branches begin to hang low and a majestic whiteness and calm overtakes the valley.

The distant firefights that still spring up among the refugees and survivors are not heard. Even the low rumble of the big generators that keep the massive complex electrified can barely be heard through the stifling snow fall.

In the communications room a staticky voice is heard. "Delayed….. Limbs down everywhere…eight inches…..stuck….."

General Adkins paces the floor. General Mays, Dan Farmer and a few other civilian and military leaders are an hour late. She knows they're coming over the mountains that will be getting hammered with snow. The softly falling snow in the Susquehanna Valley could be a blowing blizzard in the mountains. She has already sent out two five-ton trucks with snowplows to help clear the road.

* * *

Two hours late, our small convoy rolls through the front gate of Letterkenny. The six inches of snow on the ground here is significant, but more than twelve inches of snow covers the ridges to the west that we just traversed. The heavy snow is bringing down branches and trees, making travel even slower. But this meeting is important. Our fate hangs in the hands of people we barely know. Information needs to be exchanged and decisions made.

The major lake-effect snow storm will do two things. It will isolate our mountain safe-zone, keeping us safe from the renegades and refugees. But it will accelerate the deaths of millions of people unable to feed themselves, keep themselves warm and sheltered. Millions will be caught exposed and unable to take care of themselves. I'm troubled as we meet in General Adkins spacious but chilly office. I notice the thermostat is set at fifty-five degrees and that the baseboard heaters are warm, but not hot.

"Hell of a storm in the mountains, general," Colonel Fisher states. "Thanks for sending out the two plows. We sent them on, all the way to Jennerstown and back. We're not going to be able to keep all the roads open, but we need to keep a few roads passable."

"Good call colonel. We need to keep some roads open so we can meet and move supplies and troops," General Adkins replies.

"Speaking of moving troops, that's why we're all here." I state. "Let's all take a seat around the conference table and get updated. It's been two weeks since we've all met face to face." Seats are taken and a young man brings us all coffee, tea and water.

"First off, General Adkins, what's the status here and in the valley?" I ask.

"We're good to the south all the way to Waynesboro, and west all the way to Carlisle. We have even opened trade with farmers outside of Gettysburg. But the refugees coming from Harrisburg are an issue. They've come at us with violence twice. We sent people in to try and trade for scavenged goods. Finally, someone with some sense must have taken control. Last week we started trading with them. But from what we're hearing, the town is dead, literally. Maybe ten thousand people are still left in a city of three-hundred thousand. Dysentery and cholera ran rampant, then a flu bug hit them. The people were weak and starving. Their bodies couldn't fight off the bug. It's tragic Mark, tragic.

"There was nothing we could do. We couldn't take in the sick, for fear of spreading the disease. They tried to fight us, rather than trade with us. In a way, I hope this snowstorm helps to bury the past, hide the past." She shakes her head as she finishes, trying to shake away what she has had to deal with.

The room is quiet. A city of three hundred thousand people has been decimated by this attack. Maybe fifty thousand people escaped into the farmlands and mountains as refugees. A quarter of a million people have died due to violence, starvation and disease. And here we sit in warmth, with food and shelter. Outside, the snow continues to fall.

My troubled heart burns. How can this happen? I know the answer. God didn't make it happen, man did. But that rings hollow. How can God let this happen? How can we be so helpless in stopping the chaos? If we're God's people, we should be able to stop the chaos and starvation. We should be able to cure the sick and heal the injured. But we were helpless as a quarter million people died. I know in the larger cities these numbers are amplified. The thought makes me sick.

"Do we have quarters to help those in need?" I ask.

"We're getting full sir," General Adkins replies. "The local folks have taken in thousands. We have converted parts of the local college into a hospital and infirmary. The gymnasium is being used as a quarantine unit. The dorms are filled to double occupancy. Sanitation is becoming an issue. Fortunately, we have enough heating oil stocks and generators; we can keep the buildings warm."

"How about food?" I ask. "A lot of the farms took it hard before we arrived."

One of the general's aides responds. "The locals that have taken on refugees have worked out their own trade and barter system to keep people fed. Here on the depot we're keeping our people on a good diet, the refugees at the college are on short rations. A lot of animals died before it got cold enough to freeze the meat. We have staff dieticians and cooks making sure everyone gets enough, but it will be tough for the next few months."

I nod. Good farms have been pillaged across the country. Good farms are being pillaged as we speak. Will there be enough livestock and seed to rebuild those farms this spring when the chaos stops? Will we be able to rebuild? Will we be able to stop the chaos?

"It sounds like you're doing as well as can be expected. I'm sure the attacks by the refugees had to be hard on your people. Colonel Smith, how are you holding up? How are things back on the home front?"

The man I offered the command of the militia to a few months ago looks up. "General, small towns from here to Bradford owe you a debt of gratitude. I've got two dozen small units; squads and platoons, spread throughout the mountains. The anarchy has been quelled. Your civilian leaders along with their evangelists have helped to establish order. I don't believe in miracles, but this is close to one."

"Thank you, colonel," I say, happy to hear some good news. "But you didn't mention your hometown, State College. We could use the smarts of all those professors, scientists and engineers at Penn State. What's happening there? They have one of the best agricultural programs in the country. Those Brainiac's could be very helpful this spring."

"State College is a commune," the colonel states. "They've isolated themselves and have set up their own government and communal system. One of my captains has set up friendly relations with them, but they want nothing to do with us. They say they can make it on their own. They're waiting for the federal government to step in and restore order."

I chuckle. "That won't work out. They'll need to trade for fuel and food soon. Be ready to trade with them. I'd be glad to trade solutions for supplies. That university is full of very intelligent people. We're going to need their help. Sooner or later they're going to realize they need our help. Let's be ready when that time comes. You should head up there, colonel, make them know we care, and that we want good relations with them."

"I haven't seen my family in over a month, I like that idea." A warm smile crosses the colonel's face.

"Anyone have anything else they want to address before we head into the main reason we crossed the mountains in a snow storm?" No one responds. "Dan, would you like to inform our compatriots on what's happening around the country?"

Dan stands and walks to a map of the Eastern United States. It's a gas station type map taped to a large white board with a sheet of Plexiglas secured over top of it.

"Friends, you all have been part of a movement that is nothing less than miraculous. Through your hard work we have established a secure area from south of Winchester Virginia, all the way to Bradford and western New York." Dan draws a big oval showing our area of control.

"Thanks to the alliance we made with General Mills of the 82nd Airborne Division and Admiral Van Hollern of the third fleet, another area of stability has been established that runs from North Carolina all the way to Charlestown, South Carolina." Dan draws another oval on the map.

"With our help and influence, the Third fleet, including the aircraft carrier, George H. W. Bush, gained access to the deep-water port of Charlestown. That fleet has been able to refuel and resupply as well as provide much needed stability to Charlestown.

"Charlestown is now the only major city in the country that's not in total chaos. There's still a lot of problems that need worked out, but some semblance of order is taking place. A bunch of loyal marines out of Fort Jackson, south of the city, are helping to establish law and order.

"The Fifth Fleet is off the coast of Newport News. Newport News is the largest naval station on the east coast. They've made several attempts to secure the base; all have failed. Their admiral wants the Laurel Highlands Militia to secure Newport News the same way that we helped General Mills helped secure Charlestown."

The room is in stunned silence.

"Newport News is three hundred miles away," General Adkins states. "We would need to travel across a heavily populated coastal plain. Savanah was the closest city to Charlestown. The coastal plain between us and Newport News will be full of refugees from Washington, Baltimore, Philadelphia and Richmond. The two missions are not comparable."

"What about Fort Dix?" Colonel Smith asks. "They sent people to attack us. And there are at least five other military bases including Dover Air Force base? Whose side are those people on? Are they even still functional bases?"

"We asked those same questions," Dan responds. "I didn't get satisfactory answers. Fort Dix is trying to implement martial

89

law, and after using heavy handed tactics it has started to gain control of the decimated population. Dover is off line and presumed over run. That's a major Air Force base with serious hardened assets that may now be overrun by chaos."

I look out the window at the heavy snow coming down. By now the snow that pummeled the mountain tops is falling heavily in the Susquehanna Valley. Is this just an Alberta clipper that will blow through in a few more hours, only dropping lake effect snow? Or is this a cold front pushing in from the north, meeting a moist warm front moving out of the gulf? A few months ago, I could have looked at my phone and known how long the storm would last. An Alberta Clipper will play out very quickly and bring cold temperatures. Two fronts colliding means heavy snow across a wide area and moderate temperatures.

I turn to Larson as the debate goes on. "Go find the current temperature, son."

"Where can I find the current temp, Pap?"

"There's got to be a mercury thermometer here somewhere. Find it and get back to me as quickly as you can."

I turn my attention back to the debate about securing Newport News. Most are totally against the operation. And I agree, too much chaos to cross with the resources available.

But, if we could push through, I think of the lives that could be saved; another fleet docked with its aircraft carrier and all the assets it would bring. It would bring several nuclear-powered ships that could fire up parts of the grid, a hospital ship, thousands of loyal marines. We could start to bring stability to the eastern seaboard.

But how could a few thousand militia members traverse three hundred miles of chaos with unknown military units as foes, and rogue militias harassing us. We would be seen as a rogue militia too, as soon as we crossed the Susquehanna.

Larson comes back into the room, his hat and shoulders still bearing the wet heavy snow from being outside. "Thirty degrees Pap," he states. I already knew the answer just from looking at him.

I've let the conversation run freely, trying to collect my own thoughts on the mission. After seeing Larson and his snow laden cap, my thoughts are grim. This is not an Alberta Clipper, which would be confined to the mountains. This is a Nor'easter. This is going to bring heavy snowfall across the entire eastern seaboard. Some places will only get a few inches, some places will get a few feet. It will be life threatening to everyone in its path, because where it's not snow, it will be bone chilling rain.

General Adkins has some lines drawn on the map, showing how we can consolidate our forces. She's making a case for how we can push forward to Fredericksburg.

After she finishes up, I speak up. "Dan," I state, "what happens if we say no?"

"We talked about this, Mark. Admiral Van Hollern and General Mills think the fifth fleet will attack us."

"There is a Nor'easter blowin out there. Even if we said yes, there is no way we could do what they're asking." I go over my amateur forecast and predictions. Heads turn to the windows and side discussions erupt.

"Dan, I don't see any way we can secure Newport News until this spring at best. You need to let our allies know this. We need to know the consequences of our decision. I know Admiral Van Hollern is very concerned. Fort Dix would not have survived without the air support of the fifth fleet. Things could go bad if the fifth fleet commits to martial law."

"If we can't open Newport News for the fifth fleet, they're going to implement martial law with brute force," Dan states. "The commanding admiral is taking orders from the unelected government that is trying to implement martial law. They need a port. They need a foothold if they're to succeed."

"We'll be branded rebels if we don't help them. If we do help them, we're helping institute martial law," General Adkins states grimly.

Again, the room goes quiet. The stifling silence from the heavy snowfall outside muffles all noise. Two dozen survivors glance this way and that. Two dozen men and women, who have fought hard to establish a safe zone, are thinking about the reality that a fully equipped aircraft carrier, and its dozens of support ships, could do if it unleashes its fury on them.

Colonel Smith stands, causing us all to turn our attention to him. In a clear voice he makes a bold proclamation. "I pledge my honor, my fortune and my life to the cause of liberty. I will not let our freedom, all we have worked for, be taken down by tyrannical forces wishing to impose martial law."

Twenty-three pairs of eyes turn to the clear-eyed man who just made a bold statement.

The statement rings true to me. It's a statement made by Robert Morris during the first Continental Congress when they all realized they would be branded as rebels for signing the Declaration of Independence.

Grabbing my crutch, I stand up. "I stand with Colonel Smith. I pledge my honor, fortune and life to the cause of freedom. Just as our forefathers had to make bold decisions over two hundred years ago, we have to make bold decisions now. We have seen what martial law brings. And we know the liberty that is God's given right. We have come this far, I would rather die than see my grandchildren forced into a government work camp."

I sit back down as does Colonel Smith. I see at least half the heads in the room nodding at our pledge, including General Adkins.

As things quiet down, Dan stands. "Admiral Van Hollern and General Mills both expected that we would not be able to, nor willing to assist in clearing Newport News. They know we're against Martial Law. They expect the fifth fleet will commence to land in force and implement martial law aggressively in Newport News.

Dan continues, "Their first attempts to secure the base were designed to land with a hand of friendship. Half of their men deserted or were killed. We expect them to land aggressively this time. Their people will be more determined now that the situation across the country has degenerated even more. They will tell their Marines that occupying the homeland will be required in order to restore order."

"And the marines will follow those orders, because they want to see their loved ones." This comment comes from a marine lieutenant who is an Oath Keeper. "So, what's that mean to us here?"

"Anyone who resists martial law or helps those resisting martial law will be determined rebels to the state." Dan states quietly. "We'll be considered rebels. They know about us. We'll be attacked."

"But we're making things happen," shouts out an officer that was one of the managers of the Letterkenny Arms Depot. "We're literally saving thousands of people, making sure people are fed, that the farms will still be here next spring. For that we're going to be branded rebels?"

"We're not just going to be labeled rebels. we're going to be attacked." Dan States as he looks around the room, his normally soft gaze now grim and stern. "We have been noticed. We're having an impact. There are still powerful people out there who have survived this attack. They still want to implement a new world order, with the elites controlling everything. We're not complying with their efforts."

"What do you mean, 'we're going to be attacked.'" The Marine Lieutenant states.

"There are three areas of freedom on the east coast," Dan states. "The Laurel Highlands, inland New England and the Charlestown area. They can't implement martial law where stability has been established. So, we have to be destroyed."

Chapter 12, Drones

The Farmstead

January 7th

"Look Uncle Paul, I can scan the whole property. This drone is better than the one Pap got me for Christmas a few years ago. It's already a half mile away, look at the elevation I have."

Paul looks at the screen. The drone is very high and looking down on the eastern ridge over a mile away. The drone is one of the many electronic items stashed in Mark's Faraday cage. The Farmstead being snowed in, they have time to check out some of the items overlooked earlier.

Paul had been going over a plan to bring electricity to Winchester. He's calculating how much power they can generate and how to best configure their system. It's only busy work, they can't bring down another generator until it warms up and the winds die down. He hopes that they can be ready to resume operations in late March.

He knows that every generator they bring down helps to heat a thousand homes or more. But how can he ask the wind grinders and their recruits to risk almost certain death by trying to bring down another generator in the freezing cold. It would be an impossible task."

Even if they could bring down a generator, how would they get one to where it's needed, like Winchester? That's a hundred miles away over several ridges that now have over a foot of snow blocking all the roads. There are very few snow plows. Most roads are socked in.

"What's that?" Grace asks, which brings Paul back to focusing on the camera feed from the drone. "It looks like a campsite." Grace brings the drone lower to scan the disturbed grounds. Vague, but noticeable signs can be seen. Paths in the snow, a makeshift shelter against a rock outcrop, a fire pit, small, and snug against a cliff face. As the drone rotates, a man comes into view. In the next instant they see the man raise a shotgun and shoot the drone out of the sky. They see the tumbling picture of tree limbs, sky and rocks as the drone plummets to the earth.

Grace grabs the mic for the local network before Paul can react. "We have an unknown force on the ridge about a mile east of the farmstead. They just shot down our drone. They have an established campsite. Daneel, Buck, get up here, we need to send a patrol out."

* * *

Two hours later, Buck and three of the Special Forces soldiers assigned to protect the Farmstead return from their patrol. They scoured the clandestine camp and recovered the downed drone in hopes that its part could be scavenged. They determined that three or four skilled people had been camped there for several weeks. Their imprint was minimal, and the security disciple was very good. They also found tracks leading to an overwatch position. The hide hole had a direct line of site on the farmstead. They also found a scrap of wrapper for a lithium diode battery known to be used to power high level military surveillance equipment.

The lead of the Special Forces detail, a Master Sargent, reports to Paul and Brit. "Sometimes I wonder why we're here. But days like this reassure me that we need to be here. What we saw, and this tiny bit of scrap that they missed, tells me there is a high-level group watching us, scouting us. We should have known these people were about. My people failed you. It won't happen again."

"So, who were these people? They managed to to have a sniper position watching us?" Brit states emphatically. "You're supposed to be protecting us, yet we got some sniper crew less than a mile away? That ain't cool. We're providing for you and your crew. Maybe it's a bit to comfy here?"

Colonel Brit is pissed. She gets down into the details of the security of the farmstead. Roving patrols are increased. They have four horses and they're included into the plan. They only have two snow mobiles. They're needed for transport, so she tasks Daneel with finding two more. She issues directive after directive while taking time to field questions. And suggestions.

The meeting only lasts fifteen minutes, but the imperative is clear. Just because it's winter, the threat has not lessened. The security forces need to get more active, more vigilant.

The Master Sargent wants to respond, but he has no standing. The irate woman is right. They let the compound be spied on, they failed, they got complacent.

Chapter 13, Taken

Newport News Naval Station

January 7th

Twelve people witness the marines storming the beach. Six hover craft come on shore, skimming the waters and settling just short of the gorgeous beach homes that line the strand. Six of these people escape the marine's landing force. Three hundred marines off load trucks and hummers as they secure the area and start heading south towards the main naval station. The few civilians remaining in the area are divided. Some run towards the occupying force, thinking they're saviors, only to be killed or taken into custody. Others run away. Soon the word spreads among the survivors that they need to run away. They've survived three months of chaos. They know when to run away.

By the time the three hundred marines come close to the Newport News Naval Station, the local populace has been aroused. Over the past three months of chaos, hardened survivors have found a way to sustain themselves off the bountiful local seafood and the supplies they found at the base. They've fought more than a few bloody battles to keep themselves fed and supplied. But three-hundred well-armed Marines is like nothing they've seen before. They decide to open the base and let the Marines in, showing them how they've kept the base secure for them.

But to the Marines, these people are rebels, hoodlums. That is what their commanders have told them. Within thirty minutes of taking the main gate, many of the survivors that occupied the naval station have been locked up. The rest have fled, their source of survival taken from them.

They gather later that day at a local pub. It's really just an old out of the way fish cleaning operation that has become the local gathering place. Questions abound; how will they continue to feed their families? Who kicked them off the base? How can they take the base back?

* * *

A fit and trim woman and a scroungy looking man have managed to make their way to this meeting. In three days, they travelled three hundred miles on two quads with a trailer full of arms and ammunition. By keeping alert, and using their God given talents, they've found this group of people. Now they need to see if these people are really looking to fight against the occupiers, the forces of martial law. Will a group of local survivors, supplied by a few trailers full of small arms, be willing to take on the fire power of a Navy fleet?

Homemade beer and local moonshine pour freely as the men and women talk about how they're going to retake the base. They talk about how they've repelled previous attacks; how they can rally more fighters. Someone brings up the strength of this attack. "These are Marines, they ain't like the yahoos we've fought before."

"I don't care who they are, or how strong they are," a man states vehemently." They've taken away our ability to survive. We'll not let that happen without a fight. They'll have to spread out. That place is several hundred acres. We know that installation like the back of our hands. We'll fight back, we'll be in control of that place by the end of the day."

The two newcomers take notice of this man. He's referred to as Captain Roberts. He seems to be respected. He may be the person they need to ally with. Over the next few hours they keep a low profile as the two dozen rebels talk plans to retake the naval base. During that time, the crowd at the local tavern swells to over fifty people. Captain Shelia Mathews and her accompanying NCO mingle with the crowd, trying to find out who they're dealing with.

"What do you think, Doug?" Captain Matthews asks her compatriot.

"These people are solid, like the militia in the Laurel Highlands. There are a lot of vets here, solid people. They would have survived and eventually thrived, but they got out-gunned."

"We can help them a bit with that, but we need to find some skilled people. Those stingers we have need skilled people to properly fire them. They're the X factor. You head back to secure the quad and trailer. I'm going to approach Captain Roberts, see if we can work out a deal."

The man they figure as being the leader meets with people as the crowd dwindles. He's clearly giving instructions as a plan is being put in place. Captain Matthews knows she needs to bring this man into her confidence soon.

Two men approach her as she makes small talk with one of the waitresses. "We don't know you, you need to come with us," one of the men states.

She turns to the man and smiles. "Tell Captain Roberts that I would like a word with him in private. Let him know he has allies here to help him."

"Missy, the Captain is married, he has no interest in your tricks. Don't make a scene, just come with us. We'll make sure you get a warm bed and a meal in the morning."

She glances at the captain and sees he's looking her way. She decides to make a statement. She grabs the man's arm and spins him quickly, pulling his 9mm from his belt. Before the larger man can react, she swings her fist with the heavy gun firmly grasped in her hand and smacks him square in the temple. The larger of the two men crumples to the floor. The entire crowd turns their gaze on her, some drawing guns at the commotion.

She stands tall, hands held high, holding the pistol she took from the captain's security man. "Captain Roberts," she states, looking squarely at the man in charge. "I'm Captain Shelia Matthews of the Laurel Highlands Militia. I would like a word with you, in private. Have your men stand down before they get themselves killed. I'm here as an ambassador of good will."

"You put one of my best men on the ground and disarmed my second in command, yet you're an ambassador of good will? You have a funny way of making friends Captain Matthews."

"It's a funny world right now. Lots of people die for no reason. I don't want to die for no reason. Can we talk? I'm a friend, we're on your side."

"Why does your name sound familiar, Captain Shelia Matthews?" Captain Roberts asks.

"First woman to make it through Special Forces training. It made the news. So, let's talk. If we were here to kill you, you would already be dead. We're here to help you."

The captain looks around. "Who else is out there?" he asks.

Captain Matthews smiles, "Friends, captain, friends you want to know."

He shakes off his fear. "Stand down, men, I want to hear what Ms. Matthews has to say."

"Private room, Captain, you, me, and Hawkins," she states.

"Hawkins? Why Hawkins?"

"He has skills we need."

Captain Matthews has overheard many conversations. She knows Hawkins served four years in the Army, with two tours in Iraq. His specialty is Air Defense Artillery. He knows the Stinger system and can not only deploy the system, he can train people on how to use it. Shelia knows this from keeping her ears open for the past two hours.

Ten minutes later, as they talk in a small office, Captain Roberts is floored. Captain Matthews is offering him more arms and ammunition than he has seen since the attacks occurred. While they controlled the naval station, they were never able to break into the armories. His group has only been armed with rifles, shot guns and pistols. Now he's being offered access to M16s, SAWs, and Stinger missiles.

"Where is this stash of weapons?" Captain Roberts asks.

Captain Matthews ignores the question and turns to the twenty-six-ear old man sitting next to her. "One of your friends boasted that you could shoot down one of those planes if you had the right equipment. You know how to deploy a Stinger?"

"Yes ma'am. Two confirmed kills in the sand box. One fixed winged kill, a MIG in Syria. It was a sweet shot. Got an Army Commendation medal fort that kill."

Shelia looks back to Captain Roberts, "Our militia have established areas of stability in the Appalachian Mountains. We have been labeled rebels, just as you have. The naval force trying to enter Newport News is on the side of martial law. They will attack you and then they will attack us. I have Stinger missiles with me. The naval fleet will start attacking us soon. If they have Stingers launched at them, they will have to regroup. That will give us time to set up better defenses."

Captain Roberts leans back in his seat. "Okay, where's the camera crew? I know this is a reality show now. So, when I blink three times everything will be back to normal, right?"

"Not a reality show. This is real," Captain Matthews responds. "You've been overrun. We're offering a way to fight back."

Captain Roberts, hardened from surviving three months of chaos, is the Marine Captain who oversaw the Newport News Naval Station's security. He kept control of the base for two weeks, but he couldn't order his men to fire on the civilians when they came in force. As things collapsed around him, he did his best to make sure that he and his family survived. When the Marines came ashore today, he knew he was a dead man. He was already a rebel in their eyes. Now he sees a chance at survival.

After ordering Hawkins to find two recruits as his Stinger trainees, he opens up to Captain Matthews. The guilt he feels for not keeping the base secure is heavy. But he couldn't deny the starving civilians a chance to survive. He goes on, pouring his heart out. Everything that has been pent up inside him just gushes forth. His torment, frustration and their perilous attempt to survive is laid bare.

As he finishes, he realizes that he has set himself up to be beaten down. It has been so long since he has had even a glimmer of hope that he couldn't hold back.

Captain Matthews looks at the man, understanding what he has been through. Her team failed in their initial mission. But they found new allies and now have a new and better mission.

"Buck up, buttercup, you have a chance at redemption," Captain Matthews states. "This is ground zero. The Fifth Fleet has come ashore here and wants to secure the naval station. They want to wipe out any resistance to martial law. They're going to attack anyone who opposes them, which includes you. We're offering you a new way. We need you and your group on our side."

Captain Roberts didn't expect the humiliating rebuke, but it centers him. He has never been called a buttercup, he's a marine.

"Listen up, captain," she continues, "the fight is between free people and martial law. The Third Fleet has made port in Charlestown and has been replenished and resupplied. The City of Charlestown, what's left of it, has been secured and they're starting to set up free markets and self-rule. The Third Fleet has committed to an alliance with the free people of this country; that includes the 82nd Airborne Division, the Laurel Highlands Militia and a loose knit coalition of Oath Keepers.

"The Fifth Fleet, which is trying to secure Newport News, is against this movement. It has to be stopped."

"You're freaking nuts!" Captain Roberts exclaims. "This ain't no gameshow dream, this is a freaking nightmare that just keeps getting worse.' What's behind door number one Alex?' 'You all die.' 'Door number two Alex?' 'You become slaves!', 'and door number three Alex?' 'You die anyways. So which door do you want?'

"Captain, I saw you issuing orders to retake the port," Shelia replies. "You know what's at stake: you have not given up. Trust me, let me help you."

Captain Roberts looks at the young woman, with a bit of skepticism, but a bit of hope too. "You got some Stinger missiles and a few other small arms? That's supposed to stop the entire Fifth Fleet? That aircraft carrier has more fire power than most small countries. Hitting them with a few Stingers would be like slapping an elephant with a fly swatter."

"Which is exactly what we want you to do," replies Captain Matthews. "It will distract them, it will be an unexpected attack. They're without a port. They cannot afford to lose assets to minor attacks. It will force them to rethink all their plans. Even a delay of one day will help us set up better defenses for the homeland."

"The 'Homeland' you say. What's the 'Homeland'? You sneak into my territory and now you want me to fight for your homeland?"

Captain Matthews does not have time for this debate. "You have two choices, captain, help me, or stand in my way. I don't think you get it. The Third Fleet and the Fifth Fleet are at odds. There very well could be a battle fought right above your heads. The Fifth Fleet already wants you and yours dead. We're offering you the fourth door, liberty and resources to survive."

"If I deploy Stingers against the sorties taking off from their aircraft carrier, my people will become targets. My people will be decimated, while your 'homeland' goes untouched," Captain Roberts replies a bit disgruntled.

"Captain, you just ordered your people to harass the Fifth Fleet in any way they can. Somehow, using the best weapon to slow them down puts your people in jeopardy? Your arguing nonsense. I know what I'm saying. What I'm offering, is an unknown, but captain, what I'm offering is better than what you have right now."

Captain Matthews' security man enters the bar carrying their ham radio in one hand and the battery pack in another. She looks at her man, a skilled and well decorated Navy Seal.

"We can't break radio silence, Doug," Shelia states.

"But we can listen in, maybe that will convince this fine officer. The situation is getting intense. I got a few channels dialed in to back up what we've said." Shelia nods and the sergeant turns up the volume so they all can hear.

…broadcasting from the low country. Something is happening. We told you that forces from Fort Bragg secured Charlestown and the Third Fleet gained the port. But a runner today has told me that most of the fleet has dispersed, left the

105

harbor. The hospital ship and at least one or two nuclear ships are still in port but the aircraft carrier, the vaunted George H W Bush, has left port along with most of her support ships.

"I don't know what to tell you about that folks. My sources tell me the port is secure and there is no threat from the general populace. Maybe they're headed north to help the Fifth Fleet at Norfolk? That massive naval station was still in chaos, controlled by looters, from the last report we had." Doug turns off the radio.

Shelia looks at Captain Rodgers. "Is that enough to confirm what I've been telling you? Do you want me to break radio silence and get General Mills from the 82nd Airborne Division on the line? I know him personally. He pinned me when I graduated his Special Forces class."

"Why is the Third Fleet dispersing?" Captain Rodgers asks.

"Why are you dispersing?" Captain Matthews asks in return.

"The shit could hit the fan anytime. We need to be ready," the marine captain states.

"Planes are in the air as we speak, probing, pushing the envelope. When do missiles start to fly? I don't know. I hope they don't. I pray they don't. A lot of good people will die," Shelia replies. "My mission is to find allies here. Not only to help win the battle, but to secure the port after the battle is over."

"You're a confident Son-of-a-bitch. I'm in, captain. We'll help you."

"I'm not a son of bitch, I'm the daughter of a good woman. Now let's get some plans in place."

Doug tunes the ham radio to a designated channel. "Snatch" is the one word he states. He knows the channel is being monitored. Word will be relayed that the alliance has ground troops on their side in Newport News.

Chapter 14, Snatched

Bakersville

January 8th

I'm smoking a rolled cigarette from loose tobacco I acquired in North Carolina. It's my third cigarette of the day. I might as well quit. I ran out of rolled cigarettes a month ago, but while at Fort Bragg, General Mills hooked me up with three pounds of fresh tobacco. I roll my own now, but it's becoming clearer that I need to quit. More importantly it's becoming clear that I can quit. As a Christian, I know that my body is Christ's temple. Smoking defiles my body, I know that. It's something I have struggled with for decades.

But I have not always been a believer. I did many things to defile my body before I came to know Christ. I almost killed myself with booze and drugs in my younger years. I have given up a lot of those bad habits. I still drink a beer or two now and then, but not to excess. And I have learned to put other people's needs ahead of my own selfish desires. But I have not been able to kick my desire for nicotine. I ponder all these things as I stand outside the Bakersville Firehall in frigid temperatures, smoking a cigarette as dusk settles on the snow-covered landscape.

As I smash the butt into the sand filled coffee can, an aid comes to get me. "New updates, sir. They want you in the conference room," he states.

I take one last look around. There is a foot of fresh snow on the ground. One narrow lane of the road is plowed. The trees hang low with the heavy load of snow bearing on their naked branches. It's a beautiful scene, clean, tranquil and serene. A strong gust of wind blows as I turn to enter the firehall and large clumps of snow blow off the tree limbs, causing a mini blizzard. I shudder as the wind-blown snow gives me a chill.

Two hours later, we're waiting to hear back from our scouts that have infiltrated the survivors holding out at Newport News. Admiral Van Hollern is on edge. He expects that Admiral Barnes is going to try and take the naval station by force and then start imposing martial law. That will put the Laurel Highlands Militia, his allies, on the attack list.

Dan Farmer, our chief negotiator and power broker has gained Admiral Van Hollern's commitment to protect us and General Mills' people out of Fort Bragg. The situation is tense. Two American Aircraft Carrier groups may soon be in combat. Not against a Russian or Chinese carrier group, as they were designed for, but against each other.

Despite the chaos caused by the worldwide EMP attacks, forces committed to freedom have started to rebuild and survive. Meanwhile, the remaining elites of the world want martial law implemented, seeing the strong hand of imperial rule as the only way to restore order to the chaos.

General Mills talks to us over the secure sat phone. "These pilots, they won't do it, they won't do it. They won't fire missiles at another American pilot. The navy Captains and Lieutenants, they won't launch missiles against each other. Many of them know each other.

I don't care who issues the orders, this battle has already been won. We just have to figure out how to win it."

"We have to give them an out," I state. "They need some place to go. Some place neutral. What about Dover? Can we somehow get the word out that we don't want this fight? That they can go to Dover Airforce Base. Then we can try and work things out."

"Dover?" Dan questions. "That might work." He checks over his notes. Dan has dozens of people monitoring ham radio broadcasts and any other type of communications he can gather up.

That raw data is then sorted and compiled into useful information. Dan may have a more accurate picture of what is happening around the world than anyone else.

"From what I see it could be made accessible. It's been overrun by civilians, but not damaged. General Mills, you have air assault capabilities. If you could drop a company or two there, secure it enough to land planes, maybe we could provide the neutral space we need? Let me see if I can find the ham operator we got this info from."

"What about the civilians that occupy it?" Major Jeffers asks. "We can see what is going on at Newport News, the civilians are violently resisting the marines coming ashore. Why would we think the civilians at Dover would allow two-hundred airborne troops to just take over that base? I would fight tooth and nail to retain access to the supplies stored there."

"Can we get a liaison group there?" I ask. "To explain things, smooth the road."

"We went all out to get Captain Matthews to Newport News. The only way to get a team to Dover quickly is by air. You got three birds here General Mays. You care to assign two of them to fly to Dover?"

All eyes turn to me. I have not let our three helicopters fly except for dire circumstances. That has been for good reason, we have only a skeleton support crew and scarce supplies and spare parts for routine maintenance. But Dover is a massive air base, full of parts, supplies and equipment. Securing that base would be a major step towards our ability to provide stability. And if we could offer it as a neutral place, that seals the deal for me.

"Have two birds outfitted for the trip. Major Jeffers, you will be the lead. Let's get this organized ASAP. You'll leave at first light. Brit, I want you on that mission, along with Reverend Wysinger and a few of our local missionaries."

110

A bit surprised at the quick decision, Major Jeffers takes a moment to respond, "General, this is not a field trip, this is a military operation. I can't have my people babysitting your people because of your altruistic motives. Not only that, I've already dispatched a lot of my best people. I'll need to pull people from your detail and other missions in order to fill out two good squads."

"If we can stop an air war, Americans fighting Americans, then pull in all the people you need," I respond. "And this is as much a diplomatic mission as it's a military mission. You and your people will arrive a few hours before General Mills Air Assault forces arrive. Britt and the reverend will bring a compassionate eye that could make this whole operation go more smoothly. We have led with goodwill in everything we have done, there is no reason to stop now.

"Don't I have a say in this?" Colonel Britt states, a bit disturbed.

"No, you don't," I state matter-of-factly. "Not unless you want to resign your commission."

"Don't be such a pigheaded ass, Mark," she replies. "I ain't resignin'. I want to go. But the reverend is a civilian, he may not want to go. I was going to suggest Terry Barnes, she's a farmer's wife that has helped a lot in organizing the locals. You testosterone infested men need a few women alongside to keep you in check."

"I'm okay with that," I respond. "General Mills, can you support this mission?"

The commandant of Fort Bragg replies over our secure sat phone, "I have people gearing up right now. It's at the edge of our range but my ops people say we can do it. But what's Admiral Barnes going to do when he sees us descending on Dover? He will see our birds flying."

"What if we go nape of the earth? Could we avoid his radar?" Major Jeffers asks.

"Maybe, but that uses up a lot of fuel. I have a call into Admiral Van Hollern to see if he'll provide escort. But this may end up being the trigger point. I don't see Admiral Barnes allowing us to take Dover as a benign favor. There is a lot of tension in the air right now."

"This is a lot to fathom," I state. "Let's take a few hours to figure things out. Everyone needs to proceed as if this mission is a go; get the birds fueled up, get the man power ready. But let's talk again at twenty-four hundred hours, midnight, and see if we can make this happen. There are too many questions that need answered to green light this mission."

All agree. We need Admiral Van Hollern on board. We also need more local intelligence if we can get it. We need to find the local ham operator so we can get some insight into the local situation. The meeting breaks up with a flurry of activity as a major mission is in the works and could be in the air within hours.

* * *

In the main hall of the Bakersville Fire Hall, two dozen people in makeshift cubicles listen intently to different ham radio channels. Most monitor English speaking channels, but two monitor Spanish channels, while one monitors French channels and one Russian immigrant monitors for Russian transmissions. They have people with Chinese, Japanese and other language skills too, and when they're on shift, they monitor for broadcasts in their language specialty.

Tonight, there are a few channels that are designated for full time monitor, even if the transmissions are sparse. One of those operators hears a word. She jumps. It's the word she was told to listen for. After taking note of the time and channel on her record sheet, she jumps from her seat and runs to her supervisor.

112

The supervisor thanks the young woman. She then walks down the hall to General Mays' office. She knocks on the frame of the open door and peaks her head in.

* * *

I'm looking over a map of the east coast with Major Jeffers when I hear a timid knock on the door frame. I try to always keep the door open, as policy. I look up and recognize one of the ham radio monitor supervisors. "Nancy, right? Come on in."

"I don't mean to interrupt, sir, but I was told this is important, Mary just told me she heard 'snatch". I know that's important. Sorry to interrupt you for that." She says as she backs out of the door,

I look at Major Jeffers as a smile breaks out across my face. "Little Miss has local allies in Newport News! That's a total game changer."

"She came through!" the major states enthusiastically. "We need to let Dan and General Mills know right away. This changes the whole dynamic. Dover has to be a go now. We can tie up Barnes' fleet in Newport News while we move on Dover. It will get messy, general, but we just got the upper hand."

Chapter 15, The Ranch

Texas

January 9th

From his security post, Curt Mays watches through his scope at movement in the brush. Moments later he sees six people cross the trail, heading onto the Munsters's ranch that he's supposed to help protect. The intruders are all frail, barely surviving. He radios over the CB that six refugees just crossed onto their land. Two ATVs head out to the coordinates. It takes a few hours to track down the refugees, an Hispanic family that has managed to survive this long by living off the land, taking game and moving away from the mobs.

They're offered food, water and shelter in the barn. The refugees were expecting the worst. But they're offered a hand up. The ranch needs people to help them out, to keep the sprawling five thousand acres and three thousand head of cattle secure and operational.

Curt and his new wife along with his sister, her husband, and their newborn child arrived at his friends ranch four days ago. Since then, they've been fed, clothed and nursed back to health. Curt's sister and her newborn baby are still recovering, but both will make it, now that they're no longer on the run and have a good steady diet.

The massive ranch that they've found refuge in is a paradise in the chaos. The ranch has brought in over two hundred refugees and has set up trading partnerships that stretch to the outskirts of Dallas and Houston. They and their neighbors have food to offer, mainly beef, in large quantities. The herds were so large that they had to slaughter many steers, just to rot, because they did not have enough feed to maintain the herd.

It's a cruel irony that the beef starved and had to be slaughtered only a few hundred miles away from where people are starving, and being slaughtered as the mobs fight for survival, for food. Now, several months later, an equilibrium is being established, through primitive trade and transportation practices. But the suffering in and around the cities continues. And the chaos is in the ranchlands now. Desperate bands of refugees' rustle cattle and loot the farms on a regular basis.

A loose coalition of ranchers has been trying to make arrangements to provide security. They've sent an emissary to Fort Hood for help.

In the meantime, Curt Mays has been trying to find out what is going on in the Appalachian Mountains. A nearby ranch has an operational ham radio and has been trying to gather information. Curt has befriended the woman in charge of monitoring the transmissions.

Today, he brings the woman some pickled pigs' feet. She has some new information for him.

"I told you before, that a lot of people are loose with information over the airwaves, but that not a lot of information comes out of Western PA. We know there's militia in those mountains. There are also some freaky rumors that they restarted their power grid. Well, we got reports that there has been a lot of air activity on the east coast. We know two aircraft carriers are off the east coast, and they've been flying over the homeland. We got reports of more flights, helicopters flying about. Some of those are coming from inland, not the carrier groups, so something is happening.

"Now, Curt Mays, let me tell you something. I wrote it down so I wouldn't forget it. This is what a guy with the handle of 'Muddy Bottom' in South Carolina reported yesterday. I quote, 'General Mays from the Laurel Highlands Militia allied with

115

General Mills from Fort Bragg to help secure Charlestown so the third fleet could make harbor.'"

The large woman looks at Curt. "Mays is a pretty generic name, young man, but it caught my ear. I thought you would want to know."

Curt's mind spins. Yes, there are a lot of Mays in the world. But is there a Laurel Highlands Militia? That can be good, then he thinks of the renegade militias he has encountered; it could also be bad. A militia powerful enough to help in a mission five hundred miles away from its home base? That's no renegade group of thugs.

Curt thanks the woman before heading back home, his mind working in overdrive. A general named Mays from the Laurel Highlands is making things happen. Could it be his Mays?

Once back on the ranch he grabs his wife and sister to relay this new information. Kris, nursing her newborn child looks up and beams. "That's Uncle Mark, Curt, and dad. I know it."

"I think so too, but how do you figure?" Curt asks.

"You know how they prepped out that farm. That hundred-acre farm was better prepped than this five-thousand-acre ranch. You know Mark, he wouldn't sit on his ass. He'd make things happen. Same with dad. 'Rumors that the grid is back on.' That has dad written all over it. If anyone could figure out how to do it, dad could. We need to let the Munsters know. And we need to find a way to get word back to mom and dad that we're okay.

Chapter 16, Home Port

USS Ronald Reagan

January 9th

"Our mission is to restore order to our homeland. You all know about the devasting effects the EMP and nuclear attacks have had on the world. Now that we're back home, we have one mission, restore order to the homeland so our families might have a chance at survival. The chaos is so great that we can't even gain access to our own home port. We have been running reconnaissance missions over the east coast in order to establish a sense of what is happening and formulate a game plan. We're about to reveal to you what we have found out and our plan to restore order." The operations officer looks across the large room of somber pilots.

Another officer takes to the podium and surveys the room as the lights go dim and a projector fills the large screen with an image of what used to be Washington DC. "We believe a yatch or some other small vessel came up the Anacostia river and detonated a nuclear weapon that devasted our capital. As you can see, ground zero took out the White House, the capital building and even the pentagon. This occurred on 9/11, at the height of the remembrance ceremony. Several hundred legislators, senators and cabinet members were killed in this one attack."

A new slide is projected showing the decimated remains of lower Manhattan Island. "We think the same thing happened in New York. Almost simultaneously a massive nuclear detonation occurred in the East River. We estimate the initial loss of life at one million people. The president was in New York that day, it being his hometown. He is presumed dead."

The intelligence officer goes through a series of slides showing the devastation that has occurred to the homeland. The group of pilots is mainly quiet except for a few gasps and groans as they see first-hand how bad their country has been torn apart, decimated. The security officer also talks about the chaos that is happening and how law and order must be restored. She finishes up with showing how Weather Mountain has been unearthed by the lawless gangs. The pilots are rightfully indignant. They can see that lawlessness reins.

The operations officer takes the stand. "We have two immediate missions. First is to secure Newport News so that we can gain access to our home port. Then we'll have an expanded ability to refuel, rearm, resupply and repair. Securing Newport News is priority number one.

"Priority number two is to start to quash the rebellious militias that have fought against the legitimate government and our efforts to stabilize the country." The room is quiet for a moment as the pilots and their wing commanders absorb what has been said.

"How come we have to fight to take our home port?" A wing commander asks. "Why isn't it already secure? Can't our Marines secure the facility for us?"

"We have Marines moving on the port right now. Local refugees have occupied the port and have been looting the resources there. We have liaison people moving in to make sure the looters are taken care of."

"I hear the third fleet, with help from Fort Bragg, gained Charlestown and the city is peaceful. Do we have any local grunts that are going to help us out?" a pilot asks.

"Every situation is different. We don't have any ground support at this time, but we're working on it."

"Wouldn't it be better to wait for ground units to secure the base. If the base is occupied by civilians, then you're asking us to attack Americans. I'm not good with that," another pilot states.

"They're looters, ravaging our base. Where is your loyalty? Martial law has been imposed to help bring stability to the country. These looters occupying our base are rebels, defying the martial law."

"What about 'posse commatatis'?'' a wing commander asks. "The local law enforcement needs to take care of things. We're not to enforce law or take action on American soil. If our government has been decimated, as you said, who issued orders for Martial Law?"

"Admiral Barnes assured me that the orders come from the established chain of command," the captain states. "Look people, our country is in chaos. We can help them, but we need to gain our home port. To do that, we need to initiate martial law."

"So, we kill and imprison the people we're here to help?" the same wing commander states. "That's bullshit. Find a way to secure the port without blasting our way in. These are not jihadists trying to kill us. The people squatting on our port are Americans, trying to survive. I'm not buying your program, captain. Surely we can send people in to negotiate our safe entry."

The captain giving the briefing nods, not at the wing commander, but at a group of MPs. "We have thought about all you have said Captain and have determined that we do not have the time needed to negotiate with the refugees. They've been labeled as rebels and terrorists. Posse commatatist has been suspended. Our number one priority is to secure our home port. If you're not willing to help with that mission, then you're relieved of your command." Four MPs take hold of the wing commander and escort him from the preflight command center. A few pilots rise to protest, but realizing they have no way to stop what just happened, they quickly sit back down.

After the rebellious wing commander has been escorted from the briefing, the captain continues. "We have a secondary mission. There are militias that have resisted martial law and they've been growing in strength. Some of them are the people who unearthed Mount Weather and attacked Camp David. They're mainly located deep in the rural areas. They've fought against martial law and are bringing anarchy to America. We'll be attacking their strongholds in order to keep their anarchy from spreading."

The room is silent. They're to attack the homeland. They thought they would be welcomed as saviors, bringing power, medical help and stability. Now they've been informed that they will be attacking, fighting their fellow Americans. They now know if they even question the mission, they could be locked up like their wing commander. They're dismissed and the room empties.

Some pilots stop to talk with some of their close friends, but no one wants to talk. Their wing commander, a respected and well decorated pilot, was escorted from the room, essentially arrested, for speaking out. No one dares speak out now. What if their best friend rats on them for doubting the mission? Could someone end up in the brig for just voicing concern?

They've been given two hours to be ready for their specific mission briefs. As they walk silently back to their quarters, they can see that the carrier is in full combat mode as their F17s and F35s is being readied for combat. They hear the scream of the steam driven catapult launcher. The E3B's and AWACs are already being launched.

Some of the pilots take it in stride, orders are orders. To them it's no different than attacking a Taliban stronghold; they will follow their orders because the people they've been ordered to

120

attack are the bad guys. But other pilots walk away distressed. They wonder why they need to fight to gain their home port. They wonder why the third fleet gained port without a fight. They wonder why they need to attack the homeland. Many of them are Oath Keepers. They seriously doubt if the orders they've been given are constitutional orders. But they watched one of their leaders arrested just for questioning the situation.

Chapter 17, Neutrality

Dover Airforce Base

January 9th

"Give it up, you have been declared neutral," the hard scrabble survivalist exclaims, reading the leaflet he found on the ground. What the hell does that mean? As that question rings through his head, he hears gunfire ring out on his western flank. As he takes cover, he hears more gunfire to the east as well as what seems to be mortar rounds. His compound is under serious attack. They've been stable and secure for two months. He and his people have not had any serious battles since the last band of refugees they fought two months ago.

Now, in a matter of a few minutes, the entire base seems to be under attack. He grabs his CB. "What's going on out their L2?"

"I don't know! They came out of nowhere. We still don't have contact, just a lot of explosions."

A pit of despair grows in the man's stomach. He knows it's all about to come crashing down. Whoever is attacking the base is smart enough to use diversionary tactics. He looks to the west, knowing that is where the real attack will come from. He steps out of the door, to get a better view. As he does, a strong arm wraps around his neck. "Give it up, this base has been declared neutral. You can help me, or you can go to sleep. The choice is yours."

"What the hell!" the man exclaims. "I guess I don't have a choice, do I?" he says while gasping for air. The man holding him quickly disarms him. He sees two more figures, dressed in full combat, enter his makeshift command center. They emerge a few minutes later with two of his companions. No shots were fired.

Large explosions continue to be heard around the perimeter of the air base.

The man who disarmed him quickly turns him around, so they're face to face, standing just a few feet apart. To his surprise, the man salutes him.

"Major Jeffers, of the Laurel Highlands Militia here to support your command and negotiate the release of your base," the tough looking man states. "We need to move quickly, commander. Two companies from the 82nd Air Borne Division will be arriving soon. We don't want your people fighting them, it would turn out badly."

The man hesitates, but introduces himself, returning the salute, "Jim Robertson. What the hell is going on?"

"Pleased to meet you Jim," the major states as he shakes his hand. "In a nutshell, Jim, we need to make this base operational in the next twelve hours. Two Air Assault companies from Fort Bragg are on their way here. Me and my people are here to ensure they don't kill you all. Do you have CB radio contact with your people? Do you have some way to alert your people to stand down?"

"Wait a minute, Major. We've held this base for two months. We've survived because we keep this base secure. You want me to turn it over to you just because you got the jump on me? I don't think so. This base keeps hundreds of families alive."

"Not a problem, Jim, we need you to keep doing what you're doing. We'll help you. But we need the runways operational. We're going to turbo charge your operation. We're really on your side. I'll show you that I trust you."

Major Jeffers hands over the 45-caliber revolver that he took from the man. "You can shoot me if you want to, but I don't think you will. Now let's start getting your people to stand down. We don't want a war here, do we?"

* * *

Two hours later, two hundred rangers have secured the facility. A flight of engineers and air traffic control people are on their way in. The engineers will try to get the backup diesel generators started. The air traffic controllers will hopefully be employed bringing in reluctant pilots. Jim Robertson is baffled by what is happening to his base. He has been warned to send his people to secure quarters, which alarmed him. But his new allies have helped them at every step.

The local militia commander rolled the dice and made a quick decision to trust the man who got the jump on him and his people. He really had no choice in the matter. To fight the obviously better armed and trained team would have been suicide. The major's small team quickly integrated with his renegades. He was impressed with their skill and professionalism. But what amazed him most was that his two hundred people where so quickly taken down and infiltrated by such a small unit. He tells Major Jeffers this.

"We have trained for this for years. We have done this overseas for years. For decades, America has been safe because the people you see here have been doing the dirty work no one wants to know about. If you had not agreed to allying with us, if you had sided with martial law, things would have been ugly."

As they're talking, they hear the whomp whomp whomp of more incoming helicopters. Six Black Hawk helicopters land on the broad tarmac a few hundred feet away. They've already been informed that the base is secure, but they follow protocol and disperse in tactical formation. As the helos wind down, four men with a security detail approach Major Jeffers and the local commander.

Introductions are quickly made, and a game plan is put in place. "The locals on the base are not to be harassed. They're using the resources here to survive. They're to help you in any way they can.," Major Jeffers states. "The base is secure, have your men do what they need to do to make it operational.

"I don't believe it. I was sure we would be landing hot. Great job major. I have a few technical people with me, they'll get started with restoring power and bringing the base on line. How do we report to General Mills that we're secure? That will bring in the second flight with more technical people, radio operators and flight controllers."

Major Jeffers has his radio man relay the information using code words over the ham radio. It's all they got. They know the world is listening, but they don't have a better long-distance communications system yet.

The radio man tells him the message has been received. The flight with the technical people is four hours out. While they're talking, the LED runway lights come on. Two electrical engineers found a couple older 10k generators and got them fired up. The massive base is starting to come back to life.

* * *

"What the hell is happening?" Admiral Barnes exclaims. He's watching live as Dover Air Force Base, only a few hundred miles away, becomes active. Its radars have been turned on and its tower begins broadcasting. He throws his clipboard, knowing a step has been taken that he did not anticipate.

They're just minutes away from launching their aircraft to secure their home port. The marines that have been sent ashore have been met with stiff resistance. But they're making progress. Areas of resistance have been pinpointed. He has an aircraft carrier group up against civilian rebels. He'll show them who's the boss! He gives the order for the first flight to take off. He watches the

125

coastline only five miles away as his attack jets scream off his flight deck.

For a moment, he has second thoughts. His carrier is launching strikes against the homeland. But those denying him access to his home port are rebels. The homeland is full of rebels. Martial law is the only way. Besides, he has to follow orders.

He watches as two of his jets streak over Newport News and drop their precision bombs. Then he sees two flashes of light on the horizon, followed by two rocket trails. His two planes are low, less than five thousand feet altitude. He watches in amazement and horror as the two rockets find the heat signature of his fighter jets. The distance is too close for the jets to fire diversionary flares. In what seems like an hour, but is only seconds, the heat seeking Stinger missiles ram into the jet's engines. Admiral Barnes watches two of his precious jets explode in the night sky.

He turns his attention to where two more fighters are gaining altitude before letting their munitions hail down on the insurgents below. He sees two flashes on the horizon. He knows two more Stingers have been fired at his planes. One jet manages a barrel roll while launching a string of flares. The other plane takes a direct hit. Four more planes are on the flight line, ready for launch. He issues a stop order and has the fleet begin to move further off shore. Flight operations are ceased, and his officer corps is called to the operations center.

* * *

The Newport News Naval Station is a chaotic battle zone. A hundred Marines are trying to secure the base. At first the fight went well, but the resistance grew and developed into street fighting. Two full squads have abandoned the fight after seeing the dead Americans that they're fighting. The two bombing strikes from the attack jets invigorates the marines still engaged in the fight. But moments later, when they see their air support blown out of the sky, their enthusiasm wanes.

The Marines press on with their mission. The scouting reports are that they face a lightly armed rebel force. Suddenly, as they near the piers, they come under heavy fire. Their leader realizes that the have been caught in a deadly ambush. Two SAWs open up on them and several grenades land in their midst. Even though they're spread out, the company of a hundred men take ten casualties in the opening seconds of the ambush. All of his men, mostly experienced combat veterans, seek cover first, then rush the ambush.

The ambush that Captain Matthews has put in place expects this move. The two SAW gunners move while her riflemen lay down covering fire. Within a minute, the SAWs are firing from different locations and the Marines get separated. The Marines regroup in small squads and begin advancing on the rebels. But Captain Matthews has one more trick in her bag. Four snipers, armed with their deer rifles, 30.06's and 270's begin to snipe at the Marines.

It has been fifteen minutes since the three aircraft where shot down. The captain leading the marines is calling for more air support. He's told there will be no more air support until he secures the base.

"This base is swarming with well-armed rebels!" he screams into the mic. "Your reports were of a lightly armed group of refugees. These people are heavily armed and well organized. My people are under attack by sniper fire, automatic weapons fire and grenades. We have dispersed to avoid the incoming fire. We're two hundred yards from the piers. We do not have control of the situation. I repeat, we do not have control of the situation. We need additional resources."

"The USS Somerset is ready to support you. Give us the attack coordinates," is the response he receives. The USS Somerset has missile batteries that will devastate the entire block his men occupy. It's not a close support asset, it's an area support asset.

"We need a ship with five-inch guns, not a missile battery," the marine captain responds. "Or launch Charlie Platoon. Four tanks will silence these guys. I need help now, out."

The rebel SAW gunner has found his position and begins firing at him. The Marine captain, with his six men, scamper away from the compromised position.

* * *

Captain Rodgers, the militia commander at Newport News laughs as he watches the marine captain scurry away from their heavy fire. Captain Matthews looks at the captain. "Don't laugh. That could be us. He's an American Marine, probably a decorated vet. We want him on our side. Do you want to chase him around the corridors of this massive complex for the next six weeks? We want him on our side."

"We just ambushed him, how do you expect him to join us?"

"I'm going to ask him to," she replies. "I've seen miracles happen over the last few months. Maybe the man upstairs has another one waiting to happen here." She grabs the battery powered bull horn and steps out from her concealed position. "Cease fire. Cease fire. Cease fire," she bellows into the bullhorn. The fighting slows down and stops. No one wants to be in this fight. The Marines don't want to be here. Captain Rodgers' militia don't want to be fighting the marines, their fellow Americans. Given an order to stand down brings both sides to cease fire.

"Let's talk peace," Captain Matthews implores. "There is no reason for American Marines to be killing Americans. The people on this base need the supplies here to survive. They're not rebels, they're survivors. Let's talk this out."

"The looters need to be moved off the base," is the response she gets. "There can be no negotiations. The fifth fleet is making port and the looters will be punished under the martial law decree."

Captain Matthews takes a bold step. She walks fully out into the open. "Whoever you are, come out and let's talk," she states.

She waits a moment, fully exposed. She feels confident but shaky. She knows they need a face to face conversation or the wantless killing will continue. A hundred yards away, a man steps out from behind the corner of a building. "I'm Captain Wills, Marine expeditionary force commander."

"I'm Captain Matthews, Laurel Highlands Militia. Let's parley, Captain Wills, like in the old days. Me and two of mine with you and two of yours. I'll trust you if you trust me."

She sees the captain talking with some men hidden behind the corner of the wall. After several moments he turns back to her. "Okay, Captain Matthews, lets parley."

Shelia has Captain Robertson and another skilled soldier walk with her to the middle of the street. Captain Wills meets her there with two well equipped marines.

As they shake hands, they both hear Captain Wills open mic. "We need coordinates, Captain. We'll have assets ready to support you in five minutes."

"So, we have three minutes to work this out," Captain Matthews states.

"You are a rebel group occupying a naval base," Captain Wills responds.

"No, these are American citizens surviving on what their taxes have paid for, surviving the only way they can. They're not rebels, they're your brothers and sisters. Your orders are unconstitutional Captain Wills. Don't reply to that request. Walk away."

Captain Wills' mind spins. He's a Marine. Marines follow orders. "Leave now. It's going to get ugly. We have to gain our port. That is our mission."

"If you ally with us, you could gain port. Don't fight us," Captain Matthews implores.

Captain Wills winces, he knows she's right, but he doesn't have the authority to do what she's asking. As he turns away he hollers over his shoulder. "Run, run now."

Shelia and her escort turn and flee down the street. Aircraft are in the air, soon to be hunting them.

Chapter 18, Decisions

Bakersville

January 10th

I pace the floor of the conference room, alone in my thoughts. I have never paced the floor in my life. But I'm in a situation completely above my skill level. I'm a contractor; I build decks and additions, remodel kitchens. Now I'm overseeing a loose coalition of armed forces that are on the verge of a major combat operation. How did I get here? Lord, how did you choose me to be in this situation? What if a major battle breaks out? What if the two fleets end up in combat? How is that your work? How does that glorify you as the God of Peace? How am I loving my neighbor by being in the midst of this? My mind races. I ask God for wisdom, resolution.

My thoughts are interrupted by Colonel Fisher popping in the open door. "Major Jeffers has secured Dover. They're working to make it operational. The fifth fleet is moving away from Newport News. Van Holern has launched four fighters to escort General Mills' technical people to Dover. It's all coming together General."

"It's all coming together in a massive conflict, colonel." I state forlornly. "Barnes and Van Hollern are going to have it out. A lot of good people are going to die. Why does it always have to resort to a battle? It seems that whoever has the biggest guns wins the day. Why are we here? If we are men of God, why do we continually look for bigger and better arms? I can't quite get my arms around it. Why can't we be men of peace?"

Colonel Fisher sits down and looks at me, concern on his face. "Sit down, general," he states, "let's talk." I sit down and look at him, hoping he has answers.

Colonel Fisher retired as a First Sergeant in the First Calvary Division and served four tours in the Middle East, the first in Gulf War One as a corporal. Then three more tours, two in Afghanistan and one in Iraq. He saw the beginning of the war that overthrew Saddam Hussein. He has seen warfare upfront and personal. I promoted the retired First Sergeant to colonel and made him my second in command months ago when we were fighting drug addicts and anarchists. During my recovery from losing my leg, Colonel Fisher truly found Christ and the peace that he brings. Since then, he has continued to be a fervent warrior, for Christ and peace. He knows me well and I trust him.

We sit silently for a few moments. I notice a tear form at the corner of Colonel Fisher's eye. He wipes it away, then looks back at me, shaking his head. "You don't know what you have done, do you? You don't know how bad it would be right now if not for your leadership and bold decisions? We have seen the chaos of anarchy, and the results of the suppression of martial law. We fought against that. And we didn't always have the biggest and best guns. In fact, at almost every fight, every battle, from the ambush of the drug dealers to the fight to secure Letterkenny, we were outgunned.

"We're fighting to free men, not oppress men. We're willing to die for that cause. Many have died for that cause. 'No greater sacrifice can a man make than to lay down his life for another.'"

I look at the colonel, tears now rolling down his face as he talks of the good men who have died fighting to protect their families, friends and neighbors. He continues. "I don't know how we can love our neighbors more than to die for them in protecting them from evil. Mark, as confusing as it may be, we're doing God's work. If we had done nothing, we would now be slaves, our families and neighbors would be servants of anarchists or martial law.

"I have seen war all my life. I saw the destruction in Kuwait, Iraq and Afghanistan. Right now, those wars, those battles, were pointless compared to the battle we're fighting now. You're where God wants you to be. Have faith."

I listen, and I weep.

Chapter 19, Air Warfare

Off the East Coast

January 10th

"Captain," Admiral Barnes states to his flight officer, "we launch eight flights as soon as we're thirty miles off the coast. That will give our people enough maneuver room to gain altitude and avoid those Stinger missiles." He turns to the marine colonel in charge of the expeditionary force. "I want eyes on targets and coordinates in twenty minutes. We're not going to let a bunch of renegades and squatters keep us from our home port."

"I'll need to put Charlie Company ashore, sir. The shore unit is under heavy counterattack and needs to be reinforced."

"Authorized, Captain. The Fifth Fleet will dock before sunset, do you understand that?" The admiral states firmly.

"Aye, Aye." the marine officer responds.

A few minutes later he provides the flight officer with attack coordinates. Along with the operations officer, they put together an attack plan. Charlie Company will land within the hour and they will mount a full-scale attack on the main port by noon, fully supported by the fleet's air assets.

* * *

"What do you make of that?" Admiral Van Hollern asks his XO.

"They're moving out to sea to gain maneuverability. We have reports that three jets got shot down at low altitude by Stinger missiles. He didn't expect any defense. Now he will double down. He has a fleet that needs maintenance and resupplied. If he's going to be viable to anybody, he needs to gain his port."

"So what do we do? Do we allow him to attack our fellow Americans?"

"In his eyes, he's attacking rebels, looters. He's following someone's orders, or maybe he's just following what he feels needs to be done. I guess the question becomes, who is he taking his orders from? But then, who are we taking our orders from?"

"I have no friggin idea, commander. That's the problem. Barnes says he's taking orders from Senator Clinton. But what makes her in charge? She wants martial law. I can't follow those orders. Do we risk conflict with the fifth fleet just because we don't recognize Senator Clinton as Commander in Chief?"

The XO responds, "Our Oath Keeper allies on the ground allowed us to gain port without firing a shot. You know they're the ones fighting against the Fifth Fleet. You know the Fifth Fleet will implement martial law. I think we need to send a signal, make a statement."

"Make a statement that the Fifth Fleet can't land? That could lead to a massive battle between our two fleets. We need to avoid that at all costs. If I'm Admiral Barnes, I pull all stops to gain port. He needs refueled and rearmed."

"If you're asking me for my advice, admiral, we should send eight fully armed fighters directly north, as a scouting mission, and divert the four escort planes to the east. That puts twelve of our planes in Admiral Barnes orbit. That sends a message."

"That will just piss him off," Admiral Van Hollern states. "He'll send a full squadron of F35s' armed for air-to-air combat into the skies."

"But will they be willing to fight?" The flight commander asks. "The renegade general from the Laurel Highlands Militia, with help from General Mills, have secured Dover Air Force base.

135

From what I understand, Dover is to be a neutral base. A place for pilots to land who want to abandon the fight. Admiral, rumor has it that we have pilots that are considering that option. Some of our men trained with Admiral Barnes pilots. They don't want this fight."

"That's a new development, how does that effect our operations?" the admiral asks.

"The Laurel Highlands Militia reports that their allies control Dover and they've already started broadcasting themselves as a free zone, a safe haven for anyone, Oath Keepers, refugees, even looters, anarchists, and most importantly, pilots. If our people are tasked with attacking the Fifth Fleet unprovoked, I could see our pilots seeking this safe haven. If the Fifth Fleet attacks us, our people will fight that aggression. On the other hand, some Fifth Fleet pilots may take to Dover if they're ordered to attack us. It's a chess game, sir. With a lot of unknown variables."

The admiral ponders the large back lit electronic map that shows the situation on the ground. The Third Fleet was far enough from the EMP's to be unaffected and their high tech capabilities are intact. He looks at the ground secured by the militias and the areas still in chaos. He looks at were his fleet is and were the Fifth Fleet is. The admiral is a smart man. No one makes the rank of Fleet Admiral without both learned knowledge and strong common sense.

"If we attack, we become the bad guys. Our people will bail out and the Fifth Fleet people will rally. If we're attacked, our people will rally and the people from the Fifth Fleet will probably bail."

"That's how I see it, admiral," the flight commander states.

"So we play defense."

"Going on the attack will not win the day," The flight commander responds. "It's counter to everything we have been taught, every tactic we have employed. But we need to stay passive. This is not like any situation we have ever faced. We cannot ask our pilots and commanders to attack an American fleet. We have to play defense."

"Double the air cap mission. Have all ships on battle stations. We have been refueled and have a port; that gives us an advantage. What about Dover? My thoughts are that we send an air cap to cover Dover."

"I agree," the flight commander states. "But that starts to spread us a little thin. And I think you will need to let Admiral Barnes know that we'll be protecting that base. I don't think he will like that. It may be the trigger point."

"But that is a passive act, providing cover to an Air Force base. It does not threaten him directly. It may make him respond aggressively. Once he's the aggressor, we get the upper hand."

"I think that is a good strategy, admiral. We can have plans drawn up and initiated within the hour."

The admiral leans back in his big chair and thinks for a moment. For his entire career, being the aggressor has led to success, victory. Playing defense is against his nature. But the plan they've hashed out makes sense. He flew missions in the gulf, against a known enemy. It was not a hard decision to rain ammunitions down on a known enemy. But to fire lethal weapons at one's own country? That would be hard to do. To order his people to defend the homeland, including the newly active Dover Air Force Base, that is a solid constitutional order, even though it may provoke an attack from Admiral Barnes.

"Brief the pilots completely. Let them know that Dover is a safe haven; even for them. Under the circumstances, many of them may want to find a way home. If we're going to defend Dover as a safe place, it needs to be a safe place for everyone, including our own pilots."

"Aye aye, admiral," the flight commander states.

Minutes later, Admiral Van Hollern hears the scream on the steam catapult as jets are launched to protect his fleet. He knows an air battle like no one has ever seen could take place this very day. He talks over the placement of their ships with his XO and Operations Commander. They had dispersed the fleet the day before. Now the fleet is on high alert; battle stations.

The call for battle stations is sounded on the dozens of the fleet's escort ships; cruisers, destroyers, mine sweepers, even oilers and supply ships, as well as four attack submarines. Missile batteries are spun up and ready for launching to defend the fleet. Radars, sonars, all types of electronic devices, are attended to with heightened intensity. The fleet and it's thousands of sailors are on high alert. It's a drill they've been through many times, having been deployed everywhere from the South China Sea to the Persian Gulf. The skilled and able sailors rally to the call. But this time they're off the coast of America.

The admiral thinks about the actions his people are taking. Close to half of their air assets are committed. The other half will replace the assets in the air every six hours. They're stretched thin. But Admiral Barnes is stretched thinner. It's just a matter of time until Admiral Barnes has his forces attack. Then his people can provide the air power to win the day. His mind races at the accolades he will receive, the hero, the conquering general. A voice in the back of his head tells him to slow down, secure today's battle.

Chapter 20, On Line

Dover Air Force Base

January 10th

"Major Jeffers, I have an Air Force colonel that wants to meet with you," an aid states, as Major Jeffers is getting a report on the base's perimeter security, which is very thin.

He looks up at the young woman. "It has to wait. We have refugees overwhelming us and we need to work this out." He turns his attention back to the group of people around him. "Send word that hangar eighteen and nineteen need to be set up to accommodate refugees. The mess operation needs to be spun up as well. We need to reach out to the local farmers for food. Captain Harding, get on that right away. We don't want to confiscate, we're looking for help in return for security, got it?"

"Major Jeffers! You need to meet with this colonel," the young woman asserts. Major Jeffers turns to the sassy young woman in an Air Force BDU with corporal stripes. Before he can respond to her abrupt interruption she continues. "He's a wing commander from this base, Major. You want to talk to him. I would not have interrupted you if it wasn't important. I'll wait outside the door for your decision." She promptly salutes, turns about face and marches out the door, quietly closing it behind her.

He looks around at the leaders of the unit that just flew in from Fort Bragg. They're skilled leaders and technicians whose only job is to make the air base functional. The army learned a long time ago that they needed units that could secure and bring airports back on line. Establishing a functional airport is a key element in gaining a functional and secure foothold. It's a lesson learned way back in World War II. The small group consists of everything from air traffic controllers to security specialists. Members of this group have seen action from the Philippines to Syria. They know what to do. Their captain speaks up. "Sir, we should meet with this colonel. He will have vital information. My people know what to do. Make sure your people continue to secure the base and establish a workable perimeter."

The captain dismisses his men and tells the Air Force corporal to bring in the colonel. Colonel Tiani is a short man, with a full beard and wiry unkempt hair. He has a torn and bedraggled uniform that shows he has been on the run, surviving. He's thin and pale despite his olive colored skin. His eyes are sunken and he's easily thirty pounds under weight. But his eyes are clear and his composure is strong.

They shake hands as introductions are made. The major tells the young corporal to bring sandwiches and water. The major asks the colonel to tell his story, what he knows.

Colonel Tiani tells his tale. For two weeks after the attacks, the base remained secure, they flew air cap missions, not knowing what might happen. As word spread about the devastation of the attacks, people began to go AWOL. From privates entrusted to provide security, to skilled technicians and fighter pilots, everyday a few less people showed up for roll call.

As the manpower dwindled, they shut down the air cap missions and began to concentrate on securing the base. At the same time, refugees started showing up. They did their best to help people out, but as word spread, more refugees showed up. They tried to institute order, but as their ranks diminished, the ranks of the refugees grew. The refugees eventually overran the base. It's a story that has happened around the country.

Since then, he has been leading two dozen men and woman from his original command. They've been surviving off the land and by whatever they can beg from the local farmers. He wants to help the major bring the base back on line. He knows the details of the base. He can help them.

Major Jeffers looks at the captain in charge of reconstructing the base. He nods.

"Colonel Tiani, bring your people in. I'll have a security detail meet you and help get your people cleaned up and fed. Welcome home."

The Air Force Colonel salutes the Army Major, rank be damned. A tear forms in the colonel's eye as he finally has a real chance at regaining his home base.

Chapter 21, Take It Back

Newport News Naval Station

January 10th

Captain Roberts hunkers down in the corner of a large warehouse. He has three fighters with him, and Captain Matthews with two of her people. They've been pursuing the remaining elements of the Fifth Fleet's marine expeditionary force. With their knowledge of the base, and the ammunitions and arms that Captain Matthews brought, the locals have managed to disperse the marine unit. But marines are tough. A few fire teams have managed to hunker down, expecting relief soon. The Stinger missiles caught their air support by surprise, but the Marines are assured that support is coming.

Captain Matthews gets a strange feeling, a feeling that something is wrong. They've been engaging the enemy for several hours and have pushed them back. But something deep inside her tells her they need to pull back.

She grabs Captain Roberts by the arm, "Something is wrong, we need to pull our people back."

"What? We have them pinned down, we need to finish this," Captain Roberts responds, his eyes afire with adrenaline.

"No, there is more going on that we don't know about. We need to pull back, let the situation develop. We're only a small part of this battle. We need to pull back."

"You're telling me more of these grand schemes and big operations going on? Honey, my people survive by owning this base. Your people brought in Stingers and good arms to help us bring the fight, for that we are grateful. But right now we're about to run these bastards off our base. We're not pulling back."

"The people you're trying to run off your base are supported by an American naval fleet," Captain Matthews replies. "Do you think they're going to say 'oh well, that's too hard.' No, they're going to come in even harder. It's been two hours since those planes got shot down, long enough for the fleet to reposition. My guess is that the carrier has been moved off shore and destroyers with five-inch guns have been brought in. This base is about to see hellfire rained down on it. Your people will be the target of very precise bombs and artillery. We need to get the hell out of here now."

"What about your people's grand scheme? Have you given up on that, Captain Matthews?"

"Not at all. We have done what we can do. We have delayed them, made them change their plans. I'm good with that. I'm not suicidal. We need to get out now," she states again, vehemently.

She looks the local militia captain in the eye. She's deadly serious. Just then, a multitude of flashes are seen on the eastern horizon.

"Run now!" Captain Matthews screams. She grabs her security man and her SAW gunner and they flee to the west as fast as they can run. Captain Roberts and his two people watch them flee, dumbfounded. She calculates in her head how long it will take for the rounds to start landing. At five miles away, they have no more than twenty seconds. Her team can get no more than two hundred yards before seeking cover. She counts down the seconds in her head as they flee. At fifteen seconds she sees an alley between two brick buildings, she scoots into the alley, her two people follow her as they dive for cover.

She puts her hands over her ears as the rounds start to land. She can tell from the explosions that the position they occupied twenty seconds ago has been hit hard. Captain Roberts and his team are surely dead. Naval artillery rounds continue to fall, shaking the very ground they cling to. She has no time to mourn the death of the man that helped her. She's not suicidal, she seeks an avenue of escape. She grabs her two men and they flee through the streets, heading west, away from the battle.

Two minutes, that is the time she figures she has before air assets are overhead. Those assets will be able to see them, will seek them out and fire precision munitions that will take them out. She and her team run hard, putting almost a half mile between them and the naval bombardment. She can hear the roar of jets high in the air and knows they need to seek cover. A basement, a sewer line, an overpass, anything to hide them from the piercing eyes from the sky. Off to her left she see some oil tankers parked on a railroad siding. She turns that way, they're only a few hundred yards away. Feet pounding hard, breathing deep, she and her two people scramble under the railroad cars only seconds before two F 35s scream overhead.

She hopes the tanker cars shielded their heat signatures from the F35's infrared detectors. But she does not stop. They crawl along the railway line under the oil tankers for over two hundred yards while the naval bombardment continues. Finally, they come to an area where the wood line is only twenty yards from the rail line. They wait a few moments, trying to hash out a rhythm to the air patrol. A naval shot makes a direct hit on one of the oil tankers causing a massive fire only a few hundred yards away. The oil tankers begin to catch on fire and explode one by one, heading their way. They have to move now and move fast. They roll out from under the tanker car and head for the wood line only twenty yards away.

The wood line is a steep hillside, but they move on, heading up the hill, crossing a paved road and heading straight up the hill again. They move as quickly as they can. Silence is not a concern as the blasts from the naval bombardment continue. Five minutes later, they crest a small hill, a full mile away from the naval station. They look over the area. They see three hover craft heading into the port. Another full company of Marines. The base has been hit hard, but the piers are undamaged, and the warehouses are mainly intact.

"We need to get back to the tavern and get word to General Mays as to what's happened here. That's about three miles to the west. Buckle up boys, I qualified for nationals in cross country."

Chapter 22, The Battle

USS Ronald Reagan

January 10th

"We got them on the run now," Admiral Barnes states after receiving reports that the third Marine company landed and is starting to secure the base. "The tide is turning. We're going to secure our home port!"

"Now what do we do about this situation at Dover? We can't let that happen. Do they think we'll let them control an Air Force base barely a hundred miles away from our home port? As soon as we bring our jets home and can refuel them, I want them putting an air cap on Dover. That is going to be our base too."

"Admiral Van Holern has already put an air cap on Dover," his XO states. "They've declared it a free zone, whatever that means."

"God damn that son-of-a-bitch! Who does he think he is? Who is he taking orders from? Senator Clinton is the only rightful Commander in Chief. Set up a conference call with him and Senator Clinton. We need this hashed out. Set it up for 1700 hours EST."

He turns to his naval operations officer, a Vice Admiral on the rise with a solid reputation. "We need a plan to occupy Newport News tomorrow morning. You need to get that plan out. Prioritize which ships come in first. You'll need to find out what tug assets are available and coordinate accordingly. Make a plan in case no tug assets exist. Find derelict tugs and have our own people pilot them if necessary. That may get ugly, but you need to get it done. Any civilian resistance is to be dealt with harshly, do you understand?"

"Aye, aye admiral. Our people are anxious to be ashore. It will be done," the vice admiral responds with a salute as he turns to leave.

The admiral turns his attention back to his air operations officer. "It could be a long night. But we can't let Van Hollern and his people gain control of Dover. I don't trust him. I have no idea who he's taking orders from. As far as I can tell, he's gone rogue. If he gains control of Dover and brings those assets under his rogue command,,, We can't let that happen."

"Things are happening on the ground quickly, Admiral. Situations are developing that we don't know about. We need better intel, sir."

"How are we supposed to get better intel?" The admiral hollers. "We can scour the airwaves all we want, but electronic information does not exist anymore. The best we can do is monitor the freaks on the ham radios. Half of what they broadcast is bullshit. We have to go by the book. Martial law has been implemented for the good of the country and for the good of the people. We need to bring law and order back to this country. That is what we're going to do. Have your people ready for nonstop missions. We need to establish air superiority."

He turns back to his XO. "I need you to have our people ready to launch Tomahawks. We have rogue militias and anarchists fighting us. Our mission is to restore stability to the homeland. That may require launching strikes against these rogue units. Come up with a plan and an effective way to implement it. If we need to hit these assholes with a hammer, I want that hammer ready to fall. I'm tired of pussyfooting around, worried about attacking the Homeland. The Homeland shot down three of my planes. The Homeland is in anarchy. We'll bring law and order. No more bullshit."

"Aye aye, admiral. I already have our people working on it. I'll meet you here at 1700 hours for the conference call and give you an update. I'll be honest, asking our people to launch Tomahawks on our own people, that will be hard, but we'll work on it." The XO turns and exits the room, leaving the Admiral alone.

He walks confidently to the large and ornate chair behind his equally large and ornate desk. War ships are generally trim and sparse. But the admiral's office and quarters are spacious and luxurious. He sits in his large chair, puts his feet up on the large desk and begins to muse. He's the biggest and baddest unit on earth. He will bring the Third Fleet under his command and then he will begin to implement martial law. He will save the people from the misery they're facing, by decree if necessary. Then he will be elected president, the savior of the people. He smiles at the destiny he's thinking of. He dozes off thinking great thoughts.

Chapter 23, Fighters United

Dover Air Force Base

January 10th

The sprawling base is alive with activity. The hundreds of civilians that squatted on the base, scavenging to survive, have basically been deputized. Their squatter status has been recognized, giving them partial ownership and responsibility for the care of the base. Knowing they won't be chased off, they willingly pitch in to help.

A five-thousand-watt generator had been turned on earlier in the day, firing up some of the bases hardened systems. With Colonel Tiana's help, they locate two underground ten-thousand-watt generators, unaffected by the EMP. Soon, more hardened systems come back on line.

But the base recovery team finds a problem that they've not dealt with before. Some equipment, including a lot of the communications gear, is hardened and works well. But a lot of equipment, especially the newer equipment, is dead, the electronics fried. They need to work through the complex problem of integrating the working systems while bypassing the broken systems. Their first priority is to open the base, get the runways open and the communications systems operational. The team goes about its business and makes major headway.

The locals pitch in, happy to help the base become functional, happy to be part of something bigger than just surviving, All the while, a team of civilians, led by one of the base restoration people, clear out bomb shelters and underground bunkers. One of the helpers asks a good question, "Why are we cleaning out the bomb shelters?"

One of her team members responds sternly. "The Fifth Fleet has hundreds of Tomahawk Missiles. They could be landing

149

on this base within the next twenty-four hours. We need to be ready for that type of attack."

"What? We're Americans trying to secure an American base. Why would they attack us?" another worker responds.

"It's complicated. It seems some people want to institute martial law to control the anarchy and chaos. That includes the admiral of the Fifth Fleet. But there is a group of people called Oath Keepers. They think martial law is against the constitution. More importantly, they think free people will have a better chance at rebuilding the country." The senior sergeant responds.

The work of prepping the underground bomb shelter continues silently for a bit as the workers contemplate what the sergeant said.

"What happens if they implement martial law? We need the chaos stopped, why is that bad?"

The sergeant gives the questioner a sideways glance. "You would probably be accused of looting and shot for occupying a government base."

The woman's face goes pale. "I'm no looter! We're just trying to survive. My tax dollars paid for all these supplies. We're just using what we paid for."

"I agree with you ma'am. I think you're a patriot," the sergeant responds.

"So where do you stand?" she asks. "Do you want martial law?"

"I want an end to the chaos. That won't happen through martial law. It will only happen by good people doing what is right. I'm an Oath Keeper."

* * *

Colonel Tiani inspects the flight line. Two dozen F16's are ready to go, fueled up and fully armed. Two dozen more jets sit idle, ready to be prepped for flight operation. But he only has four pilots, including himself. The rest fled months ago, in hopes of saving their families.

He looks at the rows of jets, a prime target if they're attacked. He grabs one of the base recovery engineers. "You need to disperse the planes. Roll them into hangars, put them on elevators and drop them to the secure bunkers, roll them out into the fields if needed. Look at this, they're lined up to be taken out. Use whatever you have, but disperse those planes."

The engineer, seeing the major's point quickly assigns a team to disperse the planes. Within an hour, a once orderly looking base has planes parked haphazardly on the tarmac and pushed off into the surrounding fields and wood lines. Civilians bring out massive camouflage nets to disguise the irreplaceable jets.

While this is happening, three fighter pilots and a tanker pilot plan their first mission in months. The tanker pilot is nervous about the mission, he only has one seasoned airman to run the fuel lines. But they plow forward. The senior airman that will oversee the refueling is confident that they can do the mission. They move forward with their plans.

Major Jeffers reports this development to General Mays over the ham radio. It's not secure, but it's their only means of communications at this point.

He watches from the tower as the three jets scream into the air. The tanker sits on the tarmac. It will not take off until the jets get to 50 percent fuel levels. The base recovery commander stands next to him. He turns and gives him a high five. "We have an operational base, captain. All we need now is more pilots."

Once in the air, Colonel Tiani establishes communications with Admiral Van Hollern's four jets. Talking pilot gibberish and jargon, the navy pilots welcome them and chide them as well. The naval pilots also request the tanker be launched. They can provide hours more of air cap if they can get refueled. Tiana tells them they have a rookie crew, but the naval pilots are willing to take the chance. They were all rookies once.

Chapter 24, Choosing Sides

Fort Bragg

January 10th, 1700 hours

Using his secure and hardened sat phone, General Mills dials into the conference call. Before dialing in, he linked with General Mays and Dan Farmer in Bakersville as well as his friend and West Point classmate, General Watkins, the commandant of Fort Hood.

"Admiral Van Hollern, we're all on the line," General Mills states. "Go ahead and make contact with Admiral Barnes and Senator Clinton."

They hear a few clicks and hisses as the call transmits up to the hardened satellite and back to earth.

Finally, the connection is made and all the parties are on the same line. Before anyone can say anything, Admiral Van Hollern chimes in. "Glad to hear from you, Senator Clinton. What can we do to help you?"

This offer of help throws the young senator off guard. But she recovers and sticks to her script. "Following the chain of succession, Admiral Van Hollren, I'm now President Clinton, your Commander in Chief. Please have respect for the office that it deserves.

"Sorry about that Senator. I mean no disrespect to the Office of the President. But quite frankly, under the circumstances, I don't know the basis of your claim as Commander in Chief. We don't know the president is dead. We don't know if the vice president is dead. We do know the Secretary of Homeland Security survived the initial attacks, but we don't know her current where abouts. Your succession in command requires the entire cabinet to

153

be killed and most of congress to be verified as incapacitated as well, you being a junior senator."

"Admiral, you know full well that in fact most of the members of congress and most of the president's cabinet were killed in the nuclear explosion in D.C. The former president is presumed dead in the nuclear explosion in New York City. No one else has come forward to lead our country out of this chaos. I'm the only member of our elected officials to come forward. America needs a leader. Our military needs a civilian leader. Without civilian oversight, you would be deemed a tyrant, a rogue officer. You need me to give you legitimacy. Let's work together, general. Okay?"

"It would be okay, but what you say is not true," General Watkins states. "Ben Cruz, the Secretary of the Interior, was in Texas at the time of the attacks. He's helping us secure our state and the south west. He has not claimed status as President. He's hopeful that a more senior member of the president's cabinet will come forward. His position puts him ahead of you in the succession to the presidency."

Admiral Barnes explodes on the line. "Who the hell are you? I thought this was a conversation with us and Admiral Van Hollern."

"This is Major General Watkins, Commander of the Fourth Armored Division based in Fort Hood. I think I have every right to be involved in this conversation. We're talking about the future of the country I love and serve."

"I thank you for that information and your service, General Watkins," Shelley Clinton states, but it comes across as a snide comment, not sincere. "If Secretary Cruz is willing to lead the country, then he needs to step forward. The mere fact that he has laid low for this long shows he's not competent enough to do the job."

"General, I'm willing to step forward and make the hard decisions. Our country needs leadership. I'm willing to step forward in our time of need and make the hard decisions. I'm willing to do what is needed to restore order and save our great country."

"Does your willingness to restore order include instituting martial law?" Admiral Van Hollern asks.

There are a few moments of silence on the secure line as many people contemplate the senator's answer.

"Freedom is what has made our country great, admiral," Senator Clinton responds. "But in these extreme circumstances, I see no other way to secure the country. I ask that you, General Watkins, and General Mills join me and Admiral Barnes in securing our country's future. We cannot let chaos consume our country. If we unite, we can bring law and order to the country. We can unite the country."

It's a good speech. It has unity and security. But at its core, martial law will be imposed.

"Senator Clinton," Admiral Van Hollern states, "You know we secured Charlestown Naval Station by lifting martial law. Our people, along with General Mills' people have just secured Dover Air Force Base by ensuring the locals that there will be no martial law. Meanwhile, in Chicago, Atlanta and Houston, where martial law has been implemented, the chaos is worse. Your claims as president are sketchy and your plans are not compatible to the American way of life. Stifling freedom won't lead to recovery. I don't see how we can just roll over and say yes to you as commander in chief."

Rather than letting the open rebellion to Senator Clinton's claim lay festering, General Watkins jumps into the conversation again. "Senator Clinton, your claim to the presidency has no merit. You have desires to implement martial law. If you gave such orders, we would deem them unconstitutional. Senator, we thank you for your willingness to step forward. But we need to truly establish the rightful chain of command and follow constitutional orders."

"You don't understand," Senator Clinton almost yells over the secure coms network. "I'm not asking for your permission, I'm telling you what needs to be done. Have you all gone rogue? Is our country now to become a military dictatorship! God damn you all!"

A click is heard, followed by several more clicks. Senator Clinton and Admiral Barnes are no longer on the call, as well as a few of her silent allies.

Dan Farmer makes a one word statement over the still open line. "Omega."

* * *

Admiral Van Hollern, General Mills, General Watkins and I all disconnect from that call. We reestablish communications on the same secure sat phone but on a different channel.

"General Watkins, if we ever get to meet, I'm buying. You shut her down. Do you really have the Secretary of the Interior alive and well?"

"Actually, yes we do. He showed up about a week ago. A bunch of ranchers and some native Americans he was meeting with have survived and made contact with a group we sent up towards Amarillo. But more importantly, you all need to buckle down. Senator Clinton and Admiral Barnes will not go quietly. I pray for you, brothers."

"The General is right," Admiral Van Hollern states. "Admiral Barnes is not going to accept this as a done deal. Our latest reports from Newport News show his ships are finally

156

entering Newport News. Our local militias there have been run off. That naval station is four times as big as Charlestown. There is no smooth road ahead."

"We have Dover, right?" I state.

Dan Farmer responds. "Sure do, Mark. They've even launched some of their own jets to join the air cap mission, and a refueling tanker is now in the air. It's skimpy, but it's operational."

"What if the Fifth Fleet starts launching Tomahawks" I ask.

"The base will take a pounding," Dan replies. "Major Jeffers and his people know this and have been prepping for it. But that would trigger the Third Fleet. Admiral Van Hollern is clearly on our side. But he can't order his fighters to attack the Fifth Fleet for no reason. If the Fifth Fleet starts attacking Dover or any of the Laurel Highlands Militia' positions, that would be a game changer.

"If Admiral Barnes attacks us, Admiral Van Hollern will defend us, that's what you're saying, Dan?" I ask.

"Why are you asking him?" Admiral Van Hollern responds over the sat phone. "I'm on the call, you know. If you're attacked, we'll defend. I have talked with our pilots. They would prefer to just jump ship, land at Dover and move on. But if the Fifth Fleet attacks you all, our pilots will look at that as an assault on the homeland. I've talked with them. They know we gained our port without a major conflict, partially due to your efforts and guidance. One of the pilots made a very clear statement. I quote, 'if you can't gain your home port without use of force, then it ain't your home port no more.'"

I laugh. "Well stated. But that means we need to wait for Barnes' next move. That doesn't seem like a good strategy. We need to be proactive. A first strike on Dover could be devastating."

"The way Senator Clinton talked, we're all rogue units," General Watkins states. "I think I'm mainly out of her reach, but a first strike could hit any of us. Sounds like your man Jeffers understands this. But the rest of you all need to hunker down. If they decide to let those Tomahawks fly, no one is safe, including me."

"You have Patriot Missile systems, you should be okay," General Mills states.

"Some of the wiring harnesses weren't properly hardened. Some of those batteries are dead," the Fort Hood commander responds.

I interject into the conversation. "So, our only option is to hunker down and wait for the inevitable, then watch as two hundred cruise missiles explode across the homeland? Followed by dozens of the country's best naval jets landing precision munitions! I can't accept that. We need to be proactive. Certainly there's a better alternative."

After a few moments of uncomfortable silence, General Watkins speaks up. "I can't believe I'm making this offer. Now I know why they came up with the term 'Damn Yankees!' Y'all know Texas can declare independence if we want to. But y'all need our help. I got two squadrons of F16s from the Air National Guard that are fully operational and armed.

"I ain't going to fly them into Dover. That would be suicide. But I'll fly them into Pope Air Force base there at Fort Bragg. Do you have the ability to rearm and refuel my planes? Do you have technicians and refueling units?"

"Son-of-a-bitch!" General Mills responds with enthusiasm. "That would be great! Yes, we have air-to-air missiles and refueling capacities. Send some tech specialists though. How soon can you have them here?"

158

"The squadron is on standby. It can be there in two hours. The support units will take maybe six hours."

Admiral Van Hollern chimes in again. "That definitely tips the scales in our favor. We can put more fighters in the sky and have tankers to keep them flying. But the Fifth Fleet is larger than the Third Fleet. Admiral Barnes has more cruisers and destroyers than I do. That means more fire power. We may be able to take down his air assets, but his ability to strike with lethal force on the homeland can't be stopped with air superiority alone. I don't know how we stop his capability to launch Tomahawks."

"There is another factor you all need to know," Admiral Van Hollern states. "My hospital ship and two nuclear subs are still parked in Charlestown Harbor, for relief efforts. But I have dispersed the rest of my fleet. I have a strategically placed picket around the Fifth Fleet. Meanwhile, the Third Fleet is clogging the narrows into Newport News. If a fight were to break out in the next twenty-four hours, Admiral Barnes could be decimated."

"If you're thinking of a false flag operation, stop now," I respond. "Deception won't win the day. But sitting and waiting could be devastating as well. We're at a dead end right now."

"General Watkins, get your squadron to Pope Air Force base ASAP. Admiral Van Hollern, keep your people on high alert and your air cap missions flying. General Mills, move more people into Dover and see if you can get more of your best people into Newport News to support Captain Matthews and the locals there. We both need to try to get them more Stingers. We'll spread the word around here to start hunkering down. Let's talk again at 2400 hours. Are you all in agreement with that course of action?"

The high powered leaders agree and will have their staffs start to implement these moves. The conference call winds down. Dan sits back and smiles. I'm troubled by the threat we all face. Cruise missiles could be targeted at my farmstead, here at

159

Bakersville, or worse yet, our generating stations, which are keeping thousands of people alive. Cruise missiles are deadly accurate and carry a lethal explosive warhead.

"Why are you smiling, Dan? Sometimes you can be so damn smug." I state.

"You just told a fleet admiral and two three-star generals what to do. And they said 'Yes Sir!' You don't even see it do you?"

"I don't get it. I just laid out a commonsense course of action. What's the big deal?" I respond.

"They followed your orders, General Mays, that's the big deal. Wake up brother-in-law! You're in charge of the resistance, the freedom fighters." He smiles even broader and shakes his head. "Here's the weirdest part, Mark, I'm good with it. I knew you when you were a mess. You've come a long way. I know your faith. I've seen you put your faith in action. God is working miracles every day. Right now he's working miracles through you."

"I'm a blind fool, stumbling my way through this obstacle course," I respond humbly. "The whole thing may blow up if I make one bad step. I'm in way over my head. God has a funny way of picking leaders."

My sister, Sara Farmer, has been present since the conference call broke up. She has been quiet up to this point. "Mark," she states quietly, "You're not a blind fool. God is leading you. You're never blind when you lean on Him. Bad things have already happened. You did not cause them to happen. If more destruction and mayhem happens, it's not your fault. You're trying to do good. 'If God is for us, who can stand against us.' I have heard you quote that verse many times. You need to believe it, Mark. You need to live it."

160

I think things through. My sister and brother-in-law wait quietly. I didn't want to be in the position I'm in. I have just been trying to do what is right.

It started by trying to protect my family and neighbors. That is what I'm still trying to do. The second commandment, above the ten commandments, is 'love your neighbors'. When I boil it all down, that is what I'm doing, loving my neighbors by trying to keep them safe and free. Sara is right. We pray together.

* * *

I insist on getting back to the farmstead, to my wife and family. My patrol escorts me back home.

I break the news about the threat against us and that we could have cruise missiles heading our way. The decision to evacuate our beloved farmstead is made very quickly. Brit curses up a storm, "Those bastard sons-a-bitches…"

Becca takes the news stoically. She has been through enough to not get emotional, at least on the surface. This is her family and close friends in grave danger. Inside her emotions go into turmoil. To let that turmoil blow to the surface will do no good. Action is needed, not emotional breakdowns. She can cry later. She takes charge. Within an hour, the family and our entourage are on the move. Despite the foot of snow on the ground, the darkness, and the freezing temperatures, the farmstead is vacated.

The farmstead has been violently attacked several times over the past few months; we have always stood our ground. But missiles from the sky, launched from five hundred miles away is something we cannot defend against. Even our special operators agree that we need to seek new quarters.

We take our pets, including Paul's faithful dog, Badzy. But our livestock, our stored food, our precious supplies are left behind. Grace makes sure to grab our working electronics as Becca, Eve and Janie pack clothing and cherished mementos. Our security team packs up our arms as quickly as possible, taking what is needed, leaving behind what they cannot take with them on quick notice.

As I leave, I check the temperature on our front porch thermometer, eight degrees. A light snow is falling but there is no wind. For four months we have done everything we can to make the lives of our community and the refugees easier. As I hobble down our front steps, helped by my wife and Larson, I realize that we're now refugees.

We have neighbors who will take us in. Becca and I, along with a small security detail, will head back to Bakersville. Not the firehall, it has been deemed targeted as well, but to a large farmhouse a few miles away from the firehall. We leave our family and our workers at the mercy of our neighbors as we make the twenty mile trip back through Somerset and on to Bakersville. I occasionally look up.

Larson notices and looks up too. "Air cap missions, huh pap," he says. "It's real serious, isn't it?"

"Air cap missions, and God's Grace, Larson. We just fled the Farmstead. It's as serious as it can get," I reply.

Chapter 25, Call to War

USS Ronald Reagan

January 10th

"Our AWAC picked up twelve fighters heading towards Pope Air Force base," the electronic warfare officer states. "They also picked up signatures of a tanker refueling the air cap over Dover."

It's 2100 hours, pitch black and frigid cold. The only lights seen in the massive port come from the Fifth Fleet ships and a few fires burning on the mainland. Some of the fires are people trying to stay warm. Some of the fires are from skirmishes still taking place around the base. A large fire burns in the warehouse district were the squatters have set fires in the storehouses in an attempt to deny his fleet access to the supplies stored there.

But the piers are secure. His marine unit, after many bloody battles and skirmishes, has accomplished its mission. His aviators are landing precision bombs on the rebels. Two of his destroyers and several support ships are being pushed into their berths by a few functioning tugs. Refueling and resupply operations will begin immediately. His operations team is giving each ship a twelve-hour berth time. Then the ships must put back to sea. They're on a war footing. They know they have too many ships clogged up in port. So they have to resupply the ships and get them dispersed as quickly as possible. There will be no shore leave.

The USS Ronald Reagan won't be berthed until the next morning. It will take half the available tugs to nudge the almost one-thousand-foot behemoth up to the pier. Meanwhile, flight operations continue.

"I need a command staff meeting now," Admiral Barnes states. "Get all our senior operations officers here ASAP. Van

Hollern and his friends are pushing a little too far. We need to push back."

"Aye aye," his chief of staff replies, a bead of sweat breaking out on his brow. He fears what may be coming.

Ten minutes later, Admiral Barnes' six key people meet in his spacious office. Three are physically there, three are on secure video links. Some of the people were present for the conference call held a few hours ago and know the full details of the situation. The others have been briefed.

"Men, we're on the verge of civil war. You all know of the devastation of the worldwide attacks and that Senator Clinton, now President Clinton, is the only rightful elected leader left in our chain of command. She has used her presidential powers provided by the wars act to implement martial law. The martial law is starting to gain control of the chaos, especially on the west coast.

"You also know that looters, militias and rogue military units are savaging our attempts at implementing martial law here on the east coast. Four hours ago, Admiral Van Hollern and a cabal of looters and rogue officers declared President Clinton ineligible for office. Since then, they've pressed forward with their own plans to make our country, America, their own military dictatorship.

"Not only have they besmirched and belittled the rightful president, they've expanded their operations. President Clinton has the only legitimate claim to be our Commander in Chief. She has been a friend of mine, and many of you. Many of us would not be where we are now without our loyalty to her and her parents. Decisions need to be made. Where do our loyalties lie? Will we let our country fall further into chaos and anarchy? Or will we heed the difficult call to implement martial law, even if it means we must deal with the rogue units harshly?

"The rebels already control Fort Bragg, Charlestown Naval Base, large parts of the Appalachian Mountains, and now apparently Fort Hood. There are other bases that have allied with them, including Fort Jackson and maybe Minot Air Force Base in North Dakota. Most of our military bases have been abandoned. The few that remain are in rebellion, except on the west coast. Over the past few hours, Dover Air Force base has begun flight operations including refueling missions. A squadron of F16s, presumably from Fort Hood and the Texas Air National Guard, has flown into Pope Air Force base and is now helping to support their air cap missions.

"While we have moved slowly, the anarchists have moved quickly. Men, I love our country. What has happened to our country pains me to the soul. In the midst of the suffering, we have opportunists trying to overthrow our democracy. It's time to fight back. We cannot let a few rogue military units become dictators over our families, friends and neighbors.

"We have sat by and let this happen. We have the military might to bring these rebels to their knees. We can save our country. And the time to act is now.

"I need plans to start bringing down this rebellion. We have air power, we have naval power, we have air assault and land assault capabilities. And we have the long reach of our Tomahawk missiles. I want a plan by 0600 tomorrow morning. And I expect the plan to already be moving when we meet. Put flights in the air, start setting target coordinates. Get the rest of our marines ready for quick deployment. The enemy has moved faster than we have. That all changes tomorrow. We'll take down the rebels who are bringing anarchy to our homeland. We'll not sit by idly. We'll not play defense. We'll take the offense, aggressively. I want shock and awe. Let the rebels and looters know we mean business.

"This is war, gentleman. We know how to do war."

165

"But this is war where we live, where our families and neighbors live," the air commander states.

"Do you want your family living under a military dictatorship run by rogue officers?"

"No, no I don't," is the subdued response.

"Okay then. Let's get this mission moving. Operation Roll Back. We'll roll back the looters and rebels!"

Chapter 26, Desertion

USS Somerset

January 11th, 0500 hours

(Note to naval enthusiasts and the twelve hundred Somerset county residents who went to the commissioning of the USS Somerset. In reality, the USS Somerset (LDP-52) is an amphibious transport dock that carries over a thousand marines and their equipment as well as landing craft to land them on any foreign soil. I have taken literary freedom to make the USS Somerset a high-tech missile bearing destroyer to make it fit into the story. I hope you oblige me in this aspect of the story.)

The USS Somerset is one of the navy's newest and most advanced destroyers. At three hundred and fifty feet in length, it's not large, but it's not small. Its profile is unique, streamlined, literally stealth in its design. All of its armaments are hidden inside the ship and only deploy during firing, keeping the ship sleek and stealthy. There are no gun turrets, no missile tubes that can be seen. They're only exposed when in use. Other than its new-concept exterior painting, it looks more like some billionaire's yacht than one of the most high-tech fighting ships on the sea.

The ship was authorized by congress after 9/11 in honor of Flight 93. From the start, it was designed to include all the best and most effective arms available. The USS Somerset was designed to be the start of a new generation of warship, utilizing all the newest technology.

It was commissioned in 2016, and after posting stellar results in its shake down cruises, was assigned to the powerful Fifth Fleet and deployed to the Indian Ocean. The navy decided it would be good to man the USS Somerset with as many people from Somerset County as they could. The initial crew had twenty-four seamen and three officers from Somerset County. Using that policy as a recruiting tool, a few years later that number has grown. Thirty-five sailors and four officers are Somerset County natives.

* * *

"No freaking way! I can't do this. Jonesy, look at these coordinates. Double check them for me," a young seaman asks his tech sergeant.

The tech sergeant checks the coordinates. "You're good, seaman," he responds.

"It's good? That's my neighbor's farm. It's only two miles away from where I live. I used to help that guy mow his fields and take care of his animals when he went out of town." The young tech punches in five more coordinates. They all show targets in Somerset County.

"This has to be a mistake," he states. "This is the Somerset County Courthouse, this here is the Bakersville fire hall. Is this some kind of sick joke?" The young man asks, as his stomach roils, ready to convulse.

His unit commander requests that the coordinates be verified. Within a few moments, he receives his reply. The coordinates are viable targets. "Punch up the mission ," the tech sergeant orders.

The twenty-two-year-old missile technician is in a state of shock. He knows he's sending lethal weapons on his hometown. His mind races as he delays plugging in the coordinates. Lieutenant Hastings, the ships Executive Officer and second in command is a Somerset County native. He greeted the young seaman personally when he came on board. He said to come to him at any time. That was almost a year ago. But now is the time. The USS Somerset can't fire missiles on its namesake county. This has to be a mistake.

Nervous as all get out, the young seaman uses a distress protocol to contact Lieutenant Hastings. Two minutes later, his hometown mentor is standing next to him.

"What's your concern?" the senior officer asks.

"Look at these target coordinates, sir. They're all in Somerset County. I don't understand."

The second in command of the USS Somerset looks at the targets his ship is supposed to hit. He swears under his breath. He knows his fleet is supposed to be fighting rebel units, but he had no idea that they would be launching missiles at his hometown. Zero hour is only moments away. What is about to happen is wrong, he knows it in his gut.

"Cease operations now," Lieutenant Hastings bellows. "This ship won't be part of an attack on the homeland, on its namesake county."

Moments later over a hundred Tomahawk missiles fire from the fifth fleet followed by several flights of fighter/bombers with F35 fighter escorts.

* * *

In the control tower of the USS George H. W. Bush, things are happening fast. A plan was already in place, it only needed an aggressive act to put the forces in motion. The launching of the Tomahawk missiles from the Fifth Fleet is the trigger point. The Third Fleet can no longer sit by.

Admiral Van Hollern, with the support of his air and naval commanders begin operations to secure the homeland and neutralize the Fifth Fleet. The sorties already in the air are issued a weapons free order, allowing them to engage any aircraft that threatens them or attacks the homeland. Then the aircraft carrier begins launching wave after wave of attack aircraft. Their mission is to defend the fleet and the homeland, even if it means engaging their fellow American naval fighters from the USS Ronald Reagan.

Many of the pilots have serious second thoughts about their mission. The airwaves are full of chatter. Some pilots talk among themselves. Others try to reach out to the pilots of the fifth fleet. Some are gung-ho for a fight. More are holding back, wondering what the hell is going on. Word spreads that Admiral Barnes' fleet has launched over a hundred cruise missiles on the homeland, some of them are bearing down on their fleet. For many of the fighters, this kicks in their resolve as they close on the Fifth Fleet.

But other pilots, hearing that Dover Air Force Base is functional and declared a neutral zone, head away from the fight. Unwilling to engage their fellow Americans, no matter who instigated the fight, they pilot their planes to neutral ground.

Deep in the bowels of a missile cruiser, the actual Flag Ship of the Third Fleet, the screens are lit up. They see the tracks of the cruise missiles and the flight paths of all jets in the air. Over two dozen Tomahawks are inbound to their ships. "Weapons free," the fleet defense commander states in a fleet wide broadcast. "We have incoming missiles, fire at will." Weapons systems on two dozen ships spin up and begin deploying anti-missile defense systems similar to the Patriot battery systems. Millions of dollars of missiles and high-tech gunnery systems are engaged against the deadly incoming cruise missiles

Meanwhile, the fleet operations commander issues orders to fire back. They have no shore targets to engage. They target only the warships that have launched missiles against them. The vast majority of the missiles are targeted at the narrows in Newport News where the Fifth Fleet is bottled up. The Third Fleet lets loose its own volley of cruise missiles.

* * *

Captain Sheila Matthews sits on top of a rock outcrop ten miles from the massive Newport News naval station. She's several hundred feet above sea level and watches the scene from far away.

She see's missiles screaming out from the Fifth Fleet's ships, both out at sea, and bottled up in the harbor. She watches as bombers run at the shore bases, trying to dislodge the squatters, the people she's supporting, the people she's allied with.

She watches as more missiles streak across the night sky as fighters from Dover scream into the fight. Some of the air-to-air missiles hit their targets, causing a mid-air blast. She waits as more fighters begin to engage in front of her. Jet fighters from the Fifth Fleet are trying to maintain air control. But jet fighters from the Third Fleet, Dover Air Force Base and the Texas Air National Guard, begin to take charge of the skies. She watches with a keen eye as she sees her people bring the battle home.

From her vantage point she can see the Fifth Fleet bottled up in Newport News harbor. She knows her people are winning the air war. She waits, hoping for the hammer to fall on the rest of the fleet.

Suddenly, barrages of missiles fire off from the ships stuck in the narrows. Hundreds of small rockets scream into the night and explosions rock the night skies. Then the big explosions begin as the Third Fleet's cruise missiles hit home. Three massive explosions hammer the USS Ronald Reagan despite the heavy anti-missile systems it deployed. A missile cruiser takes two direct hits, the second hit causing massive explosions and a horrific fire. Six other ships take direct hits.

* * *

In the congestion of the narrows, the missile attack is devastating. But Admiral Barnes, aboard the USS Ronald Reagan, is still adamant. "We can take our home port and reorganize. As long as we still have this ship we are a fighting force. I won't let these rebels defeat us." As he says this, one of his own destroyers, its helm and steering system disabled, careens towards his disabled aircraft carrier. Out of control, the destroyer rams the admiral's carrier at speed, slicing its hull wide open. The aircraft carrier stayed afloat after three direct hits. But the destroyer rips the ship's watertight hull wide open and water gushes in. The massive ship settles to the bottom of the shipping channel, but its flight deck is still above water.

"We're still a viable fighting unit!" the admiral tries to urge on his senior officers, issuing orders to continue the mission. "If we can secure the base, we can resume our air missions from the landside airstrip. Focus on securing the base. We cannot let these rebels defeat us. We're the last remaining hope of restoring order. We have three destroyers and a missile cruiser still afloat in the harbor. I don't care if they have to ram the piers in order to dock, get them ashore and let's start to secure our port."

In the back of the admiral's mind he recalls a staff officer recommending that they wait a few days until the fleet secured the port, refueled, resupplied and dispersed before engaging in any significant operations. But that would have allowed the rebels more time to dig in. He decides not to second guess his decisions. Right now they must put all efforts into securing the port.

* * *

Captain Matthews continues to watch the battle unfold. Even as the massive aircraft carrier settles on the bottom of the channel, she watches as it fires off dozens of cruise missiles. The carrier sits at a dangerous fifteen degree angle. Two jets, their missiles exhausted, try to line up on the beached ship. The first pilot manages to put his plane on the deck, catching the restraining cables. The second F35 does not adjust for the cant of the deck and crashes as a tip of his wing clips the edge of the carrier deck. It bursts into flames and skids sideways across the deck and slams into the tower.

She sees some of the remaining ships maneuver for the docks as the air war above her begins to die down. A few more missiles streak across the sky but most of the jets on both sides have been shot down or have abandoned the fight. She knows that her next mission will be to fight the forces that the Fifth Fleet has managed to put on shore.

She looks around at the few dozen people around her. They're survivors; but are they fighters? Can they help her fight off the invaders? She needs help. She breaks radio silence, makes a quick report on what she has seen and requests support. Then they vacate their spot as quickly as possible. They're only a hundred yards away before several five-inch shells from a destroyer start landing on the position they just vacated.

Her sergeant leads them to another concealed position on the hillside were they can watch over the port. She sends her crew of locals out to rally their people. The local unit's commander is dead. It's up to them to rally around a new leader and take advantage of the position they're in. She assures them that they will see more air support and that reinforcements are on the way. She hopes she's telling them the truth. She won't know for six more hours what to expect in terms of support.

* * *

Two hundred miles east of the battle, the USS Somerset cruises south. Lieutenant Hastings, three other officers, and fifty-four seaman are crammed into the small brig. They disobeyed direct orders and had to be brought into custody for starting a mutiny. But as the ship's commander hears the results of the battle and realizes that he's also reneging in his duties; is complicit in his ship's rebellion, he makes a decision to release the sailors and make contact with the Third Fleet. They did not fire any missiles. They're a neutral party.

* * *

Deep in the Appalachian Mountains, no missiles hit Somerset County or the Johnstown area, thanks to the mutiny on the USS Somerset. Letterkenny Arms Depot takes over a dozen direct hits. General Adkins administrative building is leveled and her communication systems takes a serious toll. A lot of their precious hardened communications equipment is destroyed. But loss of life is minimal; they had vacated the buildings, having been warned of the impending attack. Fort Bragg fairs about the same. Having been warned, they bugged out or dug in.

And most importantly, there are no following attacks. Any of the Fifth Fleet fighter/bombers that wanted to engage were shot down in the air battle. The rest of the pilots sought refuge at Dover.

Dover is now the most powerful air base on the east coast, with over a hundred operational aircraft and full capability to refuel and rearm. Colonel Tiani already has air cap missions flying and is trying to organize the base into operational squadrons. As far as he's concerned, nothing flies on the east coast that he doesn't know about.

Chapter 27, Aftermath

Somerset/Johnstown Area

January 12th

The sun rises revealing a cold and bleak terrain, bright rays glistening off the snow-covered trees and fields. The fresh snow adds three inches to the heavy accumulation already on the ground. In some places the snow lies two feet deep. The fresh snow and crisp temperatures leave a clean and serene landscape. The vast white covering is unbroken. No roads have been plowed, so there is no traffic. Salt has not been spread, there is no slush, cinders and dirt. The only disruption to the blanket of white is around the farms, were farmhands make sure the herds are fed and tended to.

In Johnstown, Somerset and the surrounding small communities, the sound of church bells begins to ring out across the frozen landscape. Word of the massive naval and air battle spreads quickly. The surviving residents have no idea that their county was on the target list; that their precious generators and their leaders' compounds were to be blown to smithereens. They only know what the rumor mill generates. And the rumor mill is mainly true, the Laurel Highlands Militia and its allies won a great battle. What generates the most talk, as the church bells ring, is how their militia now has control of an aircraft carrier.

The rumors run wild. "Mark Mays, with just one leg, led a seal team and they took over the carrier," one woman states adamantly. "My Johnny was part of the boarding team."

"That's BS, Martha, and you know it," her neighbor, a crotchety old man in his eighties states. "We got allies in Texas and they sent us help. I hear when the pilots were ordered to fight the Texans, they staged a mutiny and the battled fizzled out."

"You all are dreamers," a man in his thirties states. "This is just a lull in the storm. The wanna be dictator you all idolize is about to have a hammer come down on all of us. I don't understand how you mindlessly follow this military dictator. He's going to get us all killed."

"Carl, you need to back up your accusations with facts. You've gotten fat by selling the herbs and produce from your farm without any interference. And no one stopped you from entering the elections for county council this spring. You're not winning my vote by slandering a good man," one of the local merchants states.

A young woman, a mother of three who has supported her family by cleaning, mending, cooking and doing any menial chore offered, chimes in. "God is working here. General Mays is a man of faith. He has encouraged us all to be faithful, to pray. The fact that we're alive and free is miraculous. We could be living under martial law. Whatever happened in this far away battle, God's hand was involved. I firmly believe that."

Similar conversations range across the mountains and in the towns and villages. But the day to day need to survive takes over, animals are fed, wood is split, fires are stoked and the sick are tended to.

* * *

By noon Rebecca and I are heading east, back to Mountain Side, our homestead. A plow truck has once again made the long run on Route 30 from Letterkenny, in Chambersburg, to Bakersville and back, keeping that main route open. A few other plow trucks have 219 and some of the other main roads open.

As our convoy gets closer to home, I make sure that runners are sent off to let our family and the rest of our people know it's safe to return home. Larson restarts the fires to warm up the home as Rebecca gets a large pot of kielbasa and sauerkraut warming. The first to return to the farmstead are the eight special ops security people. After checking in, and making a plan, they head back out, to resume security patrols and help the other family members return home.

By nightfall our sprawling complex is full of people. The mood is somber, yet joyful. There are no rumors here. Many of us know full well that our complex was on the Fifth Fleet's main target list. We don't know why we were spared, but we do know that the battle between the Fifth Fleet and the Third Fleet has been won by our allies. We also know that making Dover a neutral site was successful and how that affected the battle.

Larson and Ken call me out to the front porch and point to a fast-moving object in the sky. "An air cap mission, Pap. I haven't seen one of those in months," Larson states.

"That's a good thing son, that's a very good thing," I reply. Larson smiles and nods. I know he will sleep well tonight. Ken, understanding that good things are happening says nothing, but embraces me fully. I can feel his tears on my neck.

Becca comes out on the porch with Zach, Janie and a slew of kids.

"What are you warriors getting so emotional about out here?" Becca asks, seeing our teary eyes.

Ken speaks up. "Things are getting better, that's all. Things are getting better." He looks up to the sky as he says this, then smiles while wiping the tears from his cheek.

Becca looks up. "What are we looking for? Oh my God, is this the rapture? It's so beautiful and so peaceful." She grabs my hand and gazes into the star filled night sky, the Milky way clearly visible sprawling from horizon to horizon. I see a tear form on her cheek as she takes in the beauty of billions of stars and galaxies as they light up the night sky.

Zach sees what we're looking at. He turns to me and gives me a high five as his face lights up. "That's an air cap mission! Look mom, see the fast moving lights to the south. That's an air security patrol. They're flying missions to protect us from surprise attacks."

"Oh my!" she states as she picks out the fast moving lights against the vast array of stars. She turns to me. "Okay, so no rapture. But you got us an air force to protect us?" She questions me. "I think I would rather have the rapture, but I guess I'll settle for an Air Force.

"I still don't believe all that has happened," She continues. "But I have to. I'm looking at it, I've lived it. Mark, please tell me it's coming to an end. Surely these people can now take over. Tell me your mission is done. I need you here, your family needs you here."

I embrace her warmly and she buries her head in my neck. "Tell me you're going to stop playing general, Mark. Promise me you're going to stay home."

I hug her tightly. "Things are getting better, baby doll, things are getting better. But I can't promise you that my mission is done. I don't know what God has in store for us."

She steps back quickly. "You may not know what God wants, but you certainly know how to tick off your wife. Your family needs you. I need you."

She glares at me, then pushes aside her moment of anger. "Give me something old man. Tell me you're not going to lead another infantry charge against a tank battalion. Tell me you'll just issue the orders, not fight hand to hand combat. Mark, I can't bear to know you're out there on the frontline. You have done enough."

"Okay, okay," I respond. "I promise I won't charge an artillery brigade with a hunting knife."

178

She eyes me up and down, she knows me too well. "Promise me you won't put yourself on the frontline. I'll let you go to the bigwig confabs like the one we had in Fort Bragg. But no more frontline combat. You only have one freaking leg old man! You can't do that combat stuff anymore."

I grasp her by the shoulders and look directly into her eyes. "I promise, no frontline combat. God gave you to me, and I'll make sure that I'm always here for you, until the end."

She stares back at me, then smiles coyly. "Okay, General Mays. But, He gave you to me too, remember that." She kisses me warmly.

Zach speaks up. "Okay, Mom, enough with the gushy stuff. Now that we know you're going to allow Mark to continue doing his job, I want to know how the hell he got an air cap mission running."

"It has to be out of Dover," I respond, a little red faced. "Last we heard they had several squadrons land there, refusing to fight their fellow pilots. Some of those naval guys went to flight school together. Dover is a declared neutral site. By flying air cap missions over us, they're protecting us from anything Admiral Barnes might try to attempt. But at the same time, we can't use air power to attack Admiral Barnes and the Fifth Fleet."

Colonel Brit has stepped outside with a sparse plate of kielbasa and sauerkraut and a small portion of mashed potatoes. "So General Club'em is not in control of something? Get your ass down there and straighten those people out. We freaking got Dover open for them. You're losing your edge, Mark."

Becca glares at her daughter. "Just kidding, mom, just kidding. I'll go. I got my cane in case anyone acts out of sorts."

Her timely remarks bring chuckles to many on the porch.

"You're going nowhere, young lady," Becca responds. "Your family needs you too. And I've heard about your antics as well. You need to settle down. And what's with the cane?"

"Don't worry about me, Mom, I got a good security detail. And the cane gets both sympathy points and street cred. I popped a young punk in the jaw when things were about to go bad out there around Harrisburg. Turned the whole situation around, People respond when they get smacked by a crutch. It works." Brit turns and winks at me. "I learned it from a crotchety old man."

A strong breeze blows, lifting some of the freshly fallen snow off the tree limbs and sending it spiraling through the air. It also sends a chill through our front porch gathering, and we retreat inside to eat and warm up.

Chapter 28, Suffering

Everywhere

01/12

While the free people of the Laurel Highlands celebrate their allied victory over the Fifth Fleet, most of the country struggles with starvation, anarchy, violence and disease. Maybe the country would have been better off if Martial Law had been fully implemented, because anarchy and mayhem reigns, and it's ugly.

Major cities are just empty lots of high-rises with only a few hard-core survivors living off of rats, pigeons and scavenged food. In the south, the stink of the dead is almost unbearable. In the north, the dead have frozen. The stink will return in the spring. But to the city survivors, the horrors of daily living far surpasses dealing with the stink.

In the once peaceful refuge of suburbia and rural America things are the worst. It's a daily fight for survival. Any stored food is long gone; either used up, stolen or shared. The warehouses have been pillaged. Daily sustenance might be a pack of crackers or a stolen egg. A mob of starving people would quickly lay waste to a brood of backyard chickens. A one-day feast destroying a year's worth of sustainable food for some forethinking family.

Further into the rural areas, militias fight each other. One militia being a band of city refugees. The other militia being the local farmers; trying to protect their crops and herds.

By now, most of these fights have come to a close. Now the battle is against Mother Nature. The cold spell that dropped fresh snow on the Laurel Highlands is a massive artic cold front that has dropped south. It's not an Alberta Clipper, now called an Artic Vortex. It's a high-pressure system parked over the western plains that has the jet stream pumping cold air out of Canada, across the great lakes and blowing snow and cold air into the eastern half of America. The Rocky Mountains and West Coast experience warmer and dryer weather

Along with the bone chilling temperatures, the prolonged cold front brings heavy snow as the cold air moves across the great lakes. The bands of marauders and refugees that had been pillaging the farms to survive, now find themselves snowed in. Moving two miles to the next farm is no longer a simple task. As they deplete the resources of the farms they occupy, they become desperate. At the same time, the surviving farmers realized they can save themselves, maybe even work a deal with the militias.

But for most, the sick, the young, the elderly, the ill prepared, the poorly led, they suffer the most from the sustained cold weather. Family members, neighbors and friends die of starvation and exposure. Most are left where they die, their fellow travelers don't have the energy or the time to dig through the frozen ground and give them a proper burial. Across the Atlantic States., the Carolinas and New England, the effects of cold weather and heavy snow takes the lives of several million more people. And winter has just begun. The suffering and death cannot be stopped. The cold is pervasive. For most people, driven from their homes in search of food, there is no shelter.

Several hundreds of miles away from the cities, in the farmlands, the ranchers and farmers have no way to get the life sustaining food to the people who need it. Steers are slaughtered so that the breeding stock can be fed. As millions of people are dying of starvation. Tens of thousands of beef cattle, hogs, and chickens are slaughtered and left to rot.

In many remote areas around the country, in isolated enclaves like Johnstown, there is stability. But that is not the norm. For the most part chaos, anarchy and destruction are the norm.

Societal collapse is rampant. The predictions of massive loss of life are coming true.

Tens of thousands of people watched the explosions of the battle for Newport News. Very few knew why the battle happened. They don't know it yet, but many of them will be saved because patriots stood for freedom.

* * *

The family that was searching for dog meat on Christmas Eve in New Jersey is no longer alive. While stewing a feral cat with a few scavenged herbs, they were attacked and killed by another group of survivors who smelled the stew brewing from a mile away.

The towns in rural Illinois are now firmly in control of Martial Law. But their supplies and resources are diminishing. The farms have been taken over by thugs who are following the orders of people who know nothing about farming. They had great potential to form a strong and successful alliance, but that did not pan out.

In the outskirts of Roanoke, Virginia, it's a different story. The initial waves of refugees streaming out of the city caused major strife and many deadly battles. After significant loss of life and many skirmishes, an equilibrium happened between the farmers and the city folk. It's an uneasy peace, but like in Johnstown, food is traded for supplies, labor and security.

* * *

Dr. Samuel Gray, and several other local leaders meet to discuss the situation. The cold front has stalled to their north and it's a cold rainy evening.

"We got air force jets flying overhead," Dr. Gray states. "Anyone have any information on that?" he asks. The man they assigned to monitor the ham radios speaks up.

"There was a major battle at Newport News. The Fifth Fleet and the Third Fleet finally came to blows. For some reason, a lot of jets headed to Dover. Now Dover is running air cap missions. They're denying both the Fifth Fleet and the Third Fleet to use their air power. I'm not sure what to make of all that, except that the Fifth Fleet seems to have been defeated."

"So who the hell is running the country?" one of the militia leaders asks. "Two naval fleets attack each other? This is not good."

The ham radio guy speaks up again. "Ain't no one running the country. I hear Shelly Clinton, the New York Senator claims to be our rightful leader. But there are reports from some of my contacts in Texas that the Secretary of the Interior is alive and claiming the rightful seat as the President. Personally, I think they're both fools. There ain't no country left to govern. But, I have heard some pretty good rumors that there is lots of folks like us, folks who are surviving"

"What do you mean, Tom?" Dr. Gray asks.

"It's hard to get a handle on it, lots of rumors flyin' around. But a bunch of Oath Keepers along with some regular military and militias have been fighting against the people who want to instigate martial law. Seems where the militias free the people from the martial law, things go well. I got a friend in Winchester says things are looking up since a band of freedom fighters moved in."

"Winchester is only a hundred miles away," states one of the militia leaders. "Maybe we should send a scout party up there to see what's going on?"

"Send a scout party with an ambassador," Dr. Gray responds.

It takes the twelve leaders another two hours to hash it out, but they determine to send eight people in two old farm trucks and two ATVs up to Winchester to make contact with this rogue group of freedom fighters.

Chapter 29, Still fighting

Newport News

January 15th

Admiral Barnes current flagship is a missile cruiser that is stationed about ten miles off the coast. What is left of his once mighty fleet is still battling for control of the largest naval station on the east coast. He no longer has any air support other than a few Marine attack and transport helicopter squadrons. The rest of his air capacity has been grounded by the pervasive flights coming out of Dover Air Force base that have grounded all fixed wing flights.

His people have gained control of the local airport, but he does not have the air power to challenge the might of Dover. He has started focusing on securing the harbor. Small victories will lead to success. One advantage he has is that the Dover air cap has also grounded Admiral Van Hollern's flight deck as well as flights out of Pope Air Force Base.

Dover is denying any fixed wing flights that they don't control. They're maintaining their status as a neutral site. As the most powerful site, they're denying anyone else use of their air power. It seems Dover is willing to see who emerges as the victor on the ground. Admiral Barnes intends to be the victor, and then bring the air power of Dover under his command.

* * *

Thirteen miles west of the admiral's cruiser, deep in a limestone cave, Captain Shelia Matthews greets six of her teammates and two dozen additional Special Forces operators. "About time you got here, you slagerts. Was the hard cider and fast women too much to pull away from? I been busting balls just to hang on here. That bastard got control of the airport, but he can't fly, thank God. Still, the crazy bastard has naval guns. They're blasting away at our resources and costing us heavy."

"We'll work it out captain, we won't let you down, Little Miss." 'Little Miss' has been her handle since joining this group of mercenaries. She does not view it as derogatory in any way. She sees it as a title of respect and deference. They know she's a woman, and she's small, but at the same time she deserves their respect. They know she could send anyone of them to the hospital in an instant if she so chose. Like 'Red', they all have a handle.

Captain Matthews looks over her old friends and their new arrivals. She recognizes several Special Forces operators from Fort Bragg. She either trained with them or had been deployed overseas with them. They hug and high five as she walks the ranks, welcoming the support group.

After her second in command recaps the situation, she dismisses the junior ranks of the newly arrived unit to get food and sleep while she calls their six leaders into her office. Her office, and the TOC, is a dripping wet cave with a bit of communications equipment, a City of Norfolk map, and a Virginia Department of Transportation state map laid out on a couple of pieces of plywood.

She lays out the situation. "We have enough local fighters to reclaim the port. They were living off the port's supplies and are highly motivated to regain control of the warehouses. But the gun fire from Admiral Barnes' ships knock us back every step we take. So long as he has these destroyers pounding us, it's a stalemate."

"Let him take it," one of the NCO's states. "He can't fly his planes, we wouldn't be here if he could. Let him take the port. In the meantime, we rally the locals and prepare to retake everything. We wait till his ships are moored, then we flood the zone. With the help of the locals, who know all the sewers and back alleys, we can do it. All we have to do is pull back and get ready for action. We can train up the locals while we're hunkered down."

187

The room goes silent for a minute. The move is drastic, giving up everything they've fought for. But what they're doing is not working, a change in strategy is needed.

Captain Matthews' first sergeant speaks up. "The locals won't like this plan at all, unless we have a way to take care of them and their families. We don't have those resources. And the farmlands around here are in chaos. We can't count on the farms for support."

"Raid and run," a stoic and grizzled Staff Sergeant states. All eyes turn to him. "We did it in Mogadishu a few years back. We hit the supply warehouses hard and fled with enough supplies to keep our local tribesmen happy until we could be resupplied by our own people. Your locals will know what warehouses to hit. We go in heavy and pull out what we need to keep them and us supplied for a few days. Then we go underground."

"I like it," Captain Matthews states. "We'll need several different places for us to bug out to and begin staging. We'll also need to round up a few technicals and trucks with trailers to haul out our loot. We have three reliable local commanders. I'll bring them in and we can start planning. Any other suggestions?" The hardcore group of fighters throw out ideas, objections and solutions. They hash out a workable plan. Now they need to sell the locals on the idea of abandoning all they've fought for.

Chapter 30, School Is In

Mountainside

January 20th

The children kick the slush and snow from their boots as they come in from recess. The day is slightly warmer than the previous days, the sun has come out and the temperatures have reached above freezing for the first time in weeks. Two dozen children attend class today. Most are regulars from the farmstead and nearby farms. The ranks have grown from just a dozen when they first started the school in the basement of the front house.

The school is not much different than the old-fashioned one room schoolhouse. The older students help the younger students, while the teachers struggle to make sure everyone learns and progresses. For some it's dull and tedious. For others it's challenging and exciting. Until it all turns into a nightmare.

* * *

The assassin's squad has been watching, waiting. They've had to move around, keep wary, and blend in. But they've been patient, looking for an opportunity, a weakness. They knew a direct attack on the farmstead would not work. They've tracked General Mays and determined an attack on him or one of his convoys would fail as well. A new opportunity has developed, over the past few weeks the trained soldiers protecting the compound has diminished.

They're aware of all the developments and battles that have been taking place on the east coast. Because of the demand for skilled people, they've noticed that a few key people have been moved off the security detail. They also have found a weak spot in the schoolhouse. It's almost a half mile from the main house, far from immediate response. They decide that taking the children captive will force General Mays to come out. After studying their target, they know he will never let harm come to his family.

Their plan is to smash and grab the school children. Then they will demand General Mays for ransom. As soon as the general shows himself, a sharpshooter will take him down. They will leave the schoolhouse using a predetermined route set with landmines and tripwire claymores. A series of vehicles has already been staged to use for their retreat. They will be in Fredericksburg by nightfall.

* * *

The lone sentry, one of Hairys' biker friends, is a hundred yards into the wood line. He has no chance to respond as the silent crossbow dart penetrates his heart. He slumps to the ground in a puddle of blood. A Ranger standing guard at the door to the house senses that something is amiss. He stands and peers deeply into the woods as he tries to raise the dead guard on their local comm system.

The comm equipment is cheap, bought on the internet and thrown into the Faraday Cage several years ago. When the Ranger doesn't get an immediate response he's not alarmed, but he does take a secure position behind the brick wall of the front porch. He notices movement and is about to make a call back to the TOC at the main house. But an arrow pierces his head. He falls to the floor of the porch, dead.

Four deadly men, studiously avoiding the eyes of the cameras mounted to detect exactly what they're doing, join on the front porch of the sprawling ranch style house. They know at least two people will be in the kitchen, preparing to serve the children their lunch. They also expect at least one more armed guard and two or three adult teachers.

That means as many as six armed adults are inside the home. This school is not a gun free zone. Even the teachers will be

190

armed and ready to defend their young students. They follow their plan. Four skilled shooters against one armed guard, they're confident in their skills. The four assassins break in the side door and front door at the same time. They throw in flash bang grenades and wait the few seconds for the blinding explosions to burst.

* * *

The two loud booms resound over the mountain top. At the farmstead, everyone kicks into alert status, taking positions to defend the property. In less than two minutes, positions are manned and the Farmstead is in full battle status. In the comms room, Brit and Rebecca desperately try to reach the front house and the guards that are to protect it. They get no response.

"It's the front house!" Becca exclaims. "They're attacking the school. We can't reach any of our guards out there. Those bastards!" She grabs an AR15 and races out of the house. Brit is right behind her.

In the schoolhouse, the two flash bangs incapacitate the two women preparing lunch. The mercenaries rush past them, but not before firing short bursts to make sure they're down for good. Two assassins take up positions to keep watch for reinforcements coming from the main house while two more assassins storm down the stairs, throwing more flash bangs.

The assassins descend the steps, expecting the flash bangs to have put the two teachers on the ground. They need to eliminate the last guard before gathering up the children and reuniting with their compatriots on the first floor. Their sniper is already set up for when Mark Mays comes forth to negotiate. They know that is what he will do.

As the two assassins descend the steps, they're met with a fire storm of bullets. It has been less than fifteen seconds since they first breeched the house. They've moved quickly and decisively. The basement school room and its inhabitants should be

191

in shock. The intruders execute a tumble drop to the basement floor and roll up shooting.

They expected one skilled guard and a bunch of terrified children with a few teachers ready to surrender. But this is a new world. Even the youngest children have seen death and fighting. Any child older than ten or twelve is armed with a twenty-two rifle, four-ten shot gun or small pistol. Any child over fourteen has been trained to shoot, some of them have been in fierce battles to protect their farms and families. Mark's older grandsons are all battle tested. This will be the fourth time they've fought in a battle on their home grounds.

The two mercenaries die in a hail of bullets at the bottom of the stairs. Most of the shots fired by the scared children fly harmlessly. But enough connect to put the assassins down.

On the first floor, the other two assassins know things have gone upside down. The volume of fire from the basement of the schoolhouse is not what they expected. Meanwhile two women crest the hill, charging them. They expected this. They take aim on the charging women, ready to take them down. But as they're about to pull the trigger, the room they're in comes under heavy fire, fifty caliber rounds ripping through the brick and mortar, causing portions of the house to collapse. One of the assassins is hit in the shoulder, the massive round nearly severing his arm. The boom, boom, boom, from the patrol vehicle's fifty caliber machine gun continues as the remaining assassin tries to flee.

Deep in the woods, the sniper takes aim on one of the women charging the schoolhouse. He squeezes the trigger and watches with satisfaction as the taller and older woman drops to the ground. He gathers up his equipment and rushes off to their bug out bikes. He's met by their leader.

"That went to hell in a hand basket. Let's get the hell out of here." Thirty minutes later, driving in a prepositioned farm truck, they pass through a roadblock in Bedford and are back in no-man's land. But the assassins' team took a beating.

* * *

The farmstead is in a panic. The six remaining security operators start patrols while the locals attend to the wounded. Becca Mays has taken a potentially mortal chest wound. She's losing a lot of blood and needs serious medical attention. Their resident nurse, an experienced ER nurse from Baltimore, rushes to Becca's side. She's joined by a Ranger with battlefield paramedic experience.

"Blood clot, blood clot, we need blood clot now!" the Ranger hollers. Pulling his knife, he quickly cuts away her heavy coat and clothing, exposing the wound. The nurse helps in the messy task of peeling off the bloody clothing. The medic rips open his first aid kit and applies the blood clotting agent to the wound

"She needs serious medical care," the nurse states. "We got to get her to Somerset ASAP. Get on the phone and let the hospital know that we have a serious chest wound coming in." The nurse sees that the blood clot is working. But she knows the wound is bad, a sucking chest wound. She says a prayer for the woman who has taken in and cared for her and her family.

* * *

I come on the scene late. I had been down in the lower fields with Herq, discussing plans to extend our fence lines so we could take on more cattle. By the time we get to the main house, the fight is over, but the damage has been done. I'm told that Becca has been hit and the situation is critical. I don't wait for the rest of the situation report.

I nearly forget that I need crutches as I turn to race out the door. I stumble but regain my footing, hobbling along as fast as I can. Our big old GMC Suburban, brought in by my stepson Zach when he fled the airport, is backing out of the barn. I hobble along, faster than anyone could think a one-legged man could move and smack the side of the big truck. It stops and I quickly jump into the front seat. "Move, move, move!" I shout as I pull my crutches inside the door.

The big truck lurches forward through the slushy snow. I turn to see Daneel is the driver. He has a look of dread on his face. His pregnant wife was one of the teachers. He speeds down the narrow drive, skidding to a stop where Becca has fallen.

Without a word, he flings the driver's door open and races toward the schoolhouse. I'm met by Brit, trying to be calm, but about to break. "Mom's been shot. It's a chest wound, it's bad. We need to get her to the hospital now."

I hobble to Becca's side, where she's laying by the side of the driveway, the crisp white snow blemished by her crimson blood. "Dear Lord, please don't take her from me. Please, dear Lord, hear my prayers," I say out loud as I fall to my knees and begin sobbing. I kiss my wife's already cold lips,

"Out of the way old man," the nurse hollers. "We have a patient to move!" Things seem to slow down. I feel like I'm moving in slow motion as I literally crawl away from my stricken wife. Someone helps me back into the Suburban and before I know it, we're heading down the road. I'm reeling, sick to my stomach. I know that my life-mate has been shot, may be bleeding out, because of me.

Despite my queasiness, I urge the driver to go faster. I look over to see my son-in-law, Ken, is driving. Brit, and our nurse are in the back, tending to Becca. "Step on it, Ken, if she bleeds out..." I can't finish the thought.

"She ain't gonna bleed out old man," the nurse shouts. "We got her stabilized. We need you to get back in the game. Grab that CB and get a radio relay going to let Somerset Hospital know we have critical patients coming in. Tell them that Becca has a severe chest wound with a drainage tube inserted to let the blood drain out of her lung. Let them know we need an operating room fully staffed. Put those folks on alert so they can get geared up. When we have direct contact with the hospital, give me the mic so I can help them get prepped."

I fumble for the CB mic and relay the information. I'm normally calm, but right now I'm distressed, yelling into the mic, demanding confirmation. My distress is causing everyone in the whole vehicle to be distressed. Ken takes a snow covered turn too fast and starts to slide sideways down the deeply snow-covered road. We're headed for a snow filled drainage ditch. At the last moment, the tires gain traction and the large vehicle straightens out.

"Dear Lord, don't take her from me. She is my strength, my reason for being. Be with us, grant us peace in this time of chaos," I pray out loud.

I calm down, no longer egging Ken to drive faster. We continue to talk over the CBs, relaying updates as we get closer to the hospital. My wife is still alive. Panicking won't save her. I need to rely on God's peace. If God takes her from me, she will be in a better place. This is not something I say to myself to make myself feel better. This is something I know in the deepest depths of my heart. Becca knows Jesus as her Lord and Savior. If she leaves this world, she will go to a better place. But our will to live, our desire to see our loved ones live, is an overpowering urge. Why do we mourn and stress about death when we know we have salvation? I guess that is an ever-lingering doubt. I'm experiencing that doubt right now.

Ken slows down to negotiate the big turn off Route 30 to take Route 281 to Somerset. After negotiating through the foot-deep snow of the turn, we're soon moving as fast as we can down the long straight road leading to one of the only semi-functional hospitals on the East Coast. In the back, Becca's pulse weakens, she has a punctured lung and has lost a lot of blood. Her lips begin to turn blue.

Chapter 31, The Dead

Central City

January 23rd

At the crest of a small rise, overlooking the gentling rolling mountain tops, a large group gathers. An unpleasant ritual takes place once again. The burial plot that started with my brother, his wife and two friends has grown into a small cemetery. Six more graves are dug into the frozen ground. Eight bodies will be laid to rest. Two of those who died were pregnant, their unborn children recognized on the wooden crosses marking their graves.

Two people who have played an important part in keeping the farmstead safe have lost their wives. Merciless people seeking any advantage they could find killed innocents. The violence has to stop. Man killing man has to stop. When will we unite? When will the chaos end? Comfort is offered to those who have lost loved ones. But hearts are hardened by the senseless and ruthless loss of life.

Chapter 32, Mopping up

Newport News

January 25th

"That seems to be the last of them," the MP sergeant states, as his six-man crew emerges with twelve holdouts from the destroyer that rammed the pier in a desperate attempt to secure the port.

The ploy to lure the ships into port took two days to work. The local infrastructure took a beating as the shore guns from the Fifth Fleet targeted anything that posed a threat, but most of the locals followed the plan and vacated the port, luring the fleet to begin bringing in their ships for refueling and resupply.

On the third day, with the planes from Dover keeping the air clear from attack, the locals swarmed in, supported by Oath Keepers, some Rangers, and a few Special Forces soldiers that had made their way there from Fort Bragg.

With the local's knowledge of the back alleys, and at times literally using the sewer system, they and their new allies sprang up seemingly from nowhere. The few marines remaining loyal to the fleet were outmanned and out-maneuvered. The fight was deadly. Marines do not give up. They thought they were fighting for their homeland. They were faced with a determined enemy and they fought to the death.

But the locals and their well-equipped and trained allies knew they were fighting for freedom. They fought harder and more ruthlessly than the trained Marines who opposed them. Loss of life was heavy on both sides

For two days the battle for Newport News raged. It was fought in the alleys, on the piers, in the warehouses. Admiral Barnes was out of his element. He had never had to fight to gain a port. No modern American naval fleet has had to fight to gain a port. One by one, he watched his ships that had moored fall to the insurgents. Low on fuel and depleted of ammunition, he ordered the rest of his fleet to abandon the port. Two missile cruisers, three modern destroyers and a half dozen support ships flee the harbor. A modern-day naval fleet had been decimated. It turned tail and ran.

* * *

The locals celebrate. They know where the food is stored. A few local farmers, those that have not been wiped out by the marauding hordes and the naval bombardments, contribute a few steers and pigs to the celebration. January 25th will be celebrated for years to come by the residents of Newport News. It will be their new Independence Day.

As Captain Matthews is devouring a plate of pulled pork and coleslaw, two F35s fly low over the sprawling naval base and turn a barrel roll. She knows they're acknowledging their victory. Dover said they would remain neutral and let the forces on the ground work things out. Well, they worked things out.

She's sitting with a retired naval captain. He was never a fighter, always on the logistics end of things. "We need to get that landside air strip open, captain. We got supplies, equipment and fuel that those planes need. I'm giving you Smitty's company to get that part of the base cleared and operational."

The older man looks at the younger woman. In the past three days he has seen more combat up close and personal than in thirty years of active duty service. He salutes the young woman smartly. "We'll get that air strip up and running Little Miss." He smiles and laughs as he walks away to make plans with Smitty. A week ago, he was sure he was going to die a miserable death. Now he's part of rebuilding his home port.

Captain Matthews leans back in her flimsy chair and takes a deep breath. She needs sleep. In the past four days she has only slept in fits as the battle has unfolded. She has been on the frontlines, in the midst of the fight. She has been meeting with the locals, rallying them, consoling them. She has been organizing the Oath Keepers and commanding the new regular army units that have been pouring in from Fort Bragg. She's exhausted. A smile comes across her face. She has completed her mission.

Her First Sergeant, who has been with her the whole time, hands her a cup of coffee. She waves him off. "Take a seat, sergeant. We won, we deserve a short break. Forget the coffee, how about two fingers of bourbon. Certainly, someone around here can round up a good bottle of bourbon. I think that's what the good General Mays would ask for at a time like this."

The sergeant sends their aid for some bourbon. "General Mays would also give thanks to the Lord, Captain. What happened here, it's miraculous. We used good strategy, don't get me wrong, but it was crazy good. I think the man upstairs had a hand in it."

"Do you believe in that sergeant? Do you believe in God?"

"I'm not devout, captain. But momma raised me in the church. I've watched and listened to General Mays. He's a flawed man, but he practices what he believes, just like my momma did, God bless her soul. My mom loved on everyone. But at the same time, she was tough. I got in trouble when I was young. She basically made me join the army. She said I needed to learn discipline. She was right.

"But she's the one who taught me the bible. And now, twenty years later, I have to say yes, I believe in God."

The room is quiet for a few moments. The aide returns with a bottle of bourbon and they each pour two fingers.

Captain Matthews breaks the silence. "I respect your views sergeant. But if there is a God, why is all this suffering going on? Why are we fighting just to survive? It doesn't make sense. I don't see how this loving God would let this happen. Millions of people are dying, why?"

"I have struggled with that question too," her sergeant replies. "My only answer is that God didn't cause this, man did. So maybe it's a wakeup call for all of us. If we become a Godless society, then Godless things will happen. I don't know, captain."

"I don't know either, sergeant. But a few weeks ago, when I walked alone up to the front gates of Letterkenny, I prayed, and I felt a peace like I have never felt before. We ended up taking Letterkenny. It was quite a battle, but we took that fort.

"I haven't prayed since then, I don't know why. Maybe I should pray again. Do you know how to pray? Would you pray with me?"

The sergeant, sipping on his bourbon, is completely taken by surprise. He does believe, and he does pray, but he's no angel, he's not an evangelist. But something stirs in him. Now is his time to be Christ's ambassador. But he has no words. From memory he says the Lord's prayer, as best as he can remember it.

"Dear Lord, who art in heaven, hallowed be thy name. Give us this day our daily bread. Forgive us our sins, as we forgive those who have sinned against us. Deliver us from temptation, for thine is the Glory and the Kingdom forever, Amen."

Captain Matthews continues with her head bowed. "Be with us God, please don't fail us. I know you exist. Give us the strength to move forward."

The sergeant says "Amen."

After a moment, the sergeant looks up at his teary-eyed commander. Did he just witness to Captain Matthews? A chill runs up his spine. A feeling of wholeness comes across him like he has never felt before. He embraces the young woman. "God loves you, and he has plans for you. Keep the faith Little Miss, embrace the faith."

After an awkward moment, they sit down, both of them wiping tears from their eyes.

"Captain, you need a good sleep. We've been running on coffee and scrap food for five days. The locals and the Oath Keepers you've recruited can keep the mission going. They know what needs to be done. I'm pulling rank. You're off duty for eight hours, maybe twelve." The sergeant makes sure their aide knows to let the captain rest.

"I have one request," Captain Matthews states, as the aide is about to leave. "If you could, find me a bible." The aide looks a bit dumbfounded, but nods and salutes before leaving.

The exhausted captain sprawls across the ragged couch that is part of her makeshift office. She has a smile on her face as she nods off. The aid returns with a Bible. Her sergeant puts it in her arms and pulls a ratty and worn comforter over her. He smiles and a warm sensation comes over him.

He grabs another worn and tattered blanket and curls up on the floor. He's exhausted too.

Outside, all around the massive harbor, families, neighbors, and friends are reunited. Many celebrate. But the celebrations are subdued as they realize how many are not with them, how many have died. They realize how many of their neighbors, friends, and family members did not make it.

During the height of the chaos, so many died that they became numb. Now that hope for the future is renewed, the loss of loved ones comes crashing down on them. Regrets on decisions made to survive weigh heavily on some. They've survived a traumatic time. They had no hope. Now that a glimmer of hope is on the horizon, they second guess the decisions they made over the past three months; the people they left behind, the people they gave up on, and the people they fought against, killed, to survive. As bad as it was in the Laurel Highlands, it was far worse here in this heavily populated area.

Chapter 33, Trains

The Laurel Highlands

January 27th

"Gramma, what are you doing up? You should be resting," Rusty exclaims. "You've only been home a few days and the doc says you need to stay in bed."

Rebecca's wound grazed her lung, causing extensive bleeding, it was a serious wound and she could have bled out if not for the fast reaction of the nurse and ranger. The blood clotting agents and drainage tube saved her life. She could have bled out or died from the blood filling her lungs, drowned in her own blood. But she is a strong woman and healed quickly.

It's now one in the morning. Rusty and Daneel are manning the control center. Rebecca wandering into the control center is completely unexpected, especially considering her recovery situation. "Something is happening," Becca states. "I'm going back to bed now, but be alert, something is happening."

* * *

Thirty miles north east of Johnstown and six hours later, as the sun begins to light the deep valleys of the Laurel Mountains, a new rumble is heard echoing off the mountains. It's more of a low growl than a rumble. The volume and pitch vary as the new sound permeates the distant valleys.

With the wave of a hand from a skilled engineer, the massive diesel-powered locomotive begins to inch forward. A small cheer goes up as over a hundred people have turned out for this big event.

"What now?" one spectator asks.

"Make a move west, try and link up with Johnstown. I hear they have food and supplies. Their people are the ones who organized and supplied our militia," one of the leaders of the group replies.

"There's a foot or two of snow on the tracks," a woman states. "How are you gonna get a train over the mountains in the dead of winter? And why west to Johnstown, we should send this train east, toward civilization, to Harrisburg. Johnstown is a dying mill town. How can they help us?"

The leader laughs. "Harrisburg is a mess, total anarchy. Johnstown is starting to rebuild. That little backward city is remote from everything else. They've managed to establish an area of security. They've secured their farms and are able to provide for themselves and are even taking in refugees. Trust us, heading east would be a bad idea. The train would be confiscated, and they would push over the mountains to put us all under martial law. This locomotive is heading west."

As they speak, a smaller yard engine chugs up with a snow plow attachment. Several technicians and engineers scurry to make sure the massive blade is securely attached to the locomotive.

* * *

Since a company of Altoona's own National Guardsmen, along with a contingent of local vets and Oath Keepers returned from the battle at Letterkenny, order has begun to be restored to the remote and once prosperous town. The town has always been a transportation hub, even from its founding in the days of the Alleghany Portage Railroad in the early eighteen hundred's. A mainline railroad passes through Altoona.

The city has many rail yards and several locomotive repair shops. As the chaos subsided and the survivors began to evaluate their situation, many started to realize the value of a working locomotive. A group of engineers and technicians began working on getting the behemoths working. After getting a few small yard engines running, they finally have a working mainline engine; they have four more locomotives being worked on.

Unfortunately, they're trapped in their small valley in central Pennsylvania. If they were in the Midwest, they could begin ferrying beef cattle to the starving people of Chicago or St. Louis. They have no large herds of cattle to transport. They do have train loads of fuel. Altoona is a fuel distribution center as well as a transportation hub. There are dozens of massive oil, gas and diesel storage tanks sitting untouched since the attacks

As the chaos subsided, and a civilian government began to form, the local leaders began to realize the fuel depots in their small valley could be a tremendous resource. And they're right. The last of the fuel available in Johnstown is being rationed. Slow moving caravans have been set up to move fuel and heating oil from Letterkenny to Johnstown.

If Altoona could move a dozen tanker cars over the mountain, they would become heroes. And if a locomotive is to make its way over the mountains, having the momentum of the tanker cars, once up to speed, will give the snow plow more force to clear the tracks.

* * *

The temperature hovers at ten degrees, even though the sun shines brightly. The snow is crusty and brittle as the locomotive begins to back away from the massive shop on the brisk January morning. A few minutes later it disappears from sight. A few in the crowd leave, not sure how this train will help them feed their starving families. They move on to the tedious chores of surviving in this chaotic world.

An hour later, a few engineers and mechanics watch as the locomotive races past them, now on the mainline, with a half dozen fuel cars in tow. They hope and pray that the strong engine will make it over the mountain. They won't know until the train returns if their mission is successful.

Snow blows off the tracks as the train barrels up the long ascent leading to the famous horseshoe curve and eventually the summit. At the lower elevations, the snow is easily blown off the tracks. But as the train gains altitude, the snow gets deeper. The engineers on the train know that navigating the one-hundred-and-eighty degree turn of the horseshoe curve at speed will be crucial to being able to push the train through the snow at the mountain's peak.

The manual states that trains are to navigate the sharp curve at no more than twenty-five miles an hour. The curve is only half way up the mountain. The engineers know from their scouts that the snow is close to two feet deep on the summit. They estimate that their short train can navigate the curve at forty miles an hour. That hopefully will give them the momentum they need to blow through the snow and continue to the summit. The lead engineer pushes the engine to gain speed as they race towards the horseshoe curve.

As they enter the curve, the two engineers and their four-man security team can barely see in front of them as the snow billows off the track. Their speed is forty-two miles an hour. The experienced engineers can feel the massive steel wheels of the locomotive slipping on the snow- and ice-covered tracks; the train leans as they enter the curve.

The chief engineer, a sixty-year-old man with over twenty-eight years of experience driving trains over this mountain, increases the throttle slightly, hoping to make up for the slippage and the friction of the curve. The snow billowing from the plow has him blind to the track, he's operating by feel and experience.

As they push further into the massive curve, the train leans tenuously. Two of the guards grasp handholds and look anxiously at the seasoned engineer as the train squeals and bucks along the steel tracks. The engineer keeps an eye on the rearview mirror, watching the wheels of the tanker cars in his small train. The wheels are running on the tracks, the lean they're experiencing is all absorbed by the train's stiff suspension system.

Three quarters of the way through the curve, the engineer glances at his speedometer, they've dropped to thirty-eight miles an hour. He nudges the throttle forward and the massive diesel engine responds, sending a jerking motion through the whole train. He quickly glances in the mirror and can see several sets of wheels start to leave the tracks. The train is leaning heavily. They're almost through the curve; the engineer knows this from experience, even though his vision forward is blinded by the billowing snow from the plow.

Looking in the mirror, he sees the third and fourth tanker cars begin to tip precariously, their wheels a full twelve inches off the tracks. The engineer knows the tracks will be shut down until spring if he rolls the train. He smacks the throttle to full speed. The locomotive screams and strains against the new stress put on its powerful diesel engine. But the tension put on the train pulls the two errant cars back onto the tracks. The train settles down as it exits the horseshoe curve and continues to roll up the long hill to the summit. They've passed their first obstacle and cleared the way for more trains. Ten minutes later the train crests the summit and rolls to a stop in the heavy snow.

* * *

Four armed men approach the idling train. The engineer and two of his security detail dismount, warily scouting the area as the four armed men approach them. As the two groups near each other, a smile breaks out on the leader of the four armed men. "Henry, you old bastard! I knew you would be the one who could get that train up this mountain."

The two men embrace. "So, we got a dead train up ahead?" Henry asks.

"Yep," his friend replies. "But we can switch you to the other track a half mile up. I've scouted all the way to South Fork. You're good as far as I've scouted. From there, you're into the heart of the Laurel Mountain Militia territory. I don't know how many rail engineers they have, but I'm positive they'll make sure you get to the Johnstown rail yard. You have precious cargo, let alone a working locomotive. Get ready for a hero's welcome Henry!"

"I'll be glad to get a shower and a hot plate of food," Henry replies.

"Expect a bath, not a shower, but they have food, and hospitality too." The armed man winks at Henry.

Henry shakes his head. "Elizabeth is still with me and she's as beautiful as ever. All the hospitality I need is a thank you and a hot meal."

Henry climbs back onto the locomotive and nudges the throttle. The wheels slip before gaining enough traction to push the heavy snow off the tracks. The train heads down the long hill, shifting tracks to avoid the stranded train. Henry and his crew stare in wonder as they pass the derelict train. It's a coastal transport full of container shipping units. Every container unit has been ripped open. Those with useful items, like clothing or food have been scavenged. Most of the containers are full of vanity items, useless in today's world. Sixty-inch LED TV's and high-tech laptop computers are discarded in piles alongside the rail line.

Henry applies more speed to help blow the heavy snow off the tracks as he approaches Portage. He blows the train's horn as he nears the crossing at Route 160. Several people come out to see the train rolling down the snow-covered tracks. Trains were a regular occurrence a few months ago, they were a nuisance, not a blessing. Now, after four months of chaos, seeing a train roll down the mainline is reason for celebration. Another bit of normalcy has showed up. The train's passing is met with cheers, smiles, and even tears.

As Henry and his train approaches South Fork, he slows down. No sense in making it this far only to plow into a dead train blocking the tracks. He lets out several long blasts of his horn, which brings many survivors out to see the train. It also brings an armed contingent to the tracks. Henry is already travelling slowly. He applies the brakes. He cannot stop before his train passes the armed guards, but the squealing of the brakes lets the armed unit know he's trying to stop.

As Henry exits his locomotive, he has his own security team take up positions of overwatch. He walks back up the tracks to where the armed group is trying to make sense of the situation.

He hollers out as he approaches the defenders, "I'm an emissary from Altoona," he hollers. "I have fuel to trade for food and other needed supplies."

The young man in charge of the South Fork security detail is dumbfounded. He got out of the army after four years with no combat experience. He's a twenty-four-year-old corporal with six men, mainly locals, under his command. Dealing with a locomotive coming into his area is not something he expected.

"Stop where you are," the scared young corporal shouts. He looks to his radio man, who has nothing better than a CB radio to talk with the people who are rebuilding Johnstown. "Jonsey, let Sergeant Hasselrig know we have a situation." The young soldier rattles off a report like he has been trained to do. An order comes back. 'Welcome the train, they've been expected. Let them know they will be welcomed in Johnstown.'

The young man walks out and greets Henry. "Mount up and get your train rolling. You all are expected in Johnstown. Don't ask me any questions, I'm just following orders."

"You are a righteous young man," Henry states. He climbs aboard the train as it begins to slowly move forward. It's only five miles to the Johnstown railyard, all downhill.

The train, heading downhill, picks up speed as it plows more snow off the tracks. Now that they're down in the valley, the snow burden is greatly reduced. As they come into the small outlying town of Franklin, they see a crew throw a switch diverting them to another track. The track workers are all smiles as Henry brings the train to a stop.

He and his security detail dismount again, wary as to why another switch is being made. They approach the track workers casually but alert; they don't know if these are bandits or friends. One of the track men, heavily bundled up against the cold weather, begins to run towards them. The security team takes up secure positions, ready for a fight.

"Johnson! Is that you!" the man hollers. "It's Smitty, buddy."

Henry's line engineer recognizes the voice, a fellow trackman. Most mainline train workers know everyone within a hundred miles of their hometown.

Johnson, a bit confused at first, runs up and greets his longtime friend. After exchanging hugs, they talk for a bit. The train is being diverted to avoid several stalled trains including an AMTRAK passenger line. The train will follow a few side lines before ending up on a spur depot in Hornerstown. That side line can take the train all the way to Kantner, only a few miles from Central City. Smitty climbs on board the train for the ride into Johnstown, only a few miles away.

"We heard rumors you were coming," Smitty states. "It should be clear from here on out, but you never know when some rogue party of refugees may show up. You always have to be on guard, you know. It's a whole new world! And there are lots of bad people out there."

They follow the tracks and switches until they're on a sideline alongside the Stoneycreek River just a stone's throw from downtown Johnstown. At each road crossing they blow the train's horn. As they enter Johnstown, people start to come out to see the train, the first they've seen in months. When they finally get to the small side depot, almost a hundred people are there.

As Henry dismounts from the massive engine he's bear hugged by a vivacious older mixed raced woman. "We're so glad you made it!" she exclaims. She looks at the train appreciatively. "Six tanker cars, nice. We're running low on fuel. What can we offer you in trade? We'll get you whatever you need if we can. That's how we do business here."

Henry is dumbfounded as he looks around. He sees a small city starting to rebuild. Just across the tracks is a large public park. It has been turned into a stockyard. Dozens of steers occupy one corner, another area has been haphazardly fenced off to contain numerous pigs. Another larger area contains dairy cows. Chickens run freely, pecking for food. All within a half mile of the downtown district. He sees that an old derelict warehouse has been turned into a makeshift barn. On a railroad sideline are a half dozen boxcars brimming with corn feed and hay.

He glances to the residential and commercial districts. The roads have been cleared of debris and stalled cars. He notices a makeshift cemetery, which helps account for the fact that he doesn't smell rotting flesh. People are healthy and well fed, smoke is rising from several chimneys. He's astonished.

"We need food, we need help. You all are starting to clean up and rebuild. We're just barely hanging on. Getting this engine running was a chore. We haven't been able to even bury our dead. But food, that is what we need the most. If we can nourish the survivors, then we can start to rebuild too."

"Sonny, you're in the right place," Alex Cashaw responds. "We need fuel and we have food. I've already sent word up the line about your arrival. Nothing happens here that we don't know about. But how are you going to haul beef cows, potatoes and cabbage back over the mountain in a bunch of oil tankers?"

The mention of beef, cabbage and potatoes sends a hunger pain to Henry's stomach, knowing how his own family is starving to death. He has already lost several close family members since the collapse. "Can we round up some box cars? Seriously, I don't know. I'm happy we made it this far," Henry responds.

"We got a few small yard engines running from the Black Lick and Conemaugh Railroad. They've been trying to clear some of the dead trains from the main line, one or two cars at a time. We'll round up some transport cars for you, so you won't return empty handed. We'll trade you one full tanker car of fuel for ten empty box cars so you can haul food and livestock back over the mountain."

Things are moving a bit too fast for Henry. He pauses for a moment. He looks around again, tears coming to his eyes. "Ma'am, I'd be happy if you got me and my people a hot plate of food and you told me what you know. The world is in chaos and you're looking to make a deal before I even know your name."

Alex steps back, embarrassed. She gains her composure and presses on. "I'm Alex Cashaw, the leader of the Johnstown reclamation effort. Welcome to Johnstown." She turns to an aid and points to her headquarters, the old YWCA building, only a few hundred yards away across the Stoneycreek River. "Let them know we have guests for lunch. Twelve people I assume. It's to be a hot meal. And have them stoke the water heaters, we'll want to draw a few baths."

* * *

Two hours later, trailing four cars, the small train heads out of Johnstown, heading south towards Kantner. They're assured the track is clear so Henry, cleaned up and with a full belly, puts the hammer down, giving the locomotive the speed it needs to blow the heavy snow off the tracks as they're once again heading uphill.

By this time, word has spread of the arrival of the locomotive and its small train of fuel cars. Gas stations and stranded cars have been pretty well depleted. The train carries a vital resource to keep the community going, growing and protecting itself. Crowds of refugees gather and cheer as the train passes through the small towns of Benson and Hooversville as it heads up the valley. The train passes one of the generating stations. Henry and his crew stare at the small dam and sluice system that turns the generator. The workers that keep the generating station running take just a moment to give a wave before returning to their duties.

A few minutes later, Henry slows the train down as they pull into the Kantner side rail. He knows that the word of his arrival has been spread far and wide; over a dozen tankers of all sizes are lined up to be topped off. The mishmash of fuel haulers is astonishing. Some are big two thousand-gallon tankers with old diesel trucks pulling the load. Others are two hundred or five hundred-gallon tanks being pulled by horses or small farm trucks. He smiles, expecting to be well rewarded for his train load of fuel.

Before the day is over, Henry has a train of ten box cars full of food; frozen sides of beef, corn, potatoes, apples, a cornucopia of food. He can't wait to return to Altoona with his bounty. But the Laurel Highlands Militia won't let him leave. "It's too dangerous at night, there will be trouble on the line. There are groups that come down and ravage the dead trains. We have control, but there are still lots of marauding bands. You have to wait until tomorrow to head back over the mountain," Alex implores.

"Can't you send a strong-armed guard with me?" Henry asks.

"It's ambush territory. There are refugees in the mountains that live off pillaging the dead trains. Your people have made it this far. Tomorrow you will return as heroes. Twelve hours. Don't let all you have done go to waste." Alex implores. "In the mean time we can come up with a plan to clear the mainline. Your name will go down in history if we can devise a system to open the railways."

That thought rings a bell with Henry. They need to start to clear the rails of the dead trains. His people have small yard locomotives already running. And they have four more mainline locomotives that are being worked on. In a couple of weeks, they will have a small fleet of diesel engines operating. From what he has learned today, if they could open up the rail system and get food from the farms to the cities, that is a mission from God That is a mission that will save millions of lives.

Henry really doesn't have a choice. His train has been impounded. So, he spends the evening with a few other train men devising a plan to clear the tracks of dead trains. The plan is ambitious. Finding side lines and rail yards is one obstacle. Getting running locomotives is another. Finding qualified people to run the engines is another hurdle that needs passed.

And it all needs to be done with virtually no communications. How do they ensure a dead train being cleared doesn't come head on to a supply train? The old fashion use of red and green lights will need to be resurrected. They send out a request for electricians to help make their plan work.

Henry finally hits the sack at two AM. His mind races. Twelve hours ago, he hoped to trade fuel for food to help his starving community. That mission will be completed in the morning. Now he has a much larger mission; bring rail transportation back on line. It's not something he thought about as he left Altoona, but it's something that rings through his brain right now.

A key to the survival of the country will be the ability to transport goods, most importantly food. The Erie Canal followed by the steamboats and then the expansion of the railroads was all driven by the need to bring food from the farming communities to the cities. The failure of the transportation infrastructure has caused more pain, suffering and death then the collapse of the banking systems, communications systems and the electrical grid combined. Reestablishing the rail lines is crucial to saving the country. Henry falls into a fitful sleep with this heavy burden weighing on his mind.

* * *

The winter sun rises late, but the community rises early. Two hours before the sun will rise, farmers along with their hired hands are up and tending to the dairy cows. Cooks are preparing the morning meal, security details are making their rounds, hunters are heading out to their posts. There is no sleeping-in during these rough times; even the children have chores, fetching eggs, feeding pigs, shoveling snow and emptying chamber pots.

Henry wakes as he hears the town begin to come alive. The smell of frying ham makes his stomach growl. He dresses quickly, he wants to see why this town is so active before the sun rises. The first thing that strikes him is that there are lights. Even his small bedside light works.

He makes his way to the communal bathroom and relieves himself. He flushes the toilet, something that he has not done in

216

months. He washes up in the sink with cold water, happy that the tap works. They have so much to learn from these people, he thinks. And yet they're relying on him to help them.

Feeling somewhat refreshed, he heads downstairs to the mess hall. Over twenty people are eating, and the cooking crew is hard at work preparing more food. As he enters the room several people stand and start to clap. One of the train engineers that he met the night before speaks up, "Give a warm welcome to Henry from Altoona who is going to help us get the rail lines working again." The applause grows louder, and several people come over to shake his hand or give him a hug. Henry is overwhelmed by the reception.

One of his new friends guides him through the mess line where he gets plenty to eat, not too much, but enough to fill his belly. While sitting at the mess table he tells his new compatriots how blessed they are. He has eaten more in the past twelve hours than he normally eats in two days. "We'll fix you up, friend," one of his mess mates states. "We got food, we need fuel. That's an easy trade. Your people will be well taken care of. Ain't you got farmers out your way?"

Henry thinks for a moment, "Yes we do, but we don't have the systems you all have put in place. There is still anarchy in many places. The cooperation here is not happening in Altoona." A smile returns to his face as he sees a few of his crew members and security people come into the mess hall and get in line for breakfast.

"Well, General Mays is coming in to meet with you. Let him know about your problems. He'll make sure we send people back with you to help you out. We have a training program set up to help out people like you. We'd rather have friendly neighbors than enemies. We'll do what we can to help you. Cripes! Listen to me. I sound like one of the do gooders. I guess they're rubbing off on me." This statement puzzles Henry, but he lets it roll off his back

Henry sits with his new friends, gathering information. He learns a lot about how the community came together and how they're loosely governed. He realizes that the bond between the two cities needs to be strengthened. He calls over some of his crew members so that they can absorb some of the ideas being exchanged. Bringing back food will make him a hero, but he will need allies, ambassadors, if Altoona is to move from anarchy to stability.

Henry and his crew are deep in conversation about recruiting refugees to be farm hands and security when the room goes quiet. Three heavily armed men enter the room. They discretely move to power positions. Two more well equipped people enter the room and get in line for chow. Hushed conversations start. It's well known throughout the community that several attempts have been made on Mark Mays life. His own wife was shot. Anywhere General Mays goes, security details go first, so this is not unusual.

Colonel Brit with her small entourage enters and gets in the mess line, followed by more nondescript people, some are locals, some are security. Colonel Brit checks over the food carefully and keeps a wary eye on the food prep areas. She greets the kitchen supervisor with a smile. "Everything looks good Miss Martha," she states.

"We do our best, Ma'am," Martha states. "Times may be bad, but we can still do our best to serve a healthy meal." Two weeks earlier, after a bout of food poisoning killed several people and sickened many others, stricter regimens were implemented at all the community mess halls at Brit's direction.

Several minutes later there is more commotion as another large party enters the mess hall. The room is almost at capacity, but no one wants to leave in the expectation that the leader of the Laurel Highlands Militia may be coming.

A tall well-built man, Colonel Fisher, enters the room followed by a gray bearded man and a beautiful but frail red headed woman. Everyone in the room stands to get a better glimpse of what's going on. An applause breaks out as those who know General Mays Recognize him.

* * *

There are more than fifty people in the mess hall as Rebecca and I enter the room. My security detail is in place and has given the all clear. I want to meet with this intrepid railroad engineer from Altoona. Meeting him here is a good place to convey the message that we're recovering. Show a starving person an abundance of food and they will follow you anywhere. But I want him to see more than an abundance of food. I want him to see civility, compassion and freedom. That cannot be shown in a secluded office. The openness of a mess hall is the right platform.

A spontaneous applause erupts as the people recognize us. This is not unusual. Larson drops a soapbox on the floor and with his help Rebecca steps up to be better seen. One of my security shadows lets out a shrill whistle and the room goes quiet. I wink at him; his talent has come in useful many times. Rebecca looks around the room, smiling. "Everyone please be seated. Yes, my husband Mark is here, and you all will hear from him shortly." I wave my hand at this comment and that brings more cheers. Rebecca frowns at me so I wink at the guard who whistles again. Becca starts speaking again. "We're here for breakfast and a short meeting. As always, we would like to have a blessing before the meal. Please bow your heads as we give thanks." Becca says a short prayer and we get in line for breakfast.

The hubbub in the crowd is loud but we ignore it as we get our food. Becca makes her way to the table where her daughter and sister are eating as I make my way to where Henry and his crew are sitting. Larson carries my plate as I hobble along on my crutches. I greet Henry with a firm handshake. He looks me over with a bit of surprise and a smile.

"Welcome to Johnstown, Henry. You're a prayer answered. We sent some patrols your way after we secured Letterkenny, hoping to help you out. But this is the first direct contact we've had. Have a seat and tell me your story while I eat." 'Tell me your story' is a common request now as people want to know what others have been through.

For twenty minutes Henry tells his story. The three well-armed squads of Oath Keepers, veterans and National Guardsmen had managed to defeat a local drug lord and his anarchists. But strife grew between the city refugees and the few farmers in the narrow valley. There was no leadership that anyone would rally behind. A second wave of disease and starvation, as winter set in, knocked out so many people that the remaining few finally gathered in a loose coalition. That's when talk of what was happening in Johnstown inspired them to get an engine running and breach the mountain. So as the senior trackman, he ended up here.

I pepper him with questions: How many survivors in the area? About 8,000. Are there armed vigilante groups? Yes. Is there any civilian governance? Yes, but it's ignored. Are there forces trying to implement martial law? Yes. If we send food back with you, will it be pillaged? Probably. This conversation goes on for half an hour. I look at Colonel Fisher, "You know what is needed. Get Colonel Brit and her people up and running. We'll send Henry on his way at noon. That gives you plenty of time to round up what you need."

"We're stretched pretty thin right now, General," Colonel Fisher states.

"When have we not been stretched pretty thin?" I reply. "These are our neighbors. We can help people in Newport News and Charlestown, but we can't help people in Altoona? Make this a priority. Look at it as a military emergency. Altoona has hundreds of thousands of gallons of gasoline, heating fuel and diesel fuel. We can help them, and they can help us."

I turn to Henry. "You're leaving here at noon. You'll have your ten box cars of food. But it will include a heavily armed guard and one of our missionary units."

"What does that mean?" Henry asks.

"We're not sending food back to Altoona just to be pillaged, so you need an armed guard," I reply.

"But what about this 'missionary' unit.?"

"They're the key to your survival. They're the people with the administrative skills to start helping you all to set up a government. And most importantly, they come with the love and compassion of God. You will never meet finer people. In the past they helped run food kitchens and homeless shelters. They do the same now, just on a bigger scale." I smile at Henry. "And most importantly they spread the word of God's love, even in these trying times."

"I used to believe in God. I still want to. I hope you're right," Henry responds.

"You are a prayer answered, Henry. I hope we're a prayer answered for you. Within a week, Altoona can be on the road to recovery. We'll supply the resources. You all need to supply the initiative and leadership."

Henry and I wrap up our discussions. After he delivers the food to Altoona, along with our security and missionaries, he will return with more fuel, heating oil and diesel. When he heads back to Altoona the second time, so long as things go well, he will take livestock, chickens, and pigs as well as several cars of feed. He will also take some Brainiac's with him to help figure out how to get the rail lines running.

For an hour this discussion has happened openly in the mess hall. No one has spoken up. No one has interrupted, A few more people have come in, but they've been shushed as they enter. Serious negotiations have taken place in an open forum. No hidden deals, no hidden agendas. A handshake seals the deal.

I nod to Larson. He brings over the soapbox and I step up on it, giving me a slight rise over the crowd. "I'll be short my friends. Our neighbors in Altoona are having troubles. We're going to help them. We need volunteers to help them. Send out the word. We need to help our neighbors. In return, we'll have access to fuel. Not just fuel for our vehicles, but heating oil for our homes. This is a mission we all need to embrace. Get moving folks, your neighbors need your help."

Chapter 34, Alliances

Dover Air Force Base

January 30th

"We're going to join in with your people," Colonel Tiani states.

I watch as Admiral Van Hollern, General Mills and General Adkins smile.

Colonel Tiani continues. "General Mays set us up as a neutral base. That was divine inspiration. It allowed a landing zone for pilots not wanting to fight against each other. It also made Dover powerful enough to put all opposing airpower off the table. We watched as you all fought it out. After Admiral Barnes was out foxed at Newport News, it became obvious that your people clearly were in control."

"In control is a squishy statement," I state. "We're starting to rebuild, but chaos reigns."

"That's the other reason we have decided to join with your group," Colonel Tiani continues. "You seem to understand the plight the country is in. Martial Law won't bring an end to the chaos. I don't know that free markets will win the day, but martial law is not the answer, it will only bring on more chaos and strife. Americans are free spirited people. The heavy boot of martial law is not the path to rebuilding this country."

"So, what is our next course of action?" The question comes from the ham radio speaker as the Fort Hood Commander chimes in. The people in the room look at me. I have been the one who has brought them this far.

I ponder the situation. My first and most important desire from the beginning was to honor God in my decisions. I think I have done that in my own flawed way. My second oath was to keep my family safe. I have somewhat failed, because I have made them and my community a target. But for the most part, I have kept them safe. My third oath is to the community and our nation. There is the conundrum that has me in this position. My family, my community, is not safe if the country is in turmoil. These principles have put me in this situation. My family and community are not safe if the country is in turmoil.

God works in ways that we don't understand. He makes things happen that are beyond our comprehension. Why have I, a carpenter with limited military experience, and no governmental leadership experience, been thrust into a position where my decisions effect the entire country? Why are admirals and generals differing to my advice? I'm humbled at the responsibility placed on my shoulders. 'Grant me wisdom and patience God. Allow that I make wise and righteous decisions. Be with me, Lord.' I pray silently before speaking

"Admiral Van Hollern, you need to set a coastal picket to protect the homeland. Captain Tiani, you need to coordinate air cap missions with him. Keep the homeland safe. Meanwhile, we'll continue with our mission to save the farms. Without the farms, it all goes bad.

"Additionally, we need to recruit and seek out engineers, technicians, and laborers who can help rebuild our country. We can eventually reboot everything if we get the right people working on the problems we face. Anyone have anything to add?

"We need governance, general," General Adkins states. "Your people's efforts to establish local councils is working, but now, as our scope of influence expands, we need a larger civilian body of governance. How are we not martial law if we don't have civilian oversight?"

"Our people have the same concerns," Colonel Tiani states. "We know nothing can be done right now. But we have to look to the future. What is going to govern us once we establish normalcy?"

"That question has been asked around here, too," I respond. "Once the chaos is reigned in, our Constitution will be put in place. I believe it was a divinely inspired document. I'm not looking for a new nation. I'm looking for renewed nation."

"That's a mission statement I can uphold," the Fort Hood commander states. "We are Oath Keepers. We'll stand with you."

"Stand for the constitution," General Adkins says thoughtfully.

"Now that's a rally call we can all stand for," Colonel Tiani states. "That is our purpose. That is what we'll fight for!"

A new mission has been put in place. But how is it to be accomplished? I ponder this. I don't know the answer.

Chapter 35, Valentine's Day Massacre

North America

February 14th

The heavy snow pushes the bows of the big hemlock close to the ground. Three deer are sleeping under the bows, huddled close for warmth and sheltered from the cold wind. They're strong animals, built to survive. The older and frail deer won't make it through the winter. Only those strong enough to survive will see the spring. Nearby are mountain laurel and hemlocks, enough food to keep them alive until the spring brings more food. A strong wind knocks some snow off a bow, depositing a clump of snow on one of the sleeping deer. It shakes its head and after a few glances around, confirming that all is secure, she puts her head down and falls back asleep.

* * *

A strong wind blasts the east coast, driven by a high-pressure system in the Atlantic. At the same time an artic low-pressure system moves south from Canada. The high-pressure system pulls moisture into the atmosphere from the Gulf of Mexico. All this moisture collides with the cold air being pushed south from Canada. It's the classic set up for a Nor'easter. They happen several times every year. In normal times the news stations tell us to buy extra food and be prepared for the power to be out for several days. People buckle down and ride it out.

These are not normal times. The power has been out for months, the world is already in chaos. Those who have survived this long are not prepared for this storm. Most can barely survive through the day.

It's not an uncommon storm. In years past, the weather channel and every other news channel would have hyped the storm and gotten people to move out of the way. There is no weather channel. And there is no way for people to move to higher ground. The winter blast trolls up the east coast inundating hundreds of miles of coastal wetlands. Fifty miles inland, the moisture falls as snow. It piles up at a rate of several inches per hour. By evening over a foot of snow has fallen across most of the Mid-Atlantic region. The storm will then move on toward New York and New England, dropping even more snow.

The storm is the tipping point. Most of those who have survived this far do not survive this event. Everyone gets socked in by the snow. Many survivors are caught without proper shelter and die of exposure. Others don't have enough food and fuel stock piled and begin to starve to death. Within days tens of millions of people die. The east coast of the United States becomes a vast wasteland of empty cities and frozen bodies, buried under a foot of snow.

* * *

The Laurel Highlands is devastated as well. The makeshift electrical grids begin to fail as over two feet of snow falls on the remote mountains. The electrical technicians scramble to repair the powerlines, but with very little resources to clear the snow, the teams have no way to get to many of the problem areas. Houses kept warm because the blowers and pumps driven by the haphazard electrical grid begin to go cold.

At the May's farmstead, all hands are working. The solar panels have been cleared of snow on an hourly basis. The generator is running at capacity. Children and farm hands have been shoveling snow since the first flakes started to fall. The livestock have been tended to. As Mark supervises the cleanup around his land, he knows that the heavy storm will be devastating

227

to most people. They're used to plows clearing the roads and cleaning up the snow. That won't happen today.

"Larson, we're taking a snowmobile run. Get a four-man guard crew together. Load up any spare diesel fuel we have into our trailers. Throw in a couple of chain saws and other needed tree moving gear. We leave in two hours. I'll be in the communications center."

"You're planning on heading out in this mess?" Rebecca exclaims. "Can't you just take care of us? Where are you going?" She stops and looks around. Our farmstead is dealing with the storm. Paths have been dug and crews are hard at work. "Don't bother answering. I know you have to go, I just worry about you."

"I worry about me too, Babe. But I need to make sure everyone is able to dig out of this mess," I reply. "I probably won't make it home tonight. I'll see you sometime tomorrow." I give my wife a kiss, then hobble into the communications room.

Grace is manning the Communications Center. "Get word to Dan that I'll be in Somerset tonight. We need a conference call. But right now, get me a ham radio line to Dover."

"Yes sir. I'll have Dover on in just a minute. We've already established a channel. They checked in twice this morning. They're concerned about the storm. All their planes are grounded. Their radar indicates the storm is a bad one."

Minutes later I'm talking to the newly promoted General Tiani, commander of the Liberated American Air Force. "How's the most powerful air force in the world handling this storm?" I ask.

"Winds are steady at thirty-five miles per hour and gusting to over sixty. I've grounded everything. Our radar shows bad weather over the entire east coast. We have mixed rain and snow here, but it's all snow just ten miles to the west. How are you handling this is the better question? You are in the bullseye from what my people say. You could get up to two feet of snow."

"I'm getting ready to head into town to help everyone dig out. You have the best radar, so I figured I check in with you. But you confirmed what I already expected. We got a nor'easter that's going to dump a lot of snow."

"You are correct general."

"You know this will put pressure on your base," I respond.

"Yes sir. We're in a position to handle any new refugees. We'll take in all we can handle, but any misfits will be rejected. We can handle ourselves. Thanks for your concern."

"Good to hear, General Tiani," I state. "I just wanted to check in with you."

I check in with Admiral Van Hollern and General Mills as well. For the most part, they're more worried about the Laurel Highlands Militia than they're about themselves. Fort Bragg will get hit with about a foot of snow, which General Mills assures me they will handle easily. But they all reiterate their concerns for the Laurel Highlands. They still have working radar which says we're in the bullseye until the storm moves into New York and New England. I let them both know that the death toll across the east coast is going to skyrocket. I know that the death toll in my own backyard could skyrocket as well.

Larson meets me in front of the barn with four fully equipped snowmobiles. Paul is there too, with Badzy sitting atop one of the trailers. We head out into the snowstorm. We'll not let what we have built fail. God has presented us with yet another challenge. We'll not cower. We'll rise to the occasion. Within minutes we're in Central City. Plows need to be put in use right away, or they will be unable to move the deep snow. Machines need to be put in service too. It takes an hour to rally the people, but before we leave, two front end loaders, a couple of good plow trucks along with a few dozen shovelers, are diligently clearing the roads.

"Stay ahead of the snow, don't let it pile up too deep," are my last words to them before we head out of town. Major Devers is running the mission and their mayor is backing him. I'm confident they will be on top of the job.

As we make our way west on Route 30, I have runners on snowmobiles stop at every farm and occupied house. 'Get out and shovel snow!' is the word that is passed along. In many instances, farm tractors and excavators are fired up to help. We disperse fuel to those who need it. Before we make it to Stoystown, we have to send two snowmobiles down the road to Kantner in search of more fuel. Paul moves forward to Somerset, wanting to see how their grid is holding up and see what he can do to help.

The CB radio operators start to spread the word of how bad the storm will be. In Stoystown, with their broader reach, I get on a CB and start to implore people to clear the snow. "If you got a backhoe, snow plow, or front-end loader, get out there and get after it. We need to clean this snow up so our electricians can get to the problem areas. If all you have is a strong back and a good shovel, well join in and help out. No one is coming to plow your road. It's up to you to clear the snow. There are additional fuel rations available in Kantner, Benson, Somerset and Johnstown. We're expecting two feet of snow, stay ahead of it."

We head out of Stoystown as the day starts to grow dark. It's not yet five o'clock, but with the heavy snow and thick clouds, it seems like dusk. The temperature is in the high twenties. The wind has started to pick up but has not yet led to blizzard conditions. As the storm moves to the east and north, the cold air will move in, bringing high winds and whiteout conditions.

Our small caravan of snowmobiles heads down Route 271 towards Somerset. The snow is falling in sheets. As we race southwest, we see several trucks and tractors out moving snow. Our call to action has been heeded. Will it work? The snow is falling at a rate of two inches an hour. Even in the best of times it would take several days to clear the roads and bring things back to normal. Now, there is no normal. Everyday survival is a struggle. Those who have made it this far are strong and resilient. I pray that they rise to the occasion once again.

We make it to Somerset as full darkness sets in and the winds begin to howl. The streets are blanketed in white, but alive with activity. Farm trucks with plows, a few larger trucks, and a few backhoes are clearing the streets, but it's a losing proposition. The snow is falling too fast, they can't keep up. There are several crews manually shoveling snow as well. My thoughts turn to the power grid. I glance around and see lights on in some of the homes. My heart rejoices. The generator is still working. How much of the makeshift grid still works is an unanswered question. But the power source is still working.

We stop at the municipal building, which is buzzing with activity. The County Courthouse has been shuttered since it would be so hard to keep heated. The smaller and modern municipal building is the new seat of government. Commissioner Hodges is there, working to organize the assets available. I stress to her to stay ahead of the storm. Once two feet of snow piles up, it's game over. Only the massive state-run snow blowers can clear that amount of snow.

"We've seen this before, General Mays," Ms. Hodges states confidently. "It's not our first big storm. We have two big snow blowing machines at our local Penn Dot depot. We have a crew working on getting them operational. The blowers are purely mechanical. We just have to get them hooked up to working trucks big enough to run them. We're on top of this, sir, as best we can be."

"I'm impressed," I state. "Coordinate with my brother, Paul, and the electricians so they can keep the grid up."

"We're on it General. No grid means no heat. We won't let that happen," she responds.

Wind rattles the windows. It's now fully dark; the height of the storm has beset our mountaintop community. As we look outside all we see is heavy snow blowing horizontally. The nor'easter is now a full-blown blizzard. The dim lights flicker and go out. Our makeshift grid has failed.

Chapter 36, Digging Out

Laurel Highlands

February 15th

I awake to total silence, total darkness. It's cold. The stump of my amputated leg throbs. A few of my fingers are numb. I try to snuggle deeper into the blankets to stay in the relative warmth that surrounds me. But I know that to respond to dilemma with despair is to admit failure. God did not put us on this earth to fail. He will test us, but if we are faithful to him, no matter how flawed we are, he will be faithful to us.

I crawl from under the covers and say a prayer, asking for God to keep us strong and grant us wisdom so that we can see our community through this storm. I find my LED flashlight and turn it on to give me some light. I'm already wearing my best thermal underwear and wool socks. I put on more layers to keep warm. The energy I expend hobbling around the small room getting dressed warms me up.

Grabbing my load bearing harness, weapon and flashlight, I head down the hallway to where the mess hall is located. Turning the corner, I see light. I make my way into the mess hall where over a dozen people are active under the dim light of several battery powered LED lights. Some diligent soldier sees me enter and calls for attention. I tell them to stand down before he's finished.

I ask around for names and find out who is there. They're all worker bees who have been out moving snow or who are getting ready to go out and move snow. No officers are present. I look at the battery powered clock on the wall. It's five-fifteen. I'm surprised that none of my shadows are up with me. Even Larson is still sleeping.

I look at the eight intrepid men and women ready to go out and tackle the task of clearing the snow. I eye each of them up. They're good people, ready to go to work. I look at their clothing and the over coats hanging on the wall. They're ready for the cold hard work ahead. I smile.

I point to the two best looking people, one well fit young man, and a wise looking sturdy woman. "Let's go take a look outside, see what God has given us." The two people look at each other a bit confused, then quickly gather their coats and gloves as I put on my kit. We all walk out the front door of the municipal building and look around.

The whiteness and purity of the scene is stunning. The low-pressure system and all of its moisture has moved on. The high-pressure system is now over us. The wind and blizzard conditions have moved to the east. The cold air has now firmly settled in. It leaves behind a scene of pristine whiteness. Not a blemish to be found. No tracks of man or animal, just snow and moonlight.

I breathe in deep and gasp, partially from the cold, partially from the beauty of the scene. My two compatriots don't say a word. I speak up, "It's beautiful yet terrifying."

"I have never seen such a beautiful landscape," the woman says.

"God gave us a marvelous and beautiful world," I state.

"But all this beauty is causing people to die. If we don't clear the roads and get the power lines back up, all this beauty will end up with my family freezing to death," the younger man states. "So, your God blankets us with snow to make everything beautiful but kills my family. How is that a loving God? Don't preach to me about your marvelous God and a beautiful world. You're nuts and that's all bullshit."

The man's harsh comments are from his heart. His family is suffering. Many families have been decimated. I state that this snow storm is beautiful. How can that be?

I pause a bit before answering the young man. "God's creation is the earth. It does what it does. It turns every day, it rotates around the sun, it has winter and summer. It's consistent, just as God is consistent. Man made this earth comfortable with all of our gadgets and gizmos. As we became more reliant on manmade comforts, our gadgets and gizmos, we turned away from God. To many people our technology became our god, constantly looking at our phones and computers for answers and fulfillment

"You think there weren't snowstorms like this a hundred years ago? A thousand years ago? This storm is not God punishing us. This storm is letting us know how reliant we are on Him. Our gizmos can't help us. Our government can't help us. Our strength, our determination, that is what will see us through. And the will to survive comes from God."

"How do you figure that, General?" the young man asks.

"We're all here for a purpose. Most of us don't know what that purpose is. But once we figure it out, whether it's to raise good children, or become a doctor or a pastor, once we figure out our mission, our purpose, we attain a will to survive. Then we can accomplish the goal that God put us here to achieve. Once we realize we're here for a purpose, we attain a will to survive.

"If you believe you are alive out of random happenstance, then you have no purpose, no will to survive. You are just a blob of cells no better than a worm, just an organism that evolved over the eons.

"You're a handsome and intelligent young man. I think you are here for a purpose. Maybe that purpose is to help clear this snow. Maybe that purpose is to have lots of babies. Maybe that purpose is to become a great leader. You are more than a mass of useless cells that magically combined six billion years ago."

"Huh, no one ever explained it to me like that. So, how did I evolve from a worm? That really doesn't make any sense. General, maybe you ain't as crazy as they say you are."

I put my arms around the young man and the older woman, who has listened to this entire exchange. "Oh no, young man, I am a bit crazy. We're about to clear two feet of snow from these streets. Go get the others and then grab a shovel, let's get at it. Our goal is to make it to the street. Then we turn left and keep going...."

Larson and one of my shadows catch up with us at daybreak, almost an hour later. By that time, we have shoveled out the municipal building and are working to clear a path up Main Street. We have several more volunteers working with us, including a high lift operator. Before breakfast is served, the main streets of Somerset have started to be opened and the crews are working north towards the PennDOT compound where the massive snow blowers are being retrofitted.

* * *

A hundred miles to the east, General Adkins looks at the aftermath of the snowstorm and treats it as a military mission. She had five plows out moving snow off the roads all night. None got farther west than Pleasantville, on the east side of White Mountain, unable to push the heavy snow off either Route 31, leading to Somerset, or Route 56, leading to Johnstown. Letterkenny is cut off from the Laurel Highlands. One plow is stuck on Sideling Hill, having lost sight of the road and run into a deep drainage ditch.

She meets with her people and assesses the situation. Her staff comes up with a prioritized mission plan. First is to clear Letterkenny, to make its assets functional. Second is to clear trade routes so that the farmers can bring in the vital food necessary to keep their people fed. Third is to open the main roads to the west, to reestablish their link with the Laurel Highlands. She makes the rare move of using the shortwave radio to let the people at the headquarters in Central City know her plans.

Before the sun has even risen, all available troops are put into action to clear out the eighteen inches of snow that blankets her base. In some places the snow has drifted to over four feet high. But hundreds of strong backs push into moving the snow, along with dozens of machines. Rotations are set to allow for her people to get warmth and food.

Meanwhile, in some of the shop bays, serious retro fits are happening. Mine clearing equipment, essentially large plow blades, are being attached to M1A3 Abrams tanks. Anything and everything that can be retrofitted to move snow is enabled. Local township and county assets are utilized to help clear the roads. Massive plows are mounted to 1980's era 5-ton military trucks. A team of mechanics is assigned to hooking up two massive snow blowers they found at the Carlisle PennDOT facility.

By noon, serious snow removal operations are underway. Many locals, already trying to dig out their own homes, cheer as they see the plows begin to clear their roads. Four tracked vehicles move methodically west, plowing the heavy snow off the mountainous highway. The progress is slow but steady.

By nightfall they've reached Bedford. In front of them is twenty miles of mountainous roads that snake through the three-thousand-foot-high ridge. The snow will be deep, and the grade will be steep. General Adkins' staff, realizing how long it will take to open the roads, have dispatched a support caravan with extra fuel and rations for the relief teams. But even with their tanks turned into bulldozers, the task is monumental.

Never has such a hodgepodge of equipment been dispatched to clear snow. And never in such a haphazard pattern.

But the job is getting done. Remote farms and towns remain isolated, but progress is being made.

* * *

I stand in a corner of the PennDOT garage watching as a few mechanics finish hooking up a snow blower to an old triaxle truck. "Engage the PTO, Hank," an older mechanic says. Hank revs the engine, then engages the PTO. Immediately the massive snow blower blade starts to turn. "Give it some speed Hank," the mechanic hollers over the din of the churning blades. Hank revs the engine and the blade spins faster as the hydraulic pressure builds.

"Move it out, let's see if it works," I holler.

Hank puts the big truck in gear, lowers the blower and heads into the partially cleared lot. The churning blades dig into the snow and the two-stage blower sends the snow flying. A cheer erupts from the dozen people gathered there. "Head on out, Hank," the older mechanic hollers, a big smile spreading across his face. Hank turns onto North Center Street, Route 601, and begins to slowly move along, blasting snow off the road. With a nod from me, four militia members mount up on an old Ford farm truck to provide security. The massive snow blower is to push all the way to Johnstown, opening Somerset Pike for travel and commerce, and reconnecting us with the vital supplies the small city has in abundance.

I jump in a well-equipped farm truck and head back to the council building, Paul is there waiting for me. "We got four big trees down on the main line from the waterwheel that powers the rest of the grid. I got two crews clearing the downed trees, but it could take two days until we restore power. Mark, that's just this grid. I have no idea how the other grids are holding up. Our power systems keep hundreds of homes warm and operational, let alone the farms and hospitals we have helped bring on line. As much as we have done already, this storm is going to set us back."

"This storm has already set us back, Paul. But it hasn't knocked us down. Take the four sleds that brought us here and use them to go assess the damage. Load up with linemen and engineers. Get our power turned back on. I don't care what it takes Paul, just get the damn power back on."

I know my motives are selfish. I know our ability to restart the grid was a significant part of the reason that we won both Fort Bragg and the fifth fleet to our side. I worry that if we lose our edge, then we may become an afterthought. Getting the power on is not only the humanitarian thing to do, it's also the political thing to do. With that thought in mind, I remember that Dan Farmer was to set up a secure conference call with our allies. I head over to Dan's complex, the communications gathering nexus of our community.

***

I arrive at Dan's commandeered office building with my security detail, commissioner Hodges, Captain Albright and Sergeant Hays. After we clear his security protocols, he greets us in the lobby and are quickly escorted into a familiar conference room we often use for secure communications.

"Tell us what you know, Dan. Give us a broad update," I state.

"It's bad, Mark. The whole east coast is socked in. From Atlanta to Boston the storm has hit hard. Roads are impassable and the free trade that had started up has ground to a halt. We've got two or three days to get the trade routes opened. A lot of cities and small towns that have started trading with the rural farmers are going to run out of food again. The reports coming in are bad. This storm would have been hard to deal with in normal times. Now, even the hardy people who have survived this long are hard pressed."

"There's not much we can do to help anyone out," I reply. "Do you have any suggestions?"

"I've relayed to anyone who will listen to dig out as fast as they can. I've told them of the things we're doing hear, retrofitting gear and using earth moving equipment, even bulldozers. At Fort Bragg, they don't even know what a road clearing snow blower is! They think of the small units you get at the local hardware store."

"If that is what they got, then have them fire them up and start clearing snow," I respond. "We know that if the farmers can't trade with the city folk, then more people die. We have to do everything we can to keep the survivors fed." This discussion goes on for a few more minutes as ideas are exchanged and news is relayed.

"How are our allies fairing?" I ask, changing the subject.

"The Naval stations are fine. Norfolk and Charlestown didn't get any snow and they're helping to clear trade routes to the farmers further inland that did get snow. Dover is shut down. They received enough snow and ice to halt all fixed winged flights. They have a half dozen rotary aircraft that are available. General Tiani says the base will be functional again in twenty-four hours. They're clearing and salting the runways and working on getting the de-icing machines operable. Forts Bragg and Benning are socked in. They're doing the same thing we're doing, using tanks as bulldozers to clear the snow."

"Can you get a conference call going?" I ask.

"They're all on standby for a call. I can have it set up in two hours," Dan responds.

"Set up a call for six o'clock, I mean 1800 hours," I state. "We need to keep this loose alliance intact. The more we talk together, help each other, the stronger the alliance will get."

* * *

Having two hours to kill, I hang around the communications hub, something I have not done enough of. I have relied too heavily on reports and not listened to the actual ham radio calls. Dan has acquired two dozen ham radios which he has his people monitor to gather information from around the world. Listening firsthand gives me a new perspective on the worldwide situation.

I eavesdrop on a woman monitoring a very active station in central Illinois. The snow there is three feet deep. Not from this storm, just from accumulated snow. The ham operator talks about a battle they just fought against the imperialists. The woman explains that imperialists have been raiding survivalist farms and food convoys. The survivalists and farmers set up a decoy convoy and fought back against the imperialists. The ambush was a great success. Now the survivalists are expecting a counterattack, a retaliatory mission. The high-pressure system that moved the low-pressure system into the Atlantic is now sitting atop the Midwest, bringing artic cold into the Midwest. And in this cold weather, violent skirmishes flare up. The woman thinks the survivalist have the upper hand, being ready to fight even in the arctic temperatures and howling wind.

I take a few steps to the next cubicle were a young man is taking notes. The channel he's monitoring is in southern California. The Ninth Fleet has landed in its home port of San Diego and has been able to implement martial law. But outside the city, lawlessness runs rampant. Refugees from the northern states have been moving south. Those ill-prepared for the cold are now seeking refuge, heading for Mexico and Central America. In the San Ysidro Mountains, those fleeing the cold meet those fleeing

241

chaos. Neither side knows why they're fighting, other than because of the barest survival instincts.

Add into this chaos the people from Central America and Mexico fleeing north from MS13 and the Mexican drug cartels that have taken over their countries. They meet the Americans that are fleeing south to seek warmer climates, having experienced the cold and snow without modern conveniences. So, the two groups meet, and spurred on by the blood-hardened narco gangs, a war has erupted. Good people die. I shiver thinking of the battles we have fought and the battles yet to come. The final words I hear are a plea for reinforcements as the Americans try to push south.

I walk a few steps and find the next cubicle is assigned to monitoring an operator in France. The talk is slow and methodical. The woman monitoring the channel takes notes in English while responding in French. Glancing at her notes, I find out she's talking to a man in the Alps that is part of a small community of farmers that have managed to survive. They're now snowed in, as we are. The man talks about how he has lost contact with several people. He's worried they haven't survived or have been overrun.

The next cubicle has a young man tuned into a ham radio operator from southern Florida. Food riots still consume the area. He's on a remote cattle ranch on the edge of the Everglades. Two weeks ago, some of his neighbors came under attack from refugees out of both Atlanta and Miami. They have over a hundred people now trying to protect three small farms. They fear being overrun soon, unable to stop the advancing army of refugees, which has at least a thousand armed men. He vows to report until they're overrun.

Sadness begins to settle in. We have tried so hard to make good things happen, but around the world, chaos still reigns. I prayed that the work we had done here was being done elsewhere, that there were pockets of stability that could unite and rebuild the country. But all I hear about is chaos, martial law and rampant violence.

I retreat to a small isolated office for some solitude. My shadows take up security outside the door. In the small office, I fall to my knees and sob. "Why, Lord? Why all the suffering? Is there no peace anywhere? Are we the only ones to establish order? Surely, Lord, we have allies. I know we're not alone, Lord, because you are with us. Tell me I'm not Noah. Surely others have been spared from this chaos. Guide me, Lord. Grant me wisdom, grant me strength, grant me the will to carry on. Please, Lord let me know that we're not alone."

Chapter 37, Going Nuclear

Minot AFB North Dakota

February 15th

The claxons ring out and pilots scramble to their planes. Within minutes four F35 Raptors join the four F16s already in the air. Meanwhile, an entire squadron of B1 bombers line up on the remote windswept runway and take flight. Six of the hardened and modern aircraft carry nuclear armed Tomahawk missiles, the other six advanced bombers are armed with high precision conventional warheads. Four more F16s launch into the air followed by two refueling tankers. The world's second largest air force is on full alert and in flight.

Reactionary missions are not unusual to the men and women that fly these missions. They often do not know the threat, the mission, until they're in the air. Their job is to be airborne as quickly as possible. They're the elite, each rotation on high alert and ready to take off at a moment's notice. When they scramble, there is no time for preflight meetings and mission preps. They will receive their mission while airborne. Their job is to be airborne in the event that their base is incapacitated. Squadrons of burning planes on the ground would be of no use if the United States was the victim of a first strike.

Once in the air, the four F35s are directed northwest, their mission is to intercept a flight of four suspected Russian Bear bombers over the Bearing Straights. The twelve B1 bombers along with their fighter escort heads due north to circle over the north pole, ready to attack Russia if given the order.

Minot Airforce base, in a remote area of South Dakota, is functional. Most of its equipment and all of its aircraft are hardened. It's one of the few functional bases in the country. Its commander, General Travis, has been in contact with all of the operational military bases and the powers claiming to be in charge of the country. He has resisted taking any action, waiting for the country's leadership to be established. His ambivalence to Shelly Clinton's claim to the presidency put him on the assassins hit list.

But he keeps his people focused on their primary mission, which is to keep America safe from foreign invasion. He has no ambitions to help any of the factions vying for control of the country. He has set up arrangements with the local farmers and his base is well stockpiled to survive an apocalypse. He's content to ride out the storm.

Meanwhile, he has listened to reports as the Ninth Fleet came to harbor in San Diego and then sent warships north to Long Beach and Los Angeles. Now they're trying to secure a port in San Francisco. The Ninth Fleet has accomplished its mission by using overwhelming force and then implementing Martial Law, as they've been ordered to do.

General Travis also knows what happened on the east coast and has been in continual contact with General Tiani and Dover Airforce base. He's encouraged by what they've accomplished, but there is no governance in his opinion. It's a loose coalition of rogue military units masquerading under a fake civilian government. The fact they were able to defeat the Fifth Fleet and take control of both Charlestown and Newport News astonished him. He and his staff considered supporting the Fifth Fleet but decided it was too far away to get involved with on short notice. He's glad he stayed neutral, because he would have been on the losing side. The largest air force in the world, Dover's air force, might be attacking him right now if he had sided with the fifth fleet.

But now he has his original mission to work. Remote radar, so far north that it was unaffected by the EMPs, shows that Russia is up to its mischievous ways. As usual he sends a force more than capable of dealing with the threat. The Russian bombers circle for a bit, then head back to the homeland. The commander's jets escort them to the rim of Russian airspace.

The incident is mainly uneventful. In normal times it happened several times a year.

As the mission winds down, he's called to his communications hub. Something is happening and his presence is required.

* * *

"We need you on board, General Travis," General Tiani states.

The conference call has been going on for an hour. The first thirty minutes was on how people are dealing with the snowstorm. Advice has been exchanged, assurances given, and steps implemented to help people survive. Admiral Van Hollern in Charlestown, is now offering to help those who are socked in by the snowstorm. In just a few short weeks, Charlestown has made significant advances in restoring stability. The death toll was abhorrent, but those who have survived are rebuilding. The assets that the Third Fleet brought in helped jump start the revival. Now they're in a position to offer us help.

The talk turned to strategic positioning, which prompted bringing General Travis on the line. Our free-thinking military commanders are looking at problems that may arise and how to circumvent them.

"General Travis, this is Admiral Van Hollern speaking. I was in your position a month ago. We were literally a fleet with no home port. This alliance helped open Charlestown harbor so my fleet could gain a safe harbor. They also opened Dover Air Force Base which led to the defeat of the Fifth Fleet. The people leading this movement are freedom loving people who are fighting the martial law movement tooth and nail."

General Tiani speaks up. "They sent a mission into Dover that freed our base. If it wasn't for them, we would still be scrounging for food, literally fighting the dogs just to eat scraps. They've given me free reign over Dover. I provide an air cap mission and they keep us fed and secure. They helped us turn part of our base into a farm. We have fresh eggs, milk, poultry and beef all harvested from our own base. Meanwhile, they've brought in people to help establish a civilian government. Their people are now making sure our farmers get a jump start this spring. These people are real. We want you in on this movement."

"The fact that I control the largest nuclear arsenal bears no consideration on your decision?" General Travis asks sarcastically.

I speak up. "General Travis, this is General Mays. Your nuclear arsenal has everything to do with this call. Dover may have more fighter jets and bombers, Fort Hood may have a solid field army, and General Mills may have the best Special Operators in the world. But with one command, you could wipe us out. Talk with your compatriots, General. We have no ambitions of martial law. We have no ambitions of conquest. We're a group of freedom loving Christians who abhor chaos. Chaos is the devil's playground."

There is a pause on the line. General Travis has all the information he needs. He can join us, join the martial law movement, or take his own path. He could be a king maker with his nuclear arsenal and accompanying advanced fighter squadrons. But to what avail? Where would that get him? King of the Dakotas? Ruler of the chaos? I'm sure these questions are rattling through his brain. Siding with the martial law element is not an option. His own people would revolt against that decision. So his only two choices are to go it alone, or join us.

"Is General Watkins still on the line," General Travis asks.

"I'm here, John. What can I do for you?" General Watkins, the Fort Hood commander, refers to his compatriot by his first name, being of equal rank and stature.

"Your base is in the boonies. Have these people helped you out?" General Travis asks.

"Quite the contrary, John. We have helped them out. We helped them take Charlestown and Dover. And we have seen the response. The only places that are not in chaos are the few places that we control. I say we, John, because I'm all in with these people. We've got plans for unifying the country this summer. We need you on board.

"I have to add one more significant item. Sam Hutchins, Secretary of the Interior, is with us. He's in bad health but is recovering. His claim as President supersedes Senator Clinton's claim. I tell you all this in confidence. If it's known that he is alive, it puts him and his family in peril. We have found his wife, and she is with him. We're searching for his two daughters. We fear they both have not made it."

There is silence once again. After a few moments General Travis responds. "Let me talk with my people. I'll be in touch."

The meeting breaks up, and the task of digging out resumes. I smile as I hobble into the knee-deep snow, joining the other hardy folk clearing the streets and sidewalks. Two high lifts move back and forth, moving snow and helping us to dig out. I'm happy to be shoveling snow with my neighbors, where I belong, and not negotiating the control of nuclear weapons.

Dan Farmer joins me. Dan rose to power and mingled with the elites, but he grew up a humble country boy. Shoveling snow is not new to him. He asks me how Rebecca is doing. We talk about her scare after being shot and her recovery. I ask him about my sister, Sarah, and how she is doing. Since waking up from the shock, she has been stoic but involved and engaged. For an hour we talk about family as we dig paths through the deep snow. The monotonous hard work is therapeutic. Without speaking about it, we're reminded of how hard work is good for the body and soul. My peg leg may slow me down a bit, but it has not stopped me.

As darkness falls Larson shows up. We talk with my two shadows, my permanent security detail, and they let me know that our four snowmobiles are gassed and ready. With no stops, we can be back at the farmstead in time for dinner.

"Let's get going then. Round up our people," I state. Just then I see the lights come back on. "I'll be cow kicked, Paul got the power back up."

"I been down there helping him, Pap," Larson states. "Several big trees and limbs came down on the line from the generating station to the power grid. We got them cleared out and the lines back up. The electricians and linesmen are checking the rest of the grid now. Paul is staying here overnight and is heading to Johnstown tomorrow. Their grid is still down. The road crew thinks they will have Somerset Pike open by tomorrow. He's going to head there with additional people and equipment to get them back on line."

I look at my maturing grandson and smile. Six months ago, I would have had to pry information out of him. Now he understands the importance of communications, even verbal.

"By the way, Pap, I think it would be a good idea to bring some good cheese home with us. Grammy would like that."

I smile again. "I know Grammy would love some good cheese, young man. It's so thoughtful of you to think of her." I decide to push a bit. "Maybe we should invite your fine young friend and her family to church and Sunday dinner?"

Larson blushes. "I don't know about that Pap, I barely know her."

"You know her good enough to sneak out of the house a few times a week, at night. I think it's time we meet the family."

"Pap!" Larson protests.

"Chill, young man, I was eighteen once. It's life, enjoy it, don't hide from it."

Dan has been listening to the entire conversation. He has two daughters, fifteen and eighteen years old. He will be involved in a similar circumstance soon.

Before we head out, Dan pulls me aside. "Minot will come our way. Our people laid out a good argument. You did good too." My thoughts were far away from Minot. That is in God's hands. I was thinking about fresh cheese.

Chapter 38, Just Do it

Roanoke

February 22nd

The snow lays heavy on the fields and mountains of central Virginia. The small city of Roanoke is almost dead. Smoke billows from the chimneys of a few homes where survivors huddle, seeking warmth. Some paths have been forced through the deep snow so that the farmers can bring in food for the few thousand survivors. The survivors are literally tearing down abandoned houses to use the wood for fuel. Any house without a wood burning stove or fireplace has been abandoned. Those houses are targeted to be torn down for fuel, useful materials are saved as potential building material. The survivors literally step over frozen bodies in search of food, fuel and supplies.

Dr. Sam Gray and his militia in the mountains and farmlands fare much better than the city proper. Once they aired their grievances and reunited under their initial mission, they've seen successes. A large swath of farmlands and rural areas north and west of the city has been secured to the point that farmers and the general populace have started to recover.

Because of the chaos, many of the farms were unable to take in all of the corn and hay needed to keep their livestock fed through the winter. Herds of dairy cows were sent to Roanoke to be butchered and eaten. The farmers and militia gained good will with the hardscrabble survivors by this act. Sam and his people asked the city dwellers to scrounge for needed supplies, fuel, tires, paper, sanitary items. It did not take long for a barter system to take place. Even the drug lords who controlled the central city saw the need for the barter system.

But the heavy snow a week ago ground everything to a halt. Farmers struggled just to get their cows to the milking barns, let alone move milk, eggs and meat twenty miles to the city. The farming community survives. But the toll on the city is heavy. As food runs scarce once again, more food riots erupt. People die in the fighting. More people starve to death or freeze to death, their depleted bodies unable to survive the cold.

Dr. Gray feels helpless as he gazes on the distant city. His home is warm. His people are well fed. But only twenty miles away, people are dying from exposure and exhaustion, cut off from the farmlands that had been supplying them with food.

How did his forefathers move food to the city? This is not a new problem. It was solved a hundred years ago. But modern technology has erased the basic solutions. Modern technology made it happen without even thinking about it. But the roads are covered in knee deep snow, making the most traditional trade routes impossible, impassable. Yet he knows if they don't deliver food to the city, everything that they have worked to establish will crumble. Chaos will reign again.

Dr. Gray maintains a small subsistence farm, but his neighbor has over eight hundred acres and milks over two-hundred cows. The diligence of his neighbor has always amazed him, milking the cows twice a day, keeping them fed, maintaining the farm, bringing in the feed corn and hay. It's hard work just to keep the herd alive, yet alone productive. His neighbor has already allowed more than a hundred cows to be driven to Roanoke to be slaughtered to help keep the survivors alive.

Dr. Gray sits in his office that overlooks the broad valley. His farming neighbor is out tending to his herd. Large rolls of hay are strewn about the valley, unable to be brought in before the chaos started. The closest hay roll to the dairy barn is a quarter mile from the barn.

Without even looking back, the farmer trudges into the field, his herd following him. Knee deep in snow, the farmer reaches the large hay roll. His herd is right behind him, plowing

252

through the snow. They know the farmer is leading them to food. The farmer slashes open the hay roll and spreads the food as best he can. The hungry cows move in. The farmer has to scamper away to avoid being caught under the hooves of the heavy cows.

As he looks at the path the cows made, Dr. Gray has a moment of clarity. In his modern way of thinking, the roads needed to be cleared in order to bring the cows to the city. His great grandfather would have laughed at him. The cows will clear the path!

Dr. Gray rushes to put on his gear, wool pants, thermal socks, heavy coat, and his kit, including is AR-15.

He plows through the knee-deep snow, hollering at his neighbor, the dairy farmer.

* * *

By nightfall a cattle drive reaches the small city. Several thousand people are saved from chaos. The recovery of the once thriving city continues. In the city hall, a few well-intentioned leaders discuss the future. They know spring is coming, a government must be formed to maintain a civil society or chaos will return.

Chapter 39, Unfathomable Suffering

North America

2/28

Winter grips the country from the Rocky Mountains to the Mid Atlantic. It's not an unusually harsh winter. Except there is no food, no electricity, no way to bring food to those who need it. The suffering is unfathomable. Those who were prepared, were quick to react, and the smart, managed to make it through the first few months of chaos. But now that winter continues on into late February and March, even the hardiest souls succumb to the ravages of the weather.

In Chicago, the militant group that was trying to implement martial law regrets their decisions. South of them is fertile farmland with thousands of heads of cattle. But after the massacre at Momence and the battles at Kankakee, they have no hope of gaining favor with the farmers to the south. Hundreds of thousands fled the major city and have allied with the farmers to the south. But millions did not. Starvation, disease, dysentery and violence has taken a heavy toll. Those who have survived fight violently for every morsel of food or scrap of wood.

Meanwhile, a mere hundred miles to the south, herds of cattle starve to death. The farmers, so dependent on GPS and other modern technologies, were unable to harvest enough food to care for their herds. They had planned to send their beef herd to market. Now those steers must be slaughtered. They have to keep the cows alive and productive. With just a few bulls, the herd can be maintained. The steers must be euthanized, their meat is left to rot in the fields. The stench of death permeates both the cities and the farmlands.

It's a very sad situation. One that is repeated across the country. In the rural lands, food is in abundance. In the cities, the few people that have survived, starve.

But not in the small city of Winchester and other isolated rural towns. Trade thrives and the people survive, even through the heavy snows of winter. These small towns and cities begin to unite and start to form a loose coalition. Communications are primitive, couriers and line of sight CB are used extensively. But distant towns begin to unite.

The west coast survives as well. The Ninth Fleet sends ships all the way to Seattle. From San Diego on north, they take every port, most by brutal force. A few willingly accept the naval ambassadors. As the Ninth Fleet takes control of the west coast, they implement martial law.

At first this works out. Stability is restored. But as people realize they're losing their freedoms, trouble starts. Even the surviving Hollywood elite start to rebel once their mansions begin to be acquired by the new ruling authority. All they've stored for themselves is opened to the masses. But the might of the Ninth Fleet cannot be assailed by an unarmed populace. By mid-winter, the coastal areas are in the firm grip of martial law.

This does not alleviate the suffering. Food is scarce. The interior lands of the west coast, where food is abundant, is out of reach of the militant government. The situation worsens as a war erupts between the coastal cities and the farming communities. The farmers wanted to establish a trading system. The martial law advocates expected to just take over the farms. Now violent skirmishes take place on a daily basis.

Shelly Clinton is unfazed. She's planning a return to America in the spring. The Ninth Fleet has gained control of enough territory for her triumphal return. She will have her people move east in the summer and gain control of the country. She knows that when she establishes her claim as President, people will flock to follow her, a true leader with righteous ideals. This is her destiny.

255

* * *

In what remains of New Orleans, a silent killer is unleashed. It travels up the Mississippi River and silently brings death as it moves north. It's a ruthless killer, praying on the young, weak and elderly. But even stout men and women are taken out by this relentless killer. Influenza begins to wreak havoc across middle America.

In the heartland, in small cities and towns where society was starting to rebuild, this new wave of death rears its ugly head. In a normal winter, influenza, the flu, would claim the lives of several thousand people. But in this state of chaos, it claims the lives of many thousands everywhere it goes. There are bar coded boxes in remote warehouses full of flu vaccines, which no one knows about. So, there is literally no medical care to fight the disease. Many families and communities who thought they made it through the hard times are laid low.

The vital trade between communities that had started has to shut down. River boats and barges had started moving goods and supplies up and down the Mississippi River and its many sprawling tributaries. Now they're shunned, even if they carry life sustaining food. But still the virus spreads, bringing more death.

* * *

The influenza makes its way to Johnstown. Word of the disease has been spread far and wide, the very people spreading the news ironically spread the disease. The Laurel Highlands border guards have been issued orders to quarantine anyone with symptoms. But the disease makes its way into the isolated community anyway. It grinds all productivity and trade to a halt. One fifth of people who get the disease do not survive. A twenty percent mortality rate is unheard of. But with limited care facilities, it's not unexpected.

The few hospitals actually open and working run out of saline solution to keep the afflicted hydrated. The disease continues to spread even as all trade is shut down. Markets are closed. Schools are shuttered. Church services are canceled. People quit moving completely. But the disease continues to spread.

Back at the Mays' homestead, Herq realizes he has a high fever and begins to panic. He's not worried about himself, he's worried about who he has had contact with. He tells Mark's wife he's not feeling well and retreats to his room. He strips down and crawls into bed as the aches overwhelm him. He experiences chills and sweats for several hours.

During a few minutes of clarity, he grabs a pen and paper and writes down everyone he has had contact with over the past day. He stares in horror as he has listed almost two dozen names. He has been in the school because his child is there. He has met with the security detail. He has been in the operations room. He has been everywhere. He tells the nurse who already is looking pale of the situation. The nurse finds Colonel Brit and relays the information, then retreats to the small room with Herq, already knowing she's infected too.

Georgeanne, the nurse, jumps into action. She sends Grace to find surgical masks. She knows they're on the property, she saw them in the stock pile of goods when she first arrived and was given a tour of the medical supplies. Then she begins a shutdown of movement on the property. But this proves problematic. The forty some people on the compound work as a unit. How can the security people be fed, and the farm hands take care of their duties if they're shut down to isolated areas?

Georgeanne rethinks her strategy. Containment is not going to work. Treatment is her best option. She has limited access to modern medicine. The compound has Tylenol and other over-the-counter drugs available. They also have some saline solution that can be used to keep the worst cases hydrated. The rest will have to be done by home remedy.

She finds Eve in the kitchen and orders chicken noodle soup for the night's meal, strong on the broth. She makes sure Eve brews lots of strong tea too. Eve is a bit flustered at the change in menu, but realizes the need and after some fuss, begins brewing and cooking as directed.

Word quickly spreads throughout the compound that the deadly virus has arrived.

Chapter 40, Suffering Hits Home

The Farmstead

March 3rd

Leesa is burning with a fever. Her frail body, already weak from the hardships of the winter, cannot withstand the ravages of the flu. In the middle of the night she has a miscarriage of her two-month-old child as her body fights to survive. The miscarriage causes additional fatigue and blood loss. The miscarriage brings great grief. She was so proud to bring Herq another child. The loss sends her to a very bad low. She gives up the will to live, the will to fight the disease that consumes her. She passes away as the sun rises over the bleak winter landscape.

Herq sobs, holding his son as they take Leesa away.

Chapter 41, Slaughter

Palestine, Texas

March 7th

Curt Mays is assigned a dismal task. The three-thousand-acre farm that he, his wife, sister and brother-in-law have fled to cannot sustain its herd of longhorns. Fresh hay and feed are not available. Over the past month they've driven off half the herd to be slaughtered by anyone needing food. They have received trade goods and goodwill for this massive amount of food that they've provided to those in need.

But the ranch still has more cattle than can be consumed. The shut down in trade due to the spread of the flu makes it even harder for them to move the vital food to a viable market. The herd must be thinned so that the best can survive to breed in the spring. They must maintain a healthy herd.

Curt is to oversee the thinning of the herd. He has experienced cowhands with him to make sure the healthiest cattle are spared. But hundreds of steers are put down. A huge hole is dug to bury the carcasses. Curt and his siblings fled Houston as starvation caused food riots and social upheaval. To slaughter steers seems senseless knowing people are still trying to survive, killing dogs and feral cats for food. But there is no way to get the meat to those who need it.

They tried once, driving fifty steers over a hundred miles to the outskirts of Houston. It caused battles all along the way, even as they offered steers to every group they came across. By the time they got to the outskirts of Houston, they were overrun by the hungry mobs. They lost three people just trying to get away from the chaos that engulfed them.

The owner of the ranch agonized over the results of his attempt to help the starving people of Houston. But one of the people killed was his own grandson. He made a decision to not venture into the chaos again. They help all those around them, but they avoid the metropolitan areas where they can be ambushed or overrun

All these thoughts run through Curt's head. But the herd must be maintained. The herd must be viable. Spring is around the corner. The cows need to be healthy and strong to repopulate the herd. Over two days, the herd is weaned, hundreds of cattle are killed. Curt is sick to his stomach, but he sees no other alternative. He comes to realize that so many people have died even though there is more food available than is needed.

Tears roll down his cheeks as the cattle are slaughtered. Not for the cattle, but for the millions of people that he knows have not survived.

Chapter 42, No Green

San Francisco

March 14th

It's Saint Patrick's Day. The Chicago river does not flow green. There is no dispute about Gay Pride marchers in the New York parade. In Savanah there is a large outdoor service for the survivors followed by a meal of cabbage and ham stew. But there is no parade.

In New Orleans, a band plays festive music and a few hundred people gather for jambalaya and strong spirits. But as the sun sets, the party dissipates.

But in San Francisco, there is a great celebration. Hogs and steers have been slaughtered and roasted. Wine has been gathered. Every available extravagance has been set up. President Shelly Clinton has arrived, and she must be celebrated. Four naval ships preceded her arrival, as well as two marine battalions. The city has been tamed, at least the areas around the piers. As Ms. Clinton declares her presidency, crowds of people cheer.

She makes a resounding speech, knowing it will be repeated by the ham radio operators not only around the country, but around the world as well.

"Today is a new day in America! Today we start to unite and rebuild. America has been laid low by the egregious attacks of last fall. But we'll rebuild. Like you, I survived the attacks and I'm here to lead us forward as our President. We need leadership. We need courage. We need resilience. As the senior surviving elected senator, I'm your new president. I'll provide the leadership our country needs.

"We'll rebuild. We'll unite. We'll overcome! Stand with me and be true Americans. Follow the dictates of your leaders.

They seek only the best for your well-being. Obey the authorities so that we may bring peace back to our land. Listen to and heed the laws that are enacted so we can replace chaos with civility. Your obedience will be the key to rebuilding our country.

"I'm honored and humbled to be your President. Do what I ask of you and our country will not only survive, we'll begin to thrive once again. We are America and we are strong." Four F17's fly overhead as she winds down her speech. The several thousand surviving residents applaud along with the faithful military. Finally, a leader has arrived willing to stop the chaos, willing to put down the opposition.

* * *

The broadcast of the speech takes only fifteen minutes to hit the airwaves of the ham radio operators. Within minutes Dan Farmer is notified. He listens to the speech several times. He shakes his head. She's offering what everyone wants, stability. And she says it with conviction, a true politician.

But there are nuances. The last part of the speech is quite clear, martial law is coming and those that oppose it are the enemy.

In normal times he would have set up a remote conference call within an hour or two, faster if needed. But dealing with his patchwork communications system, Dan sets the conference call for the next day at noon eastern time. He lets his people know to relay a code word, Truth. It's the second highest of their priority code words. It will bring every player to the table.

* * *

On the West Coast, word quickly spreads that the country finally has a President, Shelly Clinton. San Diego has already been pacified; any resistance was decimated by the Ninth Fleet and its loyal marines. But inland, where people are resisting martial law, the news comes as a heavy blow. The drug lords approach the local militias, willing to fight with them to defeat martial law. Drug lords are ruthless, but they're capitalists as well. Their trade is illegal, and horrendous to the human spirit, but their trade will die under martial law.

A loose and wary alliance is made. The Mexican cartels, who are better armed than the militias, agree to help arm the California resistance to fight the new government. The people of Southern California willing to fight against martial law, many of them Oath Keepers, gain access to more armaments than they can believe. The best armed people in their makeshift resistance had AR-15's with limited amounts of ammunition. Now they have access to M4's, SAWs, 30 caliber and 50 caliber machine guns, sniper rifles and even C4 explosives. The true irony is that most of the weapons are American arms let into Mexico through a badly executed sting operation. But now, many of those weapons are back in American hands.

Farther north, in the Los Angeles area, the chaos is so great that the Ninth Fleet didn't even try to gain port. The nuclear blast that hit the port devastated the area. The chaos after the attacks was worse than in any other west coast city. There were food wars, not food riots. Within a week all supplies were gone, and gangs formed just to survive. Gangs of middle-aged well-off civilians quickly became as ruthless as any drug gang. The established gangs had better weapons. The new gangs had more people and became desperate. The battles raged for a month. The loss of life was astronomical.

Six months after 9/11, those battles are still fought. Both sides tried to work out a peace and trade agreement, but they never held. In the wasteland that was Los Angeles, tribal warfare reigns. Each small group has control of warehouses or subsistence farming, or both, to keep alive. They fight daily. Sometimes it's just sniper fire across territorial lines. Some days it's pitched battles as one faction tries to raid another faction's supplies. A thriving and vibrant city of ten million industrious and creative people has been reduced to a few hundred thousand bloodthirsty people living day to day. Cannibalism and human sacrifice appear in some of the darker vigilante tribes.

The Ninth Fleet's scouts reported to their commanders about the horrific situation. The fleet commander left two destroyers to monitor the situation, while they moved north to San Francisco.

In San Francisco the orders for martial law had been implemented and heeded for the most part. The city has been decimated just as the rest of the country has. Lack of food, lack of pharmaceuticals and lack of medical care has taken a heavy toll. The stockpiles of food in the port city alleviated some problems. Eventually trade was established with the ranchers in the rural lands to help stave of starvation for the survivors.

A million people cling to life in the Silicon Valley, once the heart of innovation. But all their computers are fried. All of their robotic manufacturing has ground to a halt. Software engineers are as useful as a barista. But the area had enough civil and electrical engineers to start to patch things back together. And enough good business people to start working out trade deals with the ranchers in the Sacramento Valley. The compliant populace hunkered down and rode out the chaos.

If one of their children or a neighbor became ill, they were taken to the 'medical facility', usually to never be heard from again. If they heard of someone talking about resisting, they told the authorities. They would get some extra rations and a nuisance would be removed. Martial Law grew, and the population dwindled.

It's the remnants of this society, only six months old, that Shelly Clinton addressed. A compliant and beaten population. But they're survivors, which makes them strong. and they're obedient. An army can be raised from these people. An army of passionate followers. They're alive because they were obedient. Now they're obliged to the dictates of the new government, whatever those dictates may be.

Chapter 43, Governance

Somerset, PA

March 15th

"You issued code 'Truth', right, Dan?" I ask. "Everyone on line will have a civilian as well as a military representative, right?"

"I hope so," Commissioner Hodges interjects. "I respect all you have done, Mark. But we must emphasize the need for civilian control."

Dan replies. "They all know to have a senior civilian representative with them. Let's hope for the best. They've had twenty-four hours to get ready." He picks up the secure Sat Phone and begins punching numbers. Admiral Van Hollern comes on line with the Mayor of Charlestown. General Mills checks in with a surviving North Carolina state representative. General Tiani has a woman on line with him who has been elected to represent the locals around Dover Air Force base. General Watkins from Fort Hood checks in with a prominent rancher from the area. General Travis checks in with his wife."

"We just got socked in with two feet of snow," General Travis states. "Ain't no way to get the Mayor out here. Geena is active with the local relief effort. She knows what's going on."

"We got all the major players, Mark. It's a secure line." Dan states.

There is a slight pause as I compose my thoughts. I whisper a silent prayer for wisdom, the outcome of this call will determine the future course of our country. "Gray Hawk, Shelly Clinton, has landed. She has been met with rallying calls to fight the resistance and implement martial law. Her followers are innocent. They have no idea why anyone would reject her claim to be our President.

She's backed up by the might of the Ninth Fleet. It's our understanding that the remaining marines at Oceanside have sworn allegiance to her. That means she has three SEAL teams and two fully operational marine brigades at her disposal."

Major Jeffers, sitting across the room speaks up. "The SEAL teams would have broken up. I know some of the men on those teams, they would not fight for martial law. Some of the younger members may buy into Gray Hawk's bullshit, but the older members would see right through it. The trainers too. Most of their senior leadership, and I'm sure a few of the younger men, have beat feet. Some of the more savvy operators may have stayed behind, swearing loyalty to the newly proclaimed president with the idea of sabotaging her plans and the Ninth Fleet."

General Watkins from Fort hood speaks up. "What about the marine battalions? Most of those soldiers are young and impressionable, as well as their junior officer corps. Only a few senior officers will have the guts to stand against the Ninth Fleet's commander backed by Shelly Clinton and her minions. She can round up those recalcitrant officers. They can be replaced by loyal officers."

The mayor of Charlestown speaks up. "We can barely keep our own people fed and there is turmoil up and down the East Coast. Why are we concerned about this Gray Hawk person? How does this affect us?"

Commissioner Hodges responds. She gives everyone a brief bio and a bit of her current history in working with the Laurel Highlands militia. Her story gives her more credibility not only with the civilians, but also with the military men on the line. She succinctly retells the horrific failed battle for the Johnstown airport and the successful effort to defeat martial law in Somerset

She wisely explains the threat from the West Coast. "Gray Hawk, Senator Shelly Clinton is the junior senator from New

York. She may have a legitimate claim as President. She's from a well-established political family with many powerful friends, some of whom are probably still alive and waiting for a chance to reclaim their powerful positions.

"If she can make her claim stick, it will have repercussions across the country. Forces here on the East Coast will rally to her, causing new battles to enforce her martial law edict. This may seem distant right now, but I assure you, as we meet here discussing the implications, there are other groups discussing how to take us down. We are renegades. We have rejected martial law. We are the rebels."

The female representing Dover speaks up. "If you all hadn't done what you did, we would all be dead, and our families would be starving to death. Instead, Dover is now a free base, it would have been decimated if not for your intervention. We have seen what martial law brings, it's not good.

"Which is why Shelly Clinton must be stopped," I state.

"And now that bitch is trying to take control of the country," General Travis states. "She sent an assassin team to take me out before, when I refused to partner with her. She's probably dispatched another assassin team with orders to take me out. And I'm a lot closer to her base of operations than any of you are."

"What about Tom Hutchins, the Secretary of the Interior? General Watkins, I thought you had him, and he was recovering?" I ask.

"That's not a viable option. He's not dealt with the situation very well. To put it kindly, he's not in a right state of mind," the Texas State Representative responds

"Wow, that's unfortunate," I state.

"So, General Travis, you control a major Air Force base with strategic bombers, refueling capabilities and a massive nuclear stockpile of weapons," General Mills states. "You can bet Minot will be high on Shelly's priority list."

The conference call carries on for almost an hour and the situation is thoroughly hashed out. Many people, mainly the civilians listening in, get a larger view of the dire straits the country faces. Hunkering down and hoping for the best is not a viable option. Bigger forces with bad intent will eventually over run the country, the old saying that freedom is not free is coming to light.

"From what I'm hearing," I interject, "we have a consensus that Shelly Clinton and her claim as president must be stopped as soon as possible. People, we need a determination from our civilian counterparts to execute military action against the Ninth Fleet and Shelly Clinton's allies. We all know that the civilians on the line are not all duly elected officials. But I feel it would be improper to move ahead without some civilian support. "Do we need to take a break? Or can you all agree to allow the military people to come up with a plan to take out Shelly Clinton and her allies?"

The conference call goes quiet. I have basically just asked our five civilians on the line to support waging a war. We all have been at war for six months. But we're talking about a true rebellion against an armed force and the apparent president of the country.

The mayor of Charlestown speaks up. "When your allies came into our city, they brought relief. And not just food. You all brought in a system to help us start to feed ourselves, establish trade and begin to rebuild. That is what won us over. How do you implement that on the West Coast, three thousand miles away?"

Dan Farmer responds. "We don't know, mayor. We'll be operating on blind faith. Kind of how we operated when we ventured into your city. Trying to secure Charlestown could have blown up in our faces. It was a wild leap of faith. So was freeing Dover as a neutral site. There has been a lot of failures, a lot of disappointments, but the end results have been good, otherwise we would not even be having this conversation."

"So, we go forward blindly because we have faith?" the mayor asks.

"We go forward willingly because we have faith. Faith in God or faith in humanity, you choose who you have faith in," I respond. "We'll have a plan. Some of the best military leaders in the world are on our side. Nothing will happen until a solid plan is worked out."

The representative from Dover speaks up. "You all took a leap of faith in freeing our base. I'll put my trust in you. If General Tiani agrees, all of our assets will be available to you."

The prominent businessman from Texas speaks up. "We're in. I had no idea of the perilous situations across the country. But from what I'm hearing, you all are doing good. If my friend General Watkins agrees, we're with you."

Geena from Minot speaks up. "We have no other course. We cannot let Shelly Clinton run this country. Her martial law will stifle the recovery and we'll all be killed. I hope you all know that by agreeing to this action we'll be officially branded as traitors."

General Travis speaks up. "Minot Air Force Base and all of its assets will be fully available, assuming we help generate the plan."

"Help generate the plan?" I respond. "You are the plan. You have the assets to hit her. We'll do everything we can to support you, but you are the spearhead."

General Mills chimes in. "No matter what is decided here, I'll have two companies at your base tomorrow. They're good men. A select squad will be assigned to keep your ass secure, general. The rest will be available for forward deployment. You are not in this alone, General Travis.

The state senator from North Carolina, not wanting to be the naysayer, speaks up. "Sounds like a consensus to me. If General Mills is in, then I'm in. Brand me a rebel."

Five of five of the civilian representatives are all in for denying Senator Shelly Clinton the presidency. Five of five representatives have declared themselves rebels. Five of five are willing to engage militarily with the west coast and the Ninth Fleet.

Maybe it should not be unexpected. The horrors that have been experienced so far makes war look like child's play. Millions have already died. The loss of hundreds to secure the freedom of the survivors is a necessary commitment.

Plans are made, commitments are established. Planes are in the air before the conference call ends.

Chapter 44, Strangers

Roanoke

March 17th

Dr. Samuel Gray is enjoying the early spring day. He's out taking care of his few remaining animals. He still has one good bull and has traded for three dairy cows. He's hoping the bull will breed with the females. He realizes this won't give him enough calves and he thinks about who he can trade with to get more cows. He still has one boar and two sows. That should provide for plenty of new piglets to allow for the swine herd to grow. He's glad that they did not slaughter another sow over the winter, even though his belt is cinched a little tighter because of that decision.

As he spreads hay for the cows, one of his hired hands approaches. "Boss, Elmer says three refugees are coming in from the north. He thinks you need to meet with them."

"From the north?" Sam asks. "That's unusual. Coming out of the mountains. Let's entertain these guests. Tell my wife to set out a good lunch. Cheese and bread to go along with the soup."

Sam has felt something in his heart for several weeks. He has felt something big is happening that he's missing. He has helped Roanoke get back on its feet, establish trade for food programs and made sure the refugees survived. But he still feels a void in his heart. There is something he should be doing. But he can't put his finger on it.

He throws some ground corn meal to the chickens as he heads into the house.

He's met by his wife. "We have guests for lunch, dear. They're from Winchester."

Dr. Gray enters the great room were the three guests are seated, two men and one woman. One of the men is older, in his thirties. He's well-armed, a 9mm Glock on his belt, an M4 and a crossbow leaning against the arm of his chair, a fully equipped body harness strapped with reloads and first aid kit, other survival gear slung on the back of the chair. Everyone travels well-armed, so Sam is not alarmed. But the quality of the arms is noted. And the stranger keeps them right at hand, not at the door or against a wall, which is the accustomed and polite thing to do.

A younger couple is with him. They're similarly geared up. But with less weapons and more travel gear. They have packs sitting next to them, brimming with supplies. Sam takes note of their clothes. He has been duped over the past few months and has learned that looking at the clothing a person wears tells a lot. These travelers are dressed well. He can tell they're layered and can see that mends have been made where needed.

He sizes this up in just seconds. He decides to jump straight in. "What news do you have from Winchester?"

"You are very perceptive, Dr Gray," the military man states.

Dr. Gray flashes a sign that puts his people on high alert. How does this man know his name?

The military man sees this response. He lays his hands on the table, open and far from his weapons.

"Don't be alarmed, Dr. Gray. We've been watching you and the surrounding community for several days. You are the man people respect and turn to. You and your militia are the reason Roanoke is not in total chaos. We came here to meet with you, to offer an alliance."

Dr. Gray steps back. He eyes his visitors again. His initial observations are confirmed. These people are different. They're not vagrants. They're too well equipped and disciplined to be from a rogue militia.

"Why would we want an alliance with Winchester?" He asks, still wary, but curious.

"It's not just Winchester that you would be allying with. The entire Shenandoah Valley has joined with the Laurel Mountains Militia. We are their representatives."

The young woman speaks up. She introduces herself as Susan. She tells her hosts that she and her brother are the missionary leaders of the group that has come to Roanoke. "We're a freedom loving group. We have rejected the martial law edict and we embrace free trade. Our mission is to help the farming communities to unite so that we can ensure there is a future for the survivors. We have seen too many farming areas over run and decimated. We want to make sure Roanoke stays free."

Sam has heard of the Laurel Mountains Militia on some ham radio broadcasts. They've been referred to as a secretive but strong group. Some rumors have been ludicrous, like putting the grid back on line and being involved in helping the third fleet retake Charlestown. Now that three of their emissaries sit in his home, he wonders if the rumors are true.

"Tell me about Dover Air Force base," he asks. which is part of the rumor mill.

"We have been on the road for several weeks, so we don't know the latest. I can tell you what we do know. Dover is now an independent base. Our allies went in and opened it up, got it operational and then declared it a neutral site. We had to do this because a major battle took place between the Third and Fifth fleets. It was assumed that many pilots would defect from both fleets. Dover was set up to take in the fighter and bomber pilots that wished to remain neutral. It's still a neutral site, but the Fifth Fleet has been scattered and the Third Fleet controls most of the east coast."

Dr. Gray's mouth hangs slightly open. Again, he has heard these rumors from the ham radio operators. But to hear that such major battles actually occurred is shocking. He regains his composure. "And since your side lost, you are trying to make sure you control the heartland."

"No, Dr. Gray. The Third Fleet is allied with the Laurel Mountains Militia. Our allies control Charlestown and Newport News. We assume the Fifth Fleet, what remains of it has fled north, probably to Boston. Our people won. But we're not here as victors. We're here looking to help anyone of like mind to assist in making the farmlands of the Appalachian Mountains secure. Those farmlands can help feed anyone who survives this chaos.

"Sir, the coastal cities and plains are lost. Roanoke has the Blue Ridge Mountains keeping it secure, same as the Shenandoah Valley. Your city is surrounded by fertile farmlands, and the city itself has a strong manufacturing base. We want to help you reclaim the city and bring free markets back in place between the farmers and the city. Hell, Roanoke might end up being the capital of the country once this chaos all settles out."

"So, the three of you are here to help us?" Dr. Gray asks.

"Yes," the woman states. "As soon as the snow melts, we'll start trading with you. We'll make sure the route is secure and we'll bring in more cities and towns into our alliance."

The pieces begin to fall in place for Dr. Gray. He felt something was happening, and here it is. What these people say makes sense, but it seems unfathomable.

Sam's wife speaks up. "You all bring a lot to think about. Let's have lunch and hear news from your part of the country." Her heartfelt invitation takes the edge off the conversation and the group begins their lunch of hot soup with cheese and crackers. Katy, Sam's wife insists that they say grace before eating. As Sam says a short blessing, he takes a peek at the soldier, who is respectful of the prayer, but wide eyed and alert. The man is a professional, skilled and hardened.

Sam and his wife find out that the two younger people are a brother and sister from Bedford who have been working with what is called the "missionary team" for several months. They've been working to bring the word of freedom everywhere they go. As strong Christians, they feel their mission is to make friends and give people hope any way they can. By being loving neighbors, they hope to plant the seed of redemption.

They know their travels are dangerous, so they're armed, ready to defend themselves. They've seen horrific things. They've saved people from slavery, children from abhorrent acts of sexual abuse. Their military compatriot has saved them a few times as well; his skillful eye and adroit senses keeping them from harm. They don't go into detail, but it's obvious their trek from Winchester to Roanoke has been dangerous, perilous.

The military man sits quietly through lunch, only giving a sign here and there when the two missionaries are beginning to tell too much.

Sam begins to realize the man sitting next to him is a military operative, a man who has killed and will kill again. And this man is not only trying to recruit him, he's trying to protect him, he can tell by how he speaks and what he does.

The question is asked again, "Are they willing to ally with the Laurel Highlands Militia."

"I'll need to talk with the other members of our group," Sam responds. "Would you be willing to talk with them?"

"Tomorrow at City Hall, let's get this moving," the military man states.

"That's moving pretty quick for these times," Dr. Gray states.

"John Richards, with the dairy farm south of Oxford, is already moving thirty cows to town. He expects to trade most of them, but two are for slaughter to be roasted for the occasion. And Meg Jenkins from Franklinton has over three dozen prime hogs ready for market. You best get your people moving. Spread the word, Dr. Gray, we're counting on you."

Katy speaks up as the three guests get ready to leave. "You're welcome to stay here, we have plenty of room. You can help us get organized for tomorrow."

"You'll be plenty organized for tomorrow, we have no doubt," the young missionary woman states. "We have faith, and so do you. We wouldn't be here if we didn't have faith." The young woman smiles as she shoulders her backpack. "See you tomorrow," she states with a bright face.

Sam and Katy watch as the three travelers head down their driveway towards the road, watchful and alert, but seemingly unburdened despite the heavy loads they carry.

"What do you think that was all about?" Katy asks her husband.

"I think it was exactly about what they said," he replies. "And I think we better do as they ask. I've been having a feeling for quite some time, ever since we saw those helicopters fly over. I still have this feeling. Something is happening, Katy. Something big. Those people, they knew everything, they confirmed everything we've been hearing. Send Alan into town to have them start to prepare. I'll be in my office."

Katy knows that her husband will be on their CB radio, talking with their contacts. She feels a churn in her gut. Something big is going to happen. She worries that it could be something bad.

278

These visitors from Winchester could be frauds, the vanguard of a militant sect. Or they could be truthful in what they say, but the turbulent mobs that control Roanoke could turn on them, bringing more death and destruction to her city. She falls to her knees and sobs as her gut tightens.

"Dear Lord, bring us truth. Bring us peace. Bring us a path out of the chaos. I pray that your will be done, and your justice will prevail." She continues to pray, for her family, for her community, for humanity. Twenty minutes later, she rises from her knees. She needs to find Alan and send him into town.

Chapter 45, Town Meeting

Roanoke

March 18th

A new day arises in the mountain valleys on a brisk but clear morning. It starts with the deep night turning a dark blue. Eventually the purples and pinks of the sunrise turn to oranges and yellows as the sun breaks over the tops of the ridges. A fragrant aroma spreads across the small city nestled deep in the valley. Meat is being roasted.

Several cooking fires have been burning for hours, the steady heat of their coals slowly roasting the meat being turned on heavy steel spits. As the people of the town awaken, they smell the roasting meet. They instinctively move toward the alluring aroma.

Some of the citizens of Roanoke ate the day before, they're hungry, but not starving. Some people have not had a good meal in days, surviving on dog meat, scrounged canned goods, even rats or rancid garbage. No one has awakened to the smell of freshly roasted meat for many days. People literally begin to salivate at the smell. Instinctively they wake, get dressed, and follow the scent of beef and pork roasting over an open fire.

By full sunrise, a hundred people have arrived at the courtyard in front of the courthouse where the freshly slaughtered cows and pigs are being roasted. They're quickly and willingly put to work. Tables and chairs are set up from nearby churches and community buildings. Serving trays and dinnerware are gathered as well. Over the course of a few hours, the entire town square is turned into a giant banquet hall.

The spits are continually turned as the meat cooks. The crowd continues to gather. From a church tower, a well-equipped military man looks down at the gathering crowd. He breaks radio silence. "1200 hours, make it impressive." Looking at his map, he gives precise coordinates. A few months ago, it all would have been carried out electronically. Now he has to give eight-digit coordinates, and the pilots will need to find them on a map and execute the mission precisely. This was the way it was done twenty years ago. Surely it can be done again.

The sniper in the church tower leans back, going over the plan. So much relies on the two young missionaries. If they blow their mission, if they cannot hold up their end of the bargain, then the whole mission will go to waste, weeks of planning lost in an instant of chaos. He prays for his two compatriots. It shakes him. He has never prayed for anyone ever before.

* * *

Sam meets with his fellow militia members on the courthouse steps. The gathering is impressive. Several thousand people are spread out across the open green space and are spilling into the surrounding roads and walkways. Several impromptu bazaars have been set up where everything from fresh cheese to bootleg whiskey is available. In some of the more remote alleys, farther away from the courthouse, drugs, sex and slaves are discreetly traded.

At a back-alley door, a well tattooed man talks to another man who stinks of urine and whose tattered clothes have not been changed in weeks. "I don't like this one bit. That bastard, Dr. Gray, is involved. His people are a bunch of do-gooders. They just about run us out of town already. If we didn't control so many supplies, he and his militia would have hung us in the public square." He spits a long stream of tobacco juice on the ground, landing at the smelly man's feet.

"I don't like it neither, boss," the smelly man states. "But we got control of the mall and the warehouses. They need us. Whatever they got brewing, they can't leave us out of the mix. And they know we'd start cuttin' throats if they turn on us."

"They also know we're supposed to control the center of the city," Tattoo man states. "How did they get here and set all this up without us knowin'?"

"They caught us sleepin', boss. First thing I know'd, they got a bunch of cattle and hogs milling around and a bunch of people getting ready to start a big barbeque. Then more people showed up. We couldn't stop them. They'd a' over run us."

"How are we situated now?"

"We got people out and about. But no more than a hundred. There's two thousand people out there now, and most of them are armed, even though it's just a big picnic. You know how it is, boss, no one goes anywhere without a side arm or rifle."

"So, if this turns into some kind of rally to boot us out, then we're out gunned." Tattoo man feels a churn in his stomach. His people have controlled the city through shear violence and intimidation. Even after the rural militia formed and gained control of the farmlands, his cabal of thugs, reinforced by the convicts they freed from a local penitentiary, have controlled the city.

Tattoo man looks over the crowd. "Get me Smitty. We can put these people back in their place."

* * *

"So, what's this all about?" a gray-haired bespectacled man asks. His name is John Worth. He's a professor of history and has helped Dr. Gray form the fledgling group's governance, as limited as it is.

"Quite frankly, I'm not sure, Dr. Gray responds, looking over the large assembly of people. "I think our town is going to be asked to join an alliance of mountain cities to fight against the martial law that we hear is being mandated around the country."

The shorter man grabs Sam's arm. "Really? That is what's needed! We can't survive on our own, we need allies. Who are these people? Are they good people?"

"They call themselves the Laurel Highlands Militia. I don't know much about them, but I have heard rumors. They came to my farm yesterday. They told me to set all this up, so we did. My gut told me we should."

The older man smiles and nods. "So, you met with them? Are they good people? Tell me what you know," the professor insists.

"They were the nicest people you could ever meet, but armed to the teeth. Guns and knives brimming from every pocket. They've been watching us for many days. This here barbeque was put in place at least three days ago. How did they do that without us knowing?"

"Because they've done it before, Sam. Maybe not exactly this, but they sound like experienced people. What are your concerns?"

"What if they're frauds?" Dr. Gray responds. "They claim to have helped free Dover Air Force Base and that they're allied with the Third Fleet. They claim that their alliance defeated the Fifth Fleet. There are rumors that they've restarted the grid and have running locomotives. It's too much. Three people showing up in our city is going to change things? I don't get it."

"They already have changed things. Here we are, on the courthouse steps, watching two thousand people congregate. I've heard rumors of everything you've said. News did not stop when the internet went down. Where are these emissaries of revival?" the professor asks.

"I don't know," Dr Gray responds, looking around. The pit in his stomach grows. Were they frauds? They delivered the

283

promised cows and sows. And now a massive crowd awaits. Is it all left in his hands?

* * *

By mid-morning the crowd has grown even more. Farmers have come in and more trading bazaars have been set up. The bright clear skies help the temperature to rise into the mid-forties. One young entrepreneur arrives with a stockpile of wood and a cast iron bathtub and starts a brisk business offering hot baths. A woman with her three children selling soap quickly set up shop next to the hot bath. A brisk business quickly ensues.

The tattooed man sees all this. He does not like it one bit. He wants these people starving and needing his supplies to survive. Despite that, he finds two silver quarters in his pocket. He hands them to his stinky friend. "Go get a bath you smelly bastard. I'll be watching you, don't spend it on women or booze. Get a bath, you're a rank son-of-a-bitch."

The stinky man takes the coins and snarls at his friend. "My clothes will still stink, you ungrateful bastard. I ain't seen Smitty yet, but a few of his people are around, I'm sure he'll show up soon."

"We're going to need more than a few of his people. We need to take control of this crowd. We need to own this before it gets out of hand."

Stinky grunts as he heads towards the bathing booth, pushing his way to the front of the crowd with snarls and threats.

* * *

As the sun rises higher, nearing noon, the crowd starts to get unruly. They've been smelling the roasting meat for hours. For many the hunger pains grow strong in anticipation of a freshly cooked meal. They've seen farm trucks arrive towing wagons

284

brimming with potatoes and cabbages. They can see butter being churned right before their very eyes. Their stomachs growl and they press in, anticipating the meal being prepared.

Dr. Gray's militia pushes the crowd back. It causes some ruckus, most of which is fomented by Smitty's people. They want this scene to end in chaos.

Dr. Gray and the other militia leaders watch over the crowds, issuing orders as needed to try and keep the situation calm. "This is starting to get out of control," one of his compatriot's states.

"Where are the emissaries from Winchester?" another asks. "If this turns into another food riot, we'll look like fools."

The pit in Dr. Gray's stomach grows. What happened? He was sure he was doing the right thing. Is it left up to him to put it all together? Where are his allies? How can he ask this massive crowd to ally with a myth, a vision?"

He says a prayer, seeking guidance, asking for help, praying that he's not alone.

He feels a tug at his shoulder. "Nice going Dr. Gray. This is an impressive crowd. This is going to be awesome!"

He turns to see the young missionary woman. She's smiling from ear to ear. Three men are with her, they're locals, well-armed and alert.

"Wow, am I glad to see you! Where have you been? We've got this massive gathering and you just show up now?! What do you want us to do?" the questions fly.

The woman just smiles and nods. "It looks as if you are about ready to serve this awesome dinner. I'd like to address the crowd and say grace before we eat. Would you mind introducing me?"

"I barely know you, how do I introduce you?"

"Tell them what you know, I'll take it from there. You are a child of God. Let him speak through you."

Sam is dumfounded by this simple response. He's shaking his head as he hears the old crackly sound system spark to life.

"Testing, one, two, three" echoes across the park, followed by a shrill sound that is quickly negated. "Testing one, two, three," is repeated. This time it comes across clear, the thirty-year-old equipment working well.

One of his people hands him the mic. The hushed crowd is looking at him. Thousands of people, all waiting for a good meal, stare at him on the courthouse steps. The spotlight is on him, he has to respond.

"Welcome, friends. We have made it through this long, cold and frightful winter. As this warm bright sunshine comes down on us, warms us, we know that spring is coming soon." He's speaking from his heart, but he knows he's dodging the true reason for the feast.

"Many of us have lost loved ones and have barely survived the chaos that surrounds us. This chaos has stricken the entire country. We all have been wondering what will come next. What is the next disaster to come on us, a snow storm? An invasion? A plague?"

"Yesterday, I found out what comes next. Anyone with access to a ham radio has heard of the events outside our secluded mountain city. New York and Washington have been destroyed. Our federal government has been decimated. Most major cities are in turmoil or abandoned to the ruthless gangs. The farmlands of the coastal plains have been ravaged by refugees trying to escape the cities. Most of what we have heard has been bleak."

The crowd is hushed as Sam lays out what many of them have already heard by rumor or over the ham radios. To hear the devastation confirmed brings everyone to a new reality. Their life as they knew it will never return. Modern society has been turned upside down.

"You also may have heard that martial law has been implemented across the country. A senator from New York has showed up in San Francisco declaring the rightful seat as president following the constitutional line of succession. She has declared a national emergency and has requested all military forces institute martial law, suspending habeus corpus.

"I am proud to state that Martial law has not been implemented here. Our local militias, civilian leaders and business people decided that martial law was a bad policy and would lead to even worse conditions. We stick by our decision to defy the martial law edict." The crowd is further hushed by this rebellious statement

"Lately, even in all of this chaos there have been signs of a renewal. We have heard of our naval fleets returning to their home ports. Those who have an ear for news have heard rumor of a great battle between those wishing to impose martial law and those wishing to let freedom find its own course.

"It has been reported by many that the forces defying martial law won those battles. It has been heard that a group of freedom fighters, calling themselves the Laurel Mountain Militia led this insurrection.

"Yesterday, people representing these freedom fighters came to my home. They're the ones who instituted this feast. Unknown to us, they put in motion this great gathering. They represent the opposition to martial law. As far as I can tell, they represent our best hope for a free future.

"Dinner will be served soon, but please stand and welcome Susan from the Laurel Highlands Militia. She and her people organized this feast."

The applause starts a little slow, people are hungry, they don't want to hear a bunch of speeches. But they begin to realize that the sooner they welcome this person to the stage, the sooner they can eat, so the applause grows wildly as Susan steps to the dais.

She looks at her mechanical watch, two minutes. "Thank you all for coming. There is freedom available to all of you, and that freedom can only be found through love. True love can only be found through God, our Lord and Savior. I pray you seek out his love and guidance. I'm not part of the Laurel Highlands Militia. But they're the reason I'm here." She pauses for a few seconds. She can hear the distant rumble. She sees the crowd quiet as they also hear the rumble.

"Martial law will crush freedom," she states loudly as the rumble grows louder. "I stand with freedom. Stand with me for freedom!" She shouts as the rumble grows to a thundering reverberation between the mountains. The crowd stands and shouts as four F-16s followed by two B2 stealth bombers fly low over the gathering. The crowd cheers, forgetting their hunger pains for just a few moments as they take in the impressive sight.

As the echoes of the jets dissipates, Susan speaks up over the quieted crowd. "The people I know have control of those planes. But the God I know has control over everything. Please pray with me."

The crowd, in hushed silence, bows their heads as Susan speaks. "Dear Lord, bless these people, open their eyes to your glory and your power, In Christ's name I do pray, Amen."

She opens her eyes and speaks loudly, "enjoy the food, enjoy the fellowship, may God be with you."

She turns to walk off the stage when the loud crack of a rifle is heard. Susan stumbles and falls. Many people in the crowd seek cover. But there is none, they're in a large open square, there is nowhere to hide.

More rifle shots ring out. Two of Susan's security people fall dead. Dr. Gray seeks cover as do most of his compatriots. More gunshots ring out, the crowd in the square, expecting a good meal, now begins fleeing. They've survived this long by being vigilant and prepared. They seek cover from the open spaces. Many pull their own fire arms, ready to fight back.

Susan rises from the stage; her bullet proof vest having saved her from a fatal shot. She's severely bruised, but far from dead. She grabs the thirty-year-old mic up off the floor and looks out over the chaotic scene. She says what comes to her at that time. "Cease fire, cease fire, cease fire!"

Her commands echo over the large gathering.

Stunned that she's alive, the sniper pauses for just a moment, long enough for a bullet to smash through his brain from Susan's soldier escort. The pause is also just long enough for the people in the crowd to see who is causing the mayhem. It's only a few seconds. But in a few seconds survivors become heroes. In just a few seconds the world changes. The hunters become the hunted.

Susan's plea caused enough of a pause to turn everything upside down. These people had survived enough chaos. The glimmer of hope was enough for them to take down Smitty and the boss. In less than a minute, the scales change. The people of Roanoke are now free and will fervently fight for freedom. The hundred or so thugs who have imposed tyranny over the city of Roanoke are quickly overcome, some are killed, others are subdued and taken prisoner.

Susan watches for just a minute. She's a pacifist. But she knows, sometimes bad people need to be subdued. In the past few months she has had to defend her own life with violence. She always regretted it, but she and her brother would not be alive today if she had not acted in self-defense.

The crowd has endured the cruelties of the thugs for far too long. A blood bath will occur if the crowd is not stopped.

"Stop! Please stop!" she shouts over the megaphone. "We did not come to incite violence! Stop now!"

Her pleas are heard as the mob slows and turns to hear her. In the confusion a few thugs escape, but most have already been subdued or killed.

As the crowd quiets and turns to the courthouse steps, Susan heeds her calling to be a woman of God. "Stop the killing! Stop the chaos! The men who have oppressed you need to be subdued, but do not treat them as they've treated you. The Lord commands us to love our neighbors, even our enemies. You have won the day. You have won your freedom. Do not become like those you despise. Rise to the occasion and be the good people that I know you are, that God knows you are."

The crowd has grown silent as they hear her short sermon. Most of them have been brought up in Christian homes, most of them uphold Christian values. Many of them are Christians who have let their fear and hatred overcome them. Susan's short plea brings them back to their moral roots.

Without even being asked, the crowd starts to repair the damage done by the short but violent riot. Tables and chairs begin to be put back in place. The few food tables that were disrupted are repaired. In short order the square is put back in order for the feast.

Sam takes the Mic once again and announces that the celebration of freedom will start in earnest. Twelve different lines are available to get the hungry and jubilant crowd fed. As the crowd begins to celebrate in earnest, a distant rumble is heard again. A second flyover sends the crowd into wild applause and celebration. The F-16's do barrel rolls to highlight the fly over.

* * *

An hour later, Susan, her brother and their Special Forces escort sit with Sam and a dozen of the town leaders. Questions fly. They answer them as best they can.

"Where did the flyover come from? That was spectacular, just what we needed to restore our faith in the country," One enthusiastic county commissioner asks.

"The flyover came out of Dover Free Air Force base," Susan responds. "Jerimiah coordinated it. We figured that it was a good idea. It would cement the fact that despite there are only a few of us here, that we have strong allies, strong connections."

"Does the Laurel Highlands Militia control Dover Air Force base?" one of the Roanoke militia leaders asks.

"Dover Air Force Base is its own entity," Jerimiah, the Special Forces soldier responds. "They call themselves the Free American Air Force. It consists of pilots and planes from both the third and fifth fleet who refused to fight against each other, as well as the Air Force contingent normally based there. It's the largest free air force on the east coast of America. Our people coordinate with their people. Let's just say that the Laurel Highlands Militia helped them get established.

"What about other military bases around the country, are you in contact with them?"

"I'm from Fort Bragg," Jerimiah states. "My commander has allied with the Laurel Highlands Militia. So has the commander of Fort Hood in Texas. Many forts are in chaos or have been abandoned, overrun by civilians in search of food. Several midwestern forts are still intact because they're so far away from major cities. Fort Sill and Minot Air Force Base have joined in a loose alignment with the Laurel Highlands Militia."

"Who commands the Laurel Highlands Militia?" a woman asks. She's a state representative.

"We can't tell you that," Susan responds. "He has been targeted for assassination and some of his close family members and friends have been killed. I have met him. He's a kind and generous man. His ambitions are to bring stability to the country. He has established civilian control everywhere that his militia has gone. I'm part of that mission. I want to help you establish civilian governance. No use in replacing one set of thugs with another set of thugs; God would not approve."

She smiles and looks at the assembled leaders. They know she's putting them on notice. The cute bright-eyed young girl, with the most powerful air force on the east coast at her beck and call, has just laid down a marker. And from the way she talks, she believes the most powerful air force base is located in heaven.

"What about Senator Clinton? She claims to be the president," Sam asks. "She's ordering the military to implement martial law. How is that going to affect your alliance."

"That's a troublesome situation," Jerimiah responds as he ponders the full depth of the question. "Oath Keepers won't stand for it. But many military commanders and surviving politicians, bent on acquiring power, will embrace her and her policies."

"Will your alliance stand? What will happen?" Sam insists, noticing the hesitancy of the soldier.

"There will probably be another war," the soldier replies grimly.

The End of Book Five

Thank you for jumping into this epic saga. I hope you have gotten more from it then just the thrill of reading a good tale. I hope it has made you think. If so, then I have fulfilled the commission that has been set upon me.

Book Six is the final novel of this epic saga. It is now published. I know where the story ends. God has clearly imprinted on my brain the final chapter. I can't wait for you to read it. It's EPIC!

After Thoughts

America starts to rebuild! Who saw that coming? We're a country of innovators and entrepreneurs. Our self-reliance is part of what has made America great. With a moral compass, we can overcome anything.

Our moral compass is a major aspect that makes this free country great. A reliance on a moral compass is imperative for a free society to survive. I get my moral compass from God and the Bible. Find your moral compass and follow it.

There is probably a church within a few blocks of you, consider finding your moral compass there. Just a suggestion....

Jesus Changes Everything

Timothy A. Van Sickel

P.S. Please post an honest review on both Amazon and Goodreads. They're very helpful to self-published authors.

I can be contacted at: vansickelauthor@gmail.com

A special thanks to the many people who have assisted on this project over the years. First and foremost a thank you to my beautiful wife, Stephanie. She has dealt with me spending two or three hours writing almost every night, and has been a great sounding board for the story line. Other people deserving special thanks include my story advisor, Phil, specialist advisors Scott, Phil, and the unknown electrical engineer I used as a sounding board for the windmill generator solution. Additional thanks to Linc, Erica, Sharon, Wes and the Johnstown Christian Writers Guild.

Novels By Timothy A. Van Sickel

Righteous Gathering, Righteous Survival EMP Saga Book 1

Righteous Bloodshed, Righteous Survival EMP Saga Book 2

Righteous Sacrifice, Righteous Survival EMP Saga Book 3

Righteous Soldiers, Righteous Survival EMP Saga Book 4

Righteous Suffering, Righteous Survival EMP Saga Book 5

Righteous Revival, Righteous Survival EMP Saga Book 6

All are available on Amazon in both print and e-book

Made in the USA
Middletown, DE
10 September 2020